For Jane

THE PALERMO AMBUSH

Zero Hour, July 1943. The Mediterranean island of Sicily is the key to the imminent Allied invasion of Europe. It is defended by a large German army. Limitless Nazi reinforcements can be brought in by a single train ferry from Italy. Major Petrie lands with a fellow saboteur, Ed Johnson, an American, at Palermo. Together they are on a secret mission—to sink the ferry. Alone in hostile territory, they encounter the SS, the Gestapo and the German Army in their desperate bid to reach the heavily-guarded ferry. They haven't a remote hope of succeeding without local aid. So they call on the support of the Mafia underground movement. But can they trust the Mafia?

THE PALERMO AMBUSH

Colin Forbes

CHIVERS PRESS
BATH

First published 1973
by
Pan Books
This Large Print edition published by
Chivers Press
by arrangement with
Macmillan Publishers Ltd
2000

ISBN 0 7540 1393 6

British Library Cataloguing in Publication Data available

Printed and bound in Great Britain by
REDWOOD BOOKS, Trowbridge, Wiltshire

Author's Note

Certain events which form the background to this narrative are true; the characters are fictitious. In 1943 the American Government, searching for allies behind the enemy lines, took a bizarre decision—they called in the aid of the Mafia.

CHAPTER ONE

Monday. 5 July 1943

'The whole plan is a disaster—you'll be damned lucky to get back alive . . .'

The enemy coast was in sight, a blur of mountain in the night, and Major James Petrie's urgent warning echoed in Lawson's brain as the flying-boat touched down on the Mediterranean and its floats skimmed up bursts of spray. The machine lost momentum rapidly, cruising forward parallel to the shore half a mile away while Major Lawson clung to the door-frame behind the naval pilot and watched the black water rushing past below him. As the plane came to a halt, rocking gently on the swell, Lawson manhandled three dinghies over the side where they landed with a splash and then bobbed with the waves, still moored to the flying-boat. The moon came out from behind the clouds just when Lawson was praying it would remain hidden, flooding down and illuminating the eight men of the Allied landing party as they filed past Lawson and dropped into the unsteady craft while the twin props of the aircraft flickered to a halt. As he watched the coast, looped a Sten gun over his shoulder, automatically counted the shadowed figures, Lawson remembered other warning words Petrie had repeated when it was too late to alter the plan. 'Dawnay should never have approved this crazy idea. Eight men—nine with yourself—is too many for the jobs, Bill. They'll be falling over each other . . .' In his haste to leave the flying-boat one

1

man stumbled over the legs of the man in front and only the quick grab of Lawson's hand saved him; it was a good job Petrie was still in Tunis waiting anxiously for news of the raiders' progress, Lawson thought grimly.

It was ten o'clock when the nine soldiers, disguised as peasants, pushed their dinghies clear of the flying-boat and began paddling towards Axis-occupied Sicily, began their nerve-racking journey over a horribly moonlit sea which eddied gently in saucer-shapes of shadow and illuminated water. Behind them the flying-boat, piloted by Lieutenant David Gilbey, rolled in the perpetual swell with its engines silent: it was part of the plan that Gilbey should give them time to get close inshore, should not risk arousing enemy attention until the heavily-armed raiders were almost on the beach.

Lawson sat in the lead dinghy, paddling mechanically as his tiny craft rose and dipped among the waves while he scanned the deserted shore, stared at the railway embankment beyond, and then looked back at the flying-boat which had brought them all the way from Tunis to the coast of Sicily. At least Petrie had been wrong about their mode of transport. 'A flying-boat is too noisy for this type of operation,' he had insisted at the briefing conference when all his objections had been overruled by Brigadier Dawnay and the planners. 'The enemy will hear it coming—because it will have to fly in close to Sicily to off-load the dinghies and the Messina coast is crawling with troops.' Yes, it looked as though Petrie had been wrong about that—so maybe he had been wrong about the other things, too. It was a hope which gave little comfort to Lawson: Petrie, the veteran of ten raids behind the enemy lines, was rarely wrong about these things, whereas Brigadier Dawnay, 'the iron man, iron from the neck up', as Petrie called him, had arrived from London barely six weeks ago.

As they came closer to the lonely beach the only sounds in the night were the slap of wave-tops against the dinghies, a low cough as someone nervously cleared his throat, the swish of paddles entering the sea as the nine men stroked their way in to the Sicilian shore. Lawson glanced over his shoulder and the silhouette of the flying-boat still rocked slowly from side to side, the silhouette where Gilbey was sitting in front of his controls waiting for the moment to leave. In the rear dinghy Corporal Carpenter was hunched forward more than the others as he supported the wireless transmitter on his back, a cumbersome object which reminded Lawson of a further comment Petrie had made. 'For God's sake, Bill, ditch that wireless transmitter. If you run into trouble, have to make a break for it, Carpenter will hold you up horribly carrying that thing. You can always use the under-ground transmitter Gambari's operating from inside Messina . . .' But Dawnay had insisted that the transmitter should be taken, as he had insisted on plenty of equipment, on using a flying-boat 'standard procedure off the Dutch coast, you know . . .'

Suddenly they were almost on top of the beach, but this didn't surprise Lawson; it often happened when you came in over calm water. In less than a minute they'd be on firm ground, running over the thin belt of grey sand as they headed for the first

3

cover, the rail embankment which reared up
beyond the coastal highway linking Messina in the
east with distant Palermo in the west. Resting his
paddle, Lawson made a quick gesture and the
dinghies spread out, one on either side of him
spreading out the target in case they met
opposition as they landed. He gave an order in
little more than a whisper to the stony-faced British
sergeant behind him.

'When we hit the beach I want to reach that
embankment ahead of the others, so show a bit of
speed, Briggs. And you other two.'

'We'll be right behind you, sir.'

It was a detail but it could be a vital detail:
Lawson wanted his crew first on the embankment
so he could give the others covering fire if an
enemy patrol appeared at the wrong moment. He
looked back as the flying-boat's motors started up
and the sputtering roar was unnervingly loud across
the shot-silver sea. Then he was searching the
rugged landscape in front of them for the slightest
sign of movement. The mountain loomed above
him and there was not a single house in sight; only
the desolate beach hemmed in at either end by
spillages of rock, a beach too small for any major
landing, so there were no sinister wires which
would indicate it was mined. The dinghy edged
backwards, topped a crest, slithered through
foaming surf over wet sand as Lawson jumped out
and the others followed while the last man paused
briefly to haul the craft well up the beach. Lawson
crouched low as he sprinted over the sand, crossed
the ribbon of empty highway, and scrambled up the
earthen embankment. At the top he dropped flat
while he scanned the mountain slope above, a

slope littered with crags and boulders which could conceal any number of the enemy.

Then Lawson swore as a Messerschmitt streaked down out of nowhere, heading in a power-dive for a point behind him where the flying-boat was preparing to take off. Petrie had been right after all. It had taken them fifteen minutes to reach the beach from where Gilbey had waited; long enough for a wireless message to be sent to a nearby airfield to get the fighter plane aloft. He made another gesture as more men thudded flat on the embankment and three of them ran back to collect the dinghies and bring them inland. It seemed a useless precaution—hiding the dinghies now—but it was just possible that the fighter had been on a routine patrol when it observed the enemy plane lying on the sea. There was still a thread of hope that the enemy might not know of the landing, that the Messerschmitt pilot, intent on his target, sheering down from a great height, might not have seen the minute figures hauling the dinghies over the sand into the lee of the embankmcnt. 'Better get inland fast, sir,' Sergeant Briggs suggested.

The motors of Gilbey's machine were swelling into a steady roar but the aircraft still hadn't sufficient power to start taxiing over the water as the Messerschmitt continued its murderous dive, heading down at an extreme angle, its engine rising to a screaming pitch. Lawson ignored what was happening out at sea as he stared up at the numerous crags and boulders on the mountain above. Between the embankment where they lay and the nearest crag was a zone of barren, open mountain slope without any kind of cover, an area about four hundred yards wide. If there were men

5

concealed up there the landing party would be slaughtered as it crossed that open ground.

Corporal Carpenter, the wireless operator, had taken up his correct position on the extreme left flank of the line of men sprawled behind the embankment. It would be his job to bring up the rear, the least vulnerable position at present, so while he waited he looked over his shoulder out to sea. The flying-boat was moving, cruising forward as spray burst where the floats scudded over the sea, and the drum beat of its engines quickened as it turned away from the coast prior to leaving the surface. Grimly, Carpenter saw the arrow-descent of the fighter change direction a fraction, heard the spit of its guns as it flashed down over the retreating flying-boat's tail, saw a puff of smoke and a tongue of flame flicker along the fuselage. The machine was gaining height when Gilbey lost control as the fighter pulled out of its dive and soared upwards. The flying-boat wobbled uncertainly, its right wing dipped, touched the sea, then the machine cartwheeled spectacularly, swinging over through an angle of a hundred and eighty degrees. Carpenter heard the hard smack as it smashed against the water upside down. There was a hollow explosion, a cloud of dark smoke, a little wreckage, then silence as the fighter climbed out of hearing.

Lawson heard the disaster without seeing it, heard again Petrie's prophetic words. 'A flying-boat is too noisy . . .' He pushed the memory out of his mind and without further hesitation gave the signal to advance. The eight men went up the mountain in a straggled line with their automatic weapons held in front of them, their coat pockets heavy with

6

spare magazines and grenades, and two of the men bore an extra burden—thirty pounds of high-explosive apiece for the sabotage job they had come to do. They were well spaced out as they advanced up the open slope, spaced out to vary the range for any marksman who might be waiting for them up on the silent crags.

Carpenter, knowing what was expected of him, was still concealed behind the embankment, easing the load on his shoulders as he prepared to follow them, guessing Lawson's intention as he watched the receding figure of his commanding officer and waited for the uplifted hand. He heard instead the appalling rattle of small-arms fire, a mixture of rifle shots and automatic fire as a concentrated fusillade poured down from the crags and boulders above the line of advancing men. Lawson's men opened up briefly on targets they couldn't see; some darted forward, some ran back in a vain attempt to reach the shelter of the embankment, but the enemy commander on the heights had chosen his moment perfectly and the range was point-blank as men rolled in the dust and lay still while the fusillade continued. Lawson was hit almost at once, firing only a short burst from his Sten before he went down. Lying on his side, he tried to get up and knew it was impossible. More bullets struck him. In less than a minute nothing stirred on the slope as the enemy troops came cautiously out of their concealed positions.

In less than a minute—but in that brief period Carpenter had released the transmitter from his back, had opened the flap and extended the telescopic aerial. Carpenter was a London Cockney, a cab-driver in peacetime, and he

7

attended to his duty phlegmatically in spite of what he had just seen. He didn't look over the embankment again as he methodically tapped out the vital message. 'Flying-boat alerted enemy. Orpheus landing party wiped out . . .' He was still tapping out the warning when a rifle butt descended with cruel force on the back of his head, ending the message in mid-sentence. Two hours later the signal was handed to Major Petrie.

CHAPTER TWO

Wednesday Night. 7 July

Two uniformed figures hurried through the darkness of the African night towards a large square tent where the canvas whipped and billowed as the dust-storm battered it. At a distance of no closer to the tent walls than twenty yards, armed sentries stood guarding all the approaches to the meeting-place, stood twenty yards away so there could be no danger that a man might overhear a single word of what passed at the conference which had been urgently summoned for ten o'clock at night. Major James Petrie, DSO, led the way, reached the tent first and grabbed at the swaying flap to unfasten it by the time his superior, Colonel Arthur Parridge, came up behind him.

Parridge glanced up at the sky, decided the storm was worsening, then walked into the deserted interior which held a long trestle table lined with chairs. The map laid over the table was filmed with sand. He stood for a moment, brushing dust off his khaki-drill uniform as he looked round. The empty tent was illuminated by oil-lamps slung from a wire suspended over the table and the lamps were flickering uneasily, casting restless shadows across the walls as Petrie entered and Parridge spoke. 'This time, Jim, keep your damned mouth shut.'

'You're asking a lot, sir. Under the circumstances.' Petrie glanced at the colonel and the strain lines were showing at the corners of his mouth. Parridge, prematurely white-haired, but still only in his late forties, grunted. Under the circumstances. Yes, it had been a bloodbath, Lawson's raid, and he didn't feel he could convert the request into an order, so he said something else.

'Remember, you're going on leave to Algiers in the morning.'

'At least it will take me away from Dawnay. That raid was a bloody fiasco. Nine men lost the moment they arrive—and for nothing . . .'

'That's what I meant about keeping your mouth shut,' Parridge observed as he walked to the end of the tent and took a chair farthest from the head of the table where Brigadier Dawnay would sit when he arrived. 'Your place is here,' he went on and tapped the chair next to him, determined to keep Petrie as far away from the brigadier as possible.

James Petrie was twenty-nine years old, a mining engineer in peacetime, who had joined the army strictly for the duration. Since he had been attached to Parridge's Felucca Boat Squadron in the Mediterranean he had led ten raids behind the enemy lines, an activity where the casualty rate was so high that few officers survived more than a

9

couple of months. Petrie had survived for more than two years, had become an expert at staying alive in enemy territory, had recently returned from serving as liaison officer with the Sicilian underground, as vicious a gang of cut-throats as could be found in the whole Mediterranean. Two months he had spent on the island ensuring that the Sicilians looked for the right military information, arranging for this invaluable data on which the invasion plans had been based to be wirelessed back to Allied Force Headquarters. On his return to Tunis his comment on the Sicilians had been brief and to the point. 'In Sicily it wasn't the Germans who worried me—it was our so-called allies who scared the guts out of me.'

Strange, Parridge was thinking, how some of these lads who hated the war, hated the years it was taking away from them excelled in the craft of murderous combat. Perhaps it was because they came to it fresh, saw what was in front of them without minds warped by out-of-date military doctrine, minds like 'Thruster' Dawnay's . . . He put the image of the choleric brigadier firmly out of his mind; bad enough when the bastard actually walked into the tent without imagining his presence there beforehand. And the worst problem would be keeping Petrie quiet. Dark-haired and clean-shaven, his face tanned to mahogany by the African sun, Petrie was one of those rare individuals people noticed the moment he entered a room. They noticed the strong jaw-line, the firm mouth, the nose hooked at the bridge, the restless eyes which seemed to observe everything, and so arresting was the impression he made that they were inclined to overlook a turn of the mouth which suggested a

10

sardonic sense of humour. 'Look, Jim,' Parridge said, 'I wasn't going to mention this until it came through—I've recommended you for further promotion. By the time you're back from Algiers you should have your half-colonelcy.'

'Thank you, sir.' Petrie didn't seem enormously impressed by the news.

A hand clapped him on the back as Captain Edward Johnson, US Army, who had just entered the tent, took the chair next to him. 'I thought you were hellbound for the fleshpots of Algiers.'

'Tomorrow morning, Ed. Six ack emma. On the dot. This is positively my last farewell appearance.'

'Good for you! Don't get lost in the casbah chasing after those girls with veils!' Captain Johnson, two years younger than Petrie, lit a cigarette, and Parridge smiled sourly to himself. Brigadier Dawnay was a non-smoker who preferred others to share his virtue, especially those of junior rank. It would be interesting to see how the brigadier handled this problem in Anglo-American relations. The room was filling up with people as more officers came into the tent and spread themselves round the table. Someone spotted the map and groaned audibly. 'Sicily! God, another Lawson raid coming up. I'd better get a chit from the MO right away . . .'

While Petrie and Johnson talked, Parridge studied the American and decided he liked what he saw. Dark-haired, with a command of Italian as fluent as Petrie's, he seemed casual rather than formidable, a man who smiled easily and often, but as Petrie had discovered when Ed was sent to help him for a short while inside Sicily, Johnson knew what he was about. In peacetime the American had

11

served with the US Border Patrol, a special government body which watched the frontiers of the United States to keep out smugglers and even less desirable characters. And he had served on the more dangerous frontier, along the border between the States and Mexico where a knife was commonly used for more than slicing bacon. In a few months' time Johnson would make a first-rate leader of landing parties.

The babble of voices stopped suddenly and Parridge stiffened at the warning silence which could mean only one thing: Brigadier Frederick Dawnay was arriving. Petrie finished what he was saying to Johnson, leaned back in his chair and stared at the inflated ceiling as the wind shook it with a fresh blast, an appropriate enough prelude to what was coming. Captain Stoneham, one of the British planners responsible for the Lawson raid, entered the tent and took a seat near the head of the table. For a second his eye caught Petrie's, then he looked away quickly. He was followed by Colonel Lemuel Benson, Johnson's superior, and the American joined several of his fellow-officers already spaced round the table. Like so many current operations, this was an Anglo-American affair, and at this conference Benson would have co-equal status with Dawnay. Inside the tent it was becoming intolerably stuffy and several men were mopping their foreheads as the tent flap was pulled roughly aside and a short, stocky officer in a red-tabbed uniform strode in brandishing a stick which he slammed down on the table. It was immediately apparent that Brigadier Dawnay was not in the best of tempers. 'Sit down, gentlemen,' he growled. 'We haven't time for ceremony tonight!'

'But God help the man who didn't stand up,' Petrie thought cynically as he resumed his seat.

'For the benefit of those not present at the previous meeting I'll outline the situation quickly,' Dawnay went on. 'We are, of course, faced with a major emergency. The German-Italian forces have now been thrown out of Africa and we are about to launch our first attack on the European mainland . . .'

Pausing, he sniffed the air. 'There's a man smoking there.' Johnson stubbed out the cigarette as Benson put away his cigar-case with a long face. 'Lawson's raid was a failure,' the brigadier barked, 'but, in case any of you have forgotten, there's a war on and these things happen. The next thing is to put it right—and damned quick! The enemy had six enormous train-ferries plying the waters between the mainland of Italy and Sicily a few months ago. These vessels were able to carry vast quantities of men and munitions into the island. Five of them were sunk by air attack earlier, but since then the Germans have militarized the straits of Messina on a colossal scale—we know, in fact, that Jerry has placed over seven hundred guns to guard the straits—and it is the opinion of our air chiefs that they're unlikely to break through that barrage. The sixth and last train-ferry, the *Cariddi*, is still afloat shielded by the umbrella of those guns, is still available to transport large numbers of men and guns swiftly into Sicily.' He paused again. 'Lawson went in to sink the *Cariddi*. He failed. If that vessel remains afloat it could lose us the war. And we have exactly forty-eight hours left in which to send her to the bottom.'

'Isn't that rather over-dramatizing the situation,

sir?' Johnson inquired sceptically.

Dawnay glared at him, then dipped his short-cropped head to listen to Colonel Benson. Nodding, he looked at Johnson again. 'It's pretty important that you grasp the situation,' he said bluntly, 'because you may be asked to command the next team sent in to blow her up. Everything has been tried to sink that train-ferry—high-level bombers, motor-torpedo boats, and earlier this evening a flight of torpedo-bombers tried to get through to her. Like Lawson, they failed. Squadron Leader Weston was one of the casualties.'

Petrie stirred in his seat, ignored Parridge's frowning attempt to make him keep quiet. 'You mean Weston is dead, sir?' he inquired.

'It's reported that his machine blew up in mid-air. So the Navy can't get up the straits because they're too narrow, there are too many shore batteries and too many E-boats. The RAF can't get low enough through the hellish barrage to pinpoint the target when she's in Messina harbour where she ties up.' Dawnay looked grimly round the tanned faces lit by the murky oil-lamp glow. 'That leaves the Army to do the job.' His fist crashed on the table. 'We've got to send in another sabotage team and they must get there this time! Not only get to Messina—they must penetrate the dock area which is guarded by the Nazi élite, they must get aboard that train-ferry, they must plant explosive charges in her belly and send her to the bottom of the bloody straits!'

'You said we had forty-eight hours, sir,' Parridge queried. 'When is the deadline?'

'Midnight, Friday, July 9.'

There were gasps, then a hush as Dawnay stared

14

round the table and Parridge leaned forward. His tone was crisp and demanding. 'In that case the sabotage team has only *twenty-four* hours to do their job—a day and a night will be needed to make preparations. At the very least!'

'I said it was an emergency.'

'Have we had any more news from our Italian agent inside Messina, Gambari?' There was a hint of desperation in Parridge's voice as he realized for the first time how impossible the situation was.

'Only that the *Cariddi* is still afloat,' Dawnay replied woodenly. 'And now I'll explain for Captain Johnson's benefit why I have not over-dramatized the situation. Allied Forces Headquarters calculate that if we invade Sicily our amphibious forces can defeat the enemy troops at present on the island. *At present*, I said. But our intelligence people report that the 29th Panzer Division has been brought down to the Naples area and could move south to the straits at any moment. If the 29th Panzer is moved on to the island by the *Cariddi* just after we have landed it could turn the battle against us . . .'

'But could that really lose us the war?' inquired the irrepressible Johnson.

'Ed,' Colonel Benson intervened, 'the brigadier is still telling us how it could do just that.'

'If our first attempt to return to Europe fails,' Dawnay continued, 'the Germans will withdraw large forces from the Mediterranean and send them back to Russia. If that happens the Red Army will be thrown back a vast distance. Taken to its logical extreme, it could mean the end of Russia— all because one large train-ferry was still afloat. The *Cariddi* is the only vessel left capable of moving German armour across the straits in time

15

to defeat us.'

'I go along with that assessment,' Benson said laconically. 'The brigadier isn't exaggerating, Ed.'

'Just checking, sir,' Johnson replied, equally laconic. 'I gather you want that train-ferry sunk.'

'By midnight on Friday,' Dawnay repeated. And that, Petrie was thinking, gives us the invasion hour for Sicily—some time in the early morning of Saturday, July 10.

'The question is,' Benson remarked, 'how do we go about the job this time?'

'Captain Stoneham has drawn up a plan which I've personally approved,' Dawnay informed the meeting. There was no audible groan but the faces round the table became a little tauter and Parridge glanced hastily at Petrie. With his arms folded and his eyes fixed on Dawnay, Petrie waited while Stoneham began to explain the new plan. Drop in by parachute . . . very close to Messina . . . no time to come in farther away in a less heavily-defended area . . . the men must be heavily-armed to blast their way through any opposition . . . At this suggestion Dawnay nodded his strong approval; he saw war only in terms of a dog-fight. A large team would be sent to allow for casualties . . . at least nine men, including a wireless transmitter . . .

Jesus! Petrie just stopped himself intervening. This was worse, far worse than the Lawson raid plan was, an open invitation to disaster. Parridge must have sensed something of what was passing through Petrie's mind because he tapped him on the arm, warning him again not to intervene. Petrie nodded, an acknowledgement which might have meant anything as Stoneham, went on. 'The north coast of Sicily swarms with Italian MAS patrol-

16

boats . . . no good thinking of coming ashore from the sea . . . parachute drop essential . . .' Might as well drop 'em without 'chutes, Petrie thought bitterly, that way the slaughter would be over quickly. There were twenty officers assembled round the table, and half of them were staff, but the other ten, whose expressions were grimmest, glanced frequently to the foot of the table where Petrie sat like a stone figure. They want him to speak, Parridge knew without a doubt, wanted someone to get up and tell the brigadier that what was proposed was suicidal, stark, raving madness. And Petrie, the senior raider present, was elected.

'And that concludes my outline of how I see the operation,' Stoneham ended.

'Any comments?' Dawnay demanded perfunctorily. 'They'd have to be brief. None? Then it only remains to select the team . . .'

Perhaps deliberately, he was looking down at a sheet of paper as he spoke, but something in the overheated atmosphere compelled him to look up again. Everyone was staring at the foot of the table where Petrie had risen slowly as he gave Parridge an apologetic grin and then stared along the tent with a less amiable expression. 'Permission to speak, sir,' he requested quietly.

'You'll have to be very brief,' Dawnay repeated. 'The deadline's too close for a lot of gab.'

'I submit, sir, that it's also too close for another foul-up. We have to . . .'

'What the hell do you mean by that remark?'

Petrie's tone was as innocent as his expression. 'I thought you'd already assessed the Lawson raid as a complete foul-up.'

'You said "another",' the brigadier accused.

17

'I did. I was referring to Captain Stoneham's new plan. Air-dropping a sabotage team almost on top of Messina would be like dropping men on a porcupine with steel quills. It's the most heavily-defended area on the island . . .'

'We have to take that risk. The deadline is barely forty-eight hours away.'

'So we can't afford to make a mistake, can we, sir?' Petrie inquired genially. 'This second team has got to do the job or it will be too late—too late to send in another lot. This time we have to get it right. The airdrop idea is useless anyway—tantamount to failure . . .'

'Why?' Dawnay rasped.

'Because of the deadline you've mentioned, sir. First, they'll have to be dropped at night when the moon is up, so there's a chance they'd be spotted. And the first requirement is to get the team inside Sicily so the enemy doesn't even know they've arrived. Secondly, air-drop parties nearly always get scattered coming down and valuable time will be wasted while they try to form up again. In Sicily they could lose each other for good. A parachute drop is out.'

'Any other objections?' Dawnay made no attempt to conceal the biting sarcasm in his tone and then he looked at his watch as though timing the interruption.

'Plenty, sir. In fact, I'm afraid I can't find one thing I like about Captain Stoneham's plan. He suggested at least nine men should go in. That's far too many—even disguised as peasants such a large body is bound to be conspicuous; in an emergency they'll get in each other's way, you'll have trouble whipping up that number who speak fluent Italian

18

at such short notice . . .'

'We have to allow for heavy casualties,' Dawnay snapped.

'If there are *any* casualties it means they've been seen and that means they've failed . . .'

'Why this mania for all of them speaking the lingo?'

'Because that way they can move about more confidently as civilians—so they'll move faster. It all comes back to the deadline you yourself laid down.'

'How many men do you propose then, Major Petrie?' Dawnay leaned well forward as he asked the question and the atmosphere inside the tent had become electric. No one else moved, partly to catch every word, partly to escape being caught up in the duel developing between the two men.

'I'd send in a couple of men from here . . .'

'A couple!' Dawnay exploded.

'No more, sir' Petrie insisted. 'And another point—Captain Stoneham listed the equipment to be taken. Far too much of it—this is a sabotage team, not an assault party. It must slip secretly through the enemy lines, must get on board the *Cariddi* before the Germans have the remotest clue they're there . . .'

He stopped in mid-sentence as Dawnay swung round in his chair, stared at the man who had just come inside the tent, jumped to his feet and saluted. A second later every man inside the tent was also on his feet and the silence was so complete that the sound of sand rustling beyond the canvas walls was clearly heard. The new arrival, short, compact, wiry, long-nosed, carried the crossed swords of a lieutenant general on his khaki-drill shoulder-straps and wore a tank corps beret on his head. 'I'll take over now, Dawnay,' he said crisply and went to the head of the table. 'Sit down, gentlemen, we've got to get on with this. Where have you got to, Dawnay?' The small figure under the oil-lamp dominated the meeting as much by personality as by rank, and he reminded Petrie of a coiled spring as he sat listening to the brigadier while his gaze was fixed on the foot of the table. General Sir Bernard Strickland had taken charge.

With an impatient gestum he reached out a bony hand towards Captain Stoneham and that officer surrendered a sheet of paper which contained the outline of the plan he had recently expounded. Strickland read the sheet while he listened to Dawnay and then he stared towards the foot of the table a second time. Parridge shifted uncomfortably in his chair; now he knew why Petrie had been summoned to this meeting. His name had been added to the list by General Strickland. The small figure stood up, crumpled the sheet of paper slowly in his fist, dropped it on the table.

'Another time, Captain Stoneham, bring a waste-paper basket—its the only place for rubbish like this. Your plan is a complete dog's breakfast.'

'Yes, sir,' Stoneham replied nervously.

'And report to me at my caravan tomorrow morning at 0800 hours. Dawnay, you'd better be there as well. Now, Major Petrie, how would *you* sink the *Cariddi*?'

*   *   *

Petrie had explained the method of getting inside Sicily unseen; Strickland had approved it. The

20

general had walked the full length of the tent to stand close to Petrie while he listened with his arms folded behind his back; during the explanation his eyes never once left the officer's face. 'How many men do you propose for the team?' he asked. He had a slight lisp but it seemed to add to the force of his delivery and Petrie, remembering Dawnay's reaction, hesitated.

'Come on,' said Strickland, 'when I arrive in Sicily I'm going to knock the enemy for six, but I need your help to do it. When I land, that train-ferry must be forty fathoms deep.'

'Three men will be enough,' Petrie said quietly. 'More would jeopardize the success of the whole enterprise.'

'You think that's enough?'

'I'm sure it is. One is the commanding officer of the show, and he must speak fluent Italian. Two is the explosives expert—and he's already inside Sicily. I'm referring to Sergeant Len Fielding, the wireless operator I worked with while I was over there. He also happens to be a specialist with explosives—and he speaks good Italian. The third member of the team will be the second-in-command, and he must know the lingo, too. One of the two officers must also know enough about explosives to plant the charges in case anything happens to Fielding.'

'Equipment?'

'A gun for each man—one easily concealed. Knives and sixty pounds of high-explosive. That's it. That team must be able to run like rabbits, hide at a moment's notice, and not get bogged down with a load of old scrap-iron.'

'A wireless transmitter would be scrap-iron?'

21

'Definitely. In any case, our Italian agent inside Messina, Gambari, has his own transmitter. If we need to send a message we can use that.'

'And the team lands where?'

'Palermo.'

There was a muted gasp inside the tent as Petrie's finger stabbed down at the map over the Sicilian city. For the first time Strickland frowned. 'That's well over a hundred miles west of Messina.'

'The enemy will never expect a landing there—that's part of the idea, but only part of it. There are two halves to this problem,' Petrie explained forcefully. 'The first half is to get ashore unseen in an area where they'll never expect us—Messina and the whole countryside round it bristles with the enemy, Italian and German. Lawson's raid has alerted them on the north coast for a good distance west of Messina, so that's out. I have contacts in Palermo, so that's the best place to slip ashore. More important still, we can get transport there to rush us across the island . . .'

'By the coastal highway direct from Palermo to Messina?'

'No, that's too dangerous. There's half a division reported to have moved in west of Cefalù. Look, sir, they'll have to drive over this devious inland route . . .' Petrie's finger indicated a route through the heart of Sicily. 'Enemy troops are very thin on the ground here so they'll be able to keep going. And I think Gambari should be brought out from Messina to meet them halfway—here at Scopana. Gambari is important to this plan—he knows the sailing schedules of the *Cariddi*.'

'Makes sense.' Strickland bent over the map to check the route as Parridge looked at his watch. It

22

was 10.30 PM. The general normally imposed a strict routine on himself: always up at 6 AM, always in bed by 9.30 PM. The breaking of that routine underlined the supreme importance he attached to this operation. Strickland grunted his approval, stared at Petrie again. 'You mentioned getting hold of transport in Palermo. How do they manage that?'

'That's another major reason for going in at Palermo. We need help on this job.' Petrie paused. 'We're going to use the mafia.'

*　　　*　　　*

Strickland rubbed his chin thoughtfully. Petrie had given him a shock which he was careful not to show. 'Your Sicilian underground friends, you mean?' he commented.

'If they're your only friends, it might be wiser to collect a few enemies,' Petrie replied.

'But you think we can use them?'

'AFHQ have *used* them for months to collect information about enemy troop movements on the island. I spent eight weeks inside Sicily co-ordinating their activities—and the Americans have sent in their own agents to contact the mafia. They've even released top *mafiosi* inside the States from the penitentiary [Lucky Luciano, a notorious criminal, was taken from a New York upstate prison and housed in a city apartment. From there he sent orders to New York waterfront mafias and within a month all German saboteurs had been eliminated from the area—by the mafia.] to help them. I don't like the idea, but on that island they're the nearest thing there is to a resistance

23

movement—mainly because Mussolini's police battered them underground before the war. The fact is, they're all we've got.'

Colonel Benson intervened and Strickland twisted his head to stare at the American. 'Petrie is right, sir—about our sending people over there. And we may have to use some of them in the Allied Military Government set-up we've planned for later. The *mafiosi* speak Sicilian and they can keep their people under control when we need the island for future operations.'

'I know all this!' The general made an impatient gesture. 'I asked you, Major Petrie, where we are going to find transport in Palermo.'

'The mafia supplies the transport—either a vegetable truck or a car. That will take our men fast from Palermo to Messina by the cross-country route. And the third reason why I favour Palermo as the landing-point is because they'll need a guide, a reliable Sicilian who can make sure they don't get lost.'

'Such a commodity exists?' Strickland demanded. 'A reliable Sicilian? They're a gang of ruffians. Or did you meet someone in Palermo you can even half-trust?'

'I think so. There's only one man who can do that job—one man who has the guts to get the sabotage team all the way in time.' Petrie paused, wondering again what the reaction would be. 'I'm talking about Vito Scelba.'

'That villain!' Strickland was not amused. 'He's the biggest cut-throat in the Mediterranean.'

'You underestimate Scelba, sir,' Petrie replied mildly. 'He's the biggest cut-throat north of the equator. Worse than any Communist guerrilla I

24

ever met in Greece. But he's also my fourth reason for choosing Palermo. He's not only boss of the mafia underground; he also controls the waterfront *mafiosi* of every port in Sicily—including Messina.' Petrie paused to let his observation sink in.

'You're thinking of the dockside area?'

'That's exactly what I am thinking of, sir. Scelba can use his men on the waterfront to smuggle the sabotage team inside those docks—and I gather it's one of the most heavily-defended areas in Europe.'

'You're confident that Scelba will do all this for us?' Strickland rapped out.

'Perfectly confident—if you pay his price. That way you ensure his loyalty.'

'What price?'

'I know he wants an official position in the Allied set-up when we take over Sicily—wants it badly. He'll demand to be made prefect of Palermo province, but he'll settle for appointment as mayor of Palermo city.'

'The bowler hats would have to decide that. You're prepared to recommend him for such a position since you were over there?'

Petrie spread out his hands with an air of resignation. 'I wouldn't appoint him road-sweeper if I had my way. I think it's probably a major blunder having anything to do with the mafia—in the long run it may prove we'd have been far wiser to have done without them. But if you want this job done you'll have to use Scelba.'

'That's politics,' Strickland said with distaste. 'My job is to win the war. The team will have to go in tomorrow night and I can always promise him he'll be mayor and think about it later. Now! The only outstanding question is—who goes? I believe

25

that for the commander of the sabotage team you specified these requirements.' Strickland ticked them off on his fingers. 'One, he speaks fluent Italian. Two, he's familiar with Sicily. Three, he knows something about explosives. And there's a fourth qualification you haven't mentioned—he must be able to persuade this ruffian, Scelba, to co-operate. Is that right?'

'Yes, sir.'

'Do you realize, Major Petrie, that the specification you laid down exactly describes yourself?'

'I rather thought it might,' Petrie replied without great enthusiasm.

Parridge leaned round Petrie so the general could see him as he spoke. 'You doubtless haven't been informed, sir, but Major Petrie is starting a long overdue leave first thing this morning.'

'I see!' Strickland looked at Petrie critically. 'In that case he'd better decide pretty quick whether he's going on leave or whether he's still fit enough to go in and sink the *Cariddi* for us!'

'I think I can do the job,' Petrie said quietly. 'I'll take Captain Johnson as my second-in-command.'

'*Think* isn't enough!' Strickland stood with his hands on his hips and stared hard at the officer. 'The success of my invasion could depend on the sinking of that vessel!'

'I can do the job—so long as I work to my own plan.'

'Already agreed! And now I'm off to bed.' He turned to leave but Petrie spoke again and the general swung on his heel to listen.

'The 29th Panzer Division, sir. What is the latest report on its whereabouts?'

'Good question! The most recent news was that it was still laagered in the Naples area.' Strickland frowned. 'That was yesterday. Reconnaissance planes photographed the area regularly but it's been ten-tenths cloud over there for the past twenty-four hours. We assume it's still there.' As the general left the tent and a buzz of conversation sprang up behind him Petrie took particular care not to look round the crowded table; he knew, without glancing up, what their expressions would show. Sympathy, and relief—relief that they weren't going into the cauldron.

*   *   *

At the German GHQ, Southern Europe, a round-faced, well-built man sat on the balcony of a Naples *palazzo* waiting for the telephone in the room behind him to ring. Field-Marshal Albert Kesselring was one of the ablest Axis commanders—perhaps because he was also one of the most independent—and insofar as he could he ignored the more dogmatic orders which came to him from Supreme Headquarters in East Prussia. And once again he was about to take his own decision, a decision which he deemed necessary because of the intelligence reports which had reached him. The North African ports were bursting at the seams with a frightening array of troopships and warships, and elements of the vast Allied amphibious force had already put to sea from Alexandria. It was even rumoured that a huge convoy was coming close to Gibraltar direct from the United States. It was time to act, to make his dispositions.

At ten o'clock at night he sat in the darkness. No moon showed through the heavy overcast and he prayed that it would stay that way for a little longer. Then the phone rang, its insistent summons mingling with the sound of a sentry tramping the paved courtyard below. Kesselring got up quickly, went inside and picked up the receiver. 'Is that you, Klaus? How are you?'

'Ready, sir.' General Rheinhardt, commanding general of the 29th Panzer Division, never used four words where two would suffice. From his tent he could see through the opening the silhouette of a Mark IV tank with the crew sitting on the ground beside it, fully dressed, fully equipped, fully alert. Ready.

'Klaus, you're to move south at once. I know bridges are down, that you will have to make a lot of detours, but I want as much speed as you can manage. Position B is where you're headed for.'

'They've landed?'

'Not yet. But they're coming—and soon. I've no doubt where the blow will fall, so I'll keep in touch. No panics?'

'Everything normal. Is that all, sir?'

'For the moment, yes. Goodbye, Klaus.'

The phone clicked at the other end before Kesselring could replace his own receiver, and he listened a little longer to the odd atmospherics sputtering on the line. Were the Gestapo phone-tappers at work again? It couldn't be helped: he had been careful not to give away what he had in mind, and Klaus would react swiftly. In this assumption Kesselring was absolutely correct. Within sixty seconds of ending the call Rheinhardt had issued the order. Within thirty minutes a controlled flood of armoured vehicles was moving south under cover of the night and the cloud bank heading for Calabria, heading for the eastern shore of the straits of Messina.

CHAPTER THREE

Thursday. 8 July—Before Midnight

The glass was falling rapidly, the sea was churning like a boiling cauldron as mountainous waves swept towards the Italian MAS patrol-boat proceeding through the darkness, waves which lifted it to a surf-fringed crest and then plunged it down and down into a vast trough which it seemed must engulf the vessel until, at the last moment, the bows of the large craft rose wearily again to ascend the glassy wall of another comber looming above the deck, a quivering, tumbling wall of water which threatened to submerge the patrol-boat before it could surmount the next obstacle. The wind howl disappeared inside the trough, muffled by the dancing walls of sea on all sides, but the moment they reached the next crest its menacing shriek battered at the eardrums of the men aboard who were already soaked to the skin, their bodies bruised by the frequent hammering they endured as the vessel changed direction without warning, hurling them against a bulkhead, straining at already over-strained muscles tense with the struggle to hold on, to retain some sort of balance in a world which was totally without equilibrium as the ship, powered by throbbing engines, headed in

29

towards the north coast of Sicily.

'Bit of a pounder,' Petrie yelled at the top of his voice to make himself heard by Lieutenant-Commander Vosper, who was holding the wheel.

'It's getting worse—look at the glass,' Vosper shouted back.

'And to think we could have landed by parachute!' Johnson commented. The American, standing beside Petrie in the confined area of the wheelhouse, had never been over-enthusiastic about dangling from parachute cords with the ravines of Sicily below him but now Stoneham's original plan seemed infinitely preferable to this turbulent sea. Petrie didn't bother to reply as he resisted the instinct to duck his head: a curtain of dark water burst over the bows, cascaded over the window as Vosper turned the wheel a fraction and stared ahead while they crested yet another roller.

Not a man aboard the enemy patrol-boat captured by the Allies at the end of the Tunisian campaign was dressed correctly. The British naval crew under Vosper's command wore Italian naval uniform while Petrie and Johnson, each with a day's growth of beard on his chin, were dressed in the most disreputable of peasant clothes; shabby jackets and trousers underneath even shabbier coats, and in their pockets were screwed up the peaked caps Sicilian peasants wore throughout the year, no matter what the weather might be. They might have been a little less sodden had they not made regular trips out to the exposed deck in their anxiety to catch their first sight of Sicily, a routine which Vosper had recently warned them against when the American had almost vanished overboard.

30

'This isn't the boat I'd have picked for this trip,' he commented dryly. The choice of transport had been Petrie's: the MAS boat was the exact model of the numerous Italian vessels which patrolled the north Sicilian coast, vessels which were the main defence of this shore calculated by the enemy command to be the least likely target for invasion because it lay farthest from the Allies' African bases. Beside him Petrie was searching for something he prayed wasn't there—another MAS boat, a genuine enemy vessel prowling the darkness for any sign of intruders. If they were seen they would instantly be challenged to give the recognition signal changed every twenty-four hours by the Italian naval commander of Palermo, harbour. If they were seen . . .

'Tarpaulin's coming adrift . . .' Johnson shouted the warning and then left the safety of the wheelhouse before Petrie could stop him, slamming aside the door and stepping on to the slippery deck which had been awash seconds earlier. Lashed to the deck aft of the wheelhouse was a huge tarpaulin drawn over a small Sicilian fishing-craft, and one corner of the protective covering had been torn loose by the constant spillage of the sea. They were ascending towards another crest when water again surged over the boat. Then the deck was clear again, swilling sea over its side as Johnson reached the tarpaulin, grasped the loose cord, whipped it round a deck-ring and tied it while he wedged his back against the wheelhouse as once more the vessel dropped like a stone.

He had just finished his task when the ship began a fresh ascent out of the trough. He nearly

31

went overboard, grabbed at the deck-ring just in time, felt Petrie's hand lock round his forearm, then they both held on grimly as the boat's stern fell away. Sprawled on the steel deck, tilted at an extreme angle, Johnson had a horrible conviction that this time Vosper had miscalculated, that the vessel was going to cartwheel, tipping over backwards, swinging over as the stern acted as a fulcrum to turn them upside down. Staring up he saw a gyrating funnel of sea swirling round, saw Petrie staring down at him, his face a drawn mask over the bones, and then he lost his grip on the slippery deck-ring and only Petrie's hand clawed round his arm held him on the vessel as it went on climbing and heeling prior to overturning. It was a nightmare: Petrie's left arm, bent at a cruel angle behind him where his hand still gripped the rail which was their only contact with the superstructure, felt numb, was gradually losing all feeling as it took the weight of two men. Then the boat was heaving up its stern, levelling out on a crest as Petrie hauled, dragged, twisted him round and inside the wheelhouse where the American collapsed on the floor and quietly choked until his breathing began to return to normal.

'Fishing craft . . . was going . . .' He couldn't say any more as Petrie wedged him into a corner with his own body, sitting on the floor beside Johnson while he fumbled in his coat pocket and brought out a bottle of cheap Italian brandy. Removing the cap, he handed it to the American, who swallowed a few drops, started spluttering again, then took a deeper draught. Pulling a wry face, he handed back the bottle. 'Thanks . . .' He managed a caricature of a grin as he wiped his mouth. 'Filthy muck . . . not exactly French cognac.' It was pretty deadly, Petrie agreed as he took a swig and then handed the bottle to Vosper who shook his head, shouted that he never drank on duty, and then took a long swallow.

'You did a nice job there, Ed,' Petrie remarked as he recapped the bottle. Like everything they carried, such as it was, the bottle of cheap Italian brandy could be obtained inside Sicily. In case they were stopped and searched once they landed—if they ever did reach the shore—they carried nothing which would identify them as Allied raiders. Certain items they carried would certainly mark them as suspicious characters, but as suspicious Sicilian characters in the habit of stealing anything they could lay their theiving hands on. Their guns were Italian or German weapons which could have been purloined from enemy dumps on the island, weapons which had been obtained from the huge quantities of German and Italian munitions seized when a whole Axis army surrendered in Tunisia. Even the sixty pounds of high-explosive secreted in a sack inside the wheelhouse were German explosives, and the four timer mcchanisms were standard issue to the Wehrmacht.

Although the storm still battered at them with appalling violence, the waves driving at them from all directions, pitching and tossing them perpetually, the crests were becoming lower, the troughs shallower—and somewhere the moon was breaking through the clouds, casting a cold glow which made the sea seem even worse because now they saw its hideous movements more clearly. But the glass was rising. When they caught their first glimpse of Sicily, Johnson had climbed to his feet and was standing outside the wheelhouse alongside Petrie. It was Petrie who saw the coast first, no more than a nebulous shadow in the distance as he pointed and Vosper, checking the compass, swung the wheel a few degrees to starboard. 'Over there,' Petrie said. 'Looks like a low cloud but I think . . .'

'That's Sicily,' Vosper confirmed. 'We'll be there in less than an hour. On schedule to meet your friends—if they've come out on a night like this.'

'The met report said the storm would by-pass the Sicilian coast,' Johnson reminded him. 'Not that I can believe it at the moment.'

As the deck rose and fell, as the waves burst and sent up clouds of steam-like spray which drenched them again and again, Petrie scanned the unstable world for any sign of the enemy, but they had the Tyrrhenian Sea to themselves as they dipped inside shallower troughs, climbed out of them, wallowing from side to side while they headed in closer to the smudge of mountain. When Vosper handed over the wheel to a rating and came out to join Petrie, Johnson took refuge in the doorway to the wheelhouse. They were on the fringe of the storm zone now where the weather could be dangerously treacherous, seeming to calm itself and then renewing its onslaught without warning. 'That fishing fleet will never come out in this,' Johnson shouted to Petrie.

'Depends what it's like closer in,' Petrie shouted back. 'It could be quite calm just offshore.' He replied automatically as he continued scanning the sea with narrowed eyes and Vosper, who had just completed his own visual search, was turning to go back inside the wheelhouse when Petrie grasped his arm and pointed westwards. 'What's that over

34

there?'

'Over where? Can't see a thing,' Vosper said crisply.

'Keep watching where I'm pointing. I saw a shadow, something anyway. It went down in a trough . . . No, there it is again!'

'MAS boat!' Balanced in the doorway, Vosper lifted his night glasses slung from his neck, focused them quickly, watched for a long moment, then dropped them. 'Yes, that's a MAS boat and she's heading this way. I think she's spotted us. Better get under cover with those togs of yours.' Going back inside the wheelhouse, he issued orders down the voice-pipe. 'MAS boat off starboard bow. Guns to be manned. Engines to be maintained at present speed . . .' The patrol-boat came alive as men in Italian uniform took up position to convey the impression that the ship was on routine patrol, manning the 13.2-mm machine-gun, taking up depth-charge stations, and from the rear of the wheelhouse Petrie and Johnson looked at the blurred silhouette of the enemy vessel bouncing over a wave and then dropping out of sight. The tension grew minute by minute as the real MAS boat approached them broadside on from starboard, a tension which Vosper seemed impervious to as he took a signalling lamp from a locker and waited by the open window with the instrument perched on its edge.

Petrie observed the signalling lamp with some anxiety. This was the crisis they had feared, had hoped they would never face, because in this situation there were too many things to go wrong. The ship's guns were loaded, the two 17.7-inch torpedo tubes were armed, the British naval

35

personnel behind the weapons certainly knew how to use them, and under normal conditions Vosper would have given an excellent account of himself. But this was worse: they didn't want a scrap, they didn't want anything to happen which would cause the wireless operator on board the enemy vessel to start tapping out a warning to Palermo naval HQ. And even if the oncoming vessel was sunk swiftly— before any message had been transmitted—the noise of the battle would certainly be heard on shore just as though a radio message had been sent. The secret would be shattered, the operation ruined, and there could be no question of taking Petrie and Johnson to their rendezvous outside Palermo. Without any apparent sign of strain Vosper waited calmly, waited for the code signal to be flashed across the water.

'Think we'll get away with it?' Johnson inquired as he huddled down with Petrie out of sight.

'If Scelba has sent us the right answering signal for tonight we should do,' Petrie replied as he watched Vosper closely. 'His man inside the Italian naval HQ is pretty good and the Italians are supposed to use the same signal exchange for twenty-four hours.'

'Supposed to?' Johnson wasn't too happy about this somewhat qualified reply, but it was Vosper who explained the problem as he watched the real MAS boat heaving and tossing as she crossed a rougher patch of water.

'In normal times the signal does remain the same for twenty-four hours,' Vosper told Johnson. 'But at difficult moments the signal can be changed unexpectedly as an added precaution. We use the same system ourselves.'

36

'And this,' Petrie informed Johnson, 'might just qualify as a difficult moment—with the enemy knowing that large amphibious forces are already at sea and an invasion pending. So don't bet on anything—'

'I just put my money back in my pocket.'

Sitting huddled on the floor with their backs pressed into the rear of the wheelhouse, Petrie and Johnson were probably more tense than either Vosper or the helmsman because they could see what was happening. All they could do was to watch Vosper's face caught in the moonlight and the naval officer's expression gave nothing away as they sat in their cramped position, their clothes pasted to their bodies, the pounding throb of the engines vibrating under them, the horizon only appearing briefly when the patrol-boat slipped deep into a fresh trough. Vosper straightened up, told the helmsman to maintain a steady course: the low silhouette of the real MAS boat was less than a quarter of a mile away when a lamp on board began flashing the recognition signal, a signal he watched carefully as he held the lamp ready to reply. For Petrie and Johnson it was an agonizing moment when Vosper told them what was happening because they had no way of knowing whether this was the signal expected. Petrie suddenly noticed a small detail. Vosper's forehead was filmed with sweat as he stood with a frown of concentration, and this could mean only one thing: he didn't recognize the signal being flashed to him. Palermo naval HQ had changed it since Scelba's man had sent the information; now Vosper would have no idea of the signal he was supposed to flash back. Petrie glanced at Johnson and guessed from his expression that he was experiencing the same pessimistic reaction. Then Vosper started flashing his own reply. When he had finished he waited with the lamp still rested on the window edge.

'OK?' Johnson called out softly.

'It was what I expected, but they may have changed only the answering signal, in which case their next action will be a shot through this wheelhouse.'

'And a happy birthday to you, too,' the American murmured.

The waiting period when the signalling had ended was worst of all, but then the nearby engine sound changed. 'It's all right,' Vosper told them casually, 'she's pushing off.' His voice changed, took on an edge as he spoke to the helmsman. 'Full speed ahead for Palermo!'

*　　　*　　　*

The prediction of the met officer in Tunis came true as the MAS boat sped in close to the mountainous shore: the sea became calmer and soon was no more than a gentle swell in the moonlight which had broken through the clouds, calm enough for Petrie to stand with Johnson on deck without holding the rail as he stared at an isolated peak in the night. 'There's Monte Pellegrino,' he remarked. 'You'll remember it from when you were last here.'

'I reckon I'm getting my bearings—Palermo's just east of it. Hey! What the hell are all those lights bobbing about over there?'

'The fishing fleet Scelba said would be outside Palermo harbour. They fish at night here and those

38

lamps are fixed to the prows of the boats—they attract the fish into their nets. I only hope to God that Guido's somewhere out there.'

They didn't say anything else as Vosper reduced speed and every revolution of the patrol-boat's engines took them nearer the coast, so that gradually the silhouette of the mountain grew larger, the bobbing lights came closer, and the nerves of the two watchers on deck tautened. They were approaching the high-risk phase for any landing party, the time when they moved within one mile of an enemy coast, and the gap between ship and shore was narrowing minute by minute. To avoid silhouetting themselves in their peasant clothes they crouched on the deck, resting on their haunches with their backs against the wheelhouse as the bobbing lights of the fishing fleet drifted towards them, orange lights, which looked strangely festive in the moonlight. 'So far, so good!' Johnson muttered the remark as he used his coat sleeve to wipe sweat from his forehead where it had begun to drip into his eyes. It was chilly on deck but the faces of both men were coated with perspiration as they waited, still no more than cargo to be delivered by Vosper to the appointed rendezvous with the mafia.

Petrie had made no reply to the hopeful comment, his eyes were scanning the undulating sea for any sign of another MAS boat. If they were challenged a second time it might not go so well: the enemy vessel would be able to examine them more carefully in these calmer seas and the scope for further deception would be greatly diminished. This was the period he feared most of all, the interval between coming in close and losing themselves among the fishing fleet. The engine-throbs slowed to a steady tom-tom beat. Vosper edged the patrol-boat towards the vessels strung out across the sea, saw one boat, its task completed, heading back for Palermo. So far none of them had shown the least interest in the familiar torpedo-boat chugging in their direction as though on routine patrol, and Petrie was waiting for one of the orange lamps to flash on and off four times, Guido's signal which would locate the position of his own craft. The lamps remained obstinately unblinking as Vosper leaned out of the wheelhouse and called quietly to Petrie in Italian, 'No sign of a welcome yet.'

'Nothing ever happens exactly as you expect,' Petrie replied calmly. He made a gesture to Johnson as he started moving to the rear of the wheelhouse. 'We'll get round to the port side ready to go overboard.'

Petrie and Johnson worked quickly, unfastening the cords which had secured the tarpaulin over the small fishing craft underneath. Above the throb of their engines and the slap of the waves against the hull, they could hear the doleful sound of the fishermen intoning a sea shanty while they hauled in their catch. As far as was known all the fishermen belonged to Scelba's *cosca*, the mafia 'union' which secretly controlled the fishing rights off the Sicilian coast despite the efforts of the *carabinieri* to destroy it. Under the pre-war direction of Moro, [Moro was the police chief sent with extraordinary powers to Sicily by Mussolini to curb the mafia.] the *carabinieri* had driven the mafia underground, but like an octopus it was still holding on with its tentacles under the surface,

40

fighting to retain its power over the local population. Vosper certainly didn't envy Petrie his job of dealing with these people.

The ropes for lowering the fishing craft over the side were already laid under the boat, and more men appeared as the craft was eased to the edge and then, under Petrie's guidance, lowered to the surface of the sea. It was a tricky operation because the MAS boat was still moving slowly in case a second enemy vessel appeared, observed what was happening and wirelessed Palermo. In that case the landing would have to be abandoned. The fishing craft slid gently into the sea, all ropes except one were released, and then Vosper changed course to take them close to the fleet. For a moment he left the wheel with a rating, stepping out to the port side to clap a hand on Petrie's shabby back as Johnson shouldered the sack containing the explosives and supplies. 'Good luck, Jim. There's been no signal from Guido, but I still think you'll make it.'

'This one we have to make,' Petrie replied quietly. 'And thanks for the ride . . .'

He followed the American down into the swaying fishing-boat where Johnson had dropped the sack and was fiddling with the motor controls. In less than a minute, still hauled along under the lee of the patrol-boat, their own motor ticked over gently and Vosper performed a delicate manoeuvre: he signalled to the rating crouched close to the wheelhouse and the man released the last rope. Petrie whipped the loose rope aboard, coiled it swiftly under the orange lamp he had lit at the prow while Johnson gripped the wheel as the crucial moment arrived. Moving slowly under their

41

own power, they watched the protective hull of the MAS boat sliding past them like a wall, then they were exposed to full view.

The nearest Sicilian vessel was less than a score of yards away. Men were crouched over its side as they hauled in a net, and their orange lamp tilted dangerously as the vessel heeled over under the weight of their catch. Vosper had contrived his departure so that he appeared to have slipped between two vessels of the fishing fleet—Petrie's and another—as he increased speed and the wake from his boat glowed whitely in the moonlight. They were completely on their own, less than half a mile from the enemy shore, coming in on the eastern fringe of the fleet.

'Slow her a bit, Ed,' Petrie whispered in Italian. 'We don't want to get too close until Guido's contacted us.'

'If Guido's here.'

'He'll be here.'

Petrie fell silent as he watched the nearest vessel where the crew was apparently absorbed in its task. They were not the most desirable of neighbours, these swarthy fishermen with bony faces and the look of men who would put a knife in your back for the price of a meal, and Petrie was still disturbed by the thought that Guido might have been caught. A sound made him turn his head quickly. As he looked, Johnson stiffened. 'What's the matter?'

'We have company—at the wrong moment.'

It was the sudden surge of power from Vosper's patrol-boat which warned him; the naval officer's burst of speed indicated that he had decided it might be a good idea to get to hell out of here. The wake of the retreating vessel surged in the

42

moonlight as Vosper continued his sweeping turn and then headed due north away from Palermo. The spur to this burst of speed was only too obvious: another MAS boat was rearing in from the east, heading directly for the fishing fleet. Petrie looked round quickly for any sign of one of the fishing craft approaching them; Guido, if he was there, had left the moment of contact too late. 'Ed, give me the Schnellfeur,' he snapped as he watched a fishing-boat edging towards them. Johnson held the wheel with one hand, dipped the other into the mouth of the sack, passed the gun to Petrie as the MAS boat thundered towards them.

*   *   *

The German Schnellfeur—fast-fire—Mauser 7.63-mm automatic is a deadly weapon which can be used either as a handgun or an automatic machine-pistol. It takes a twenty-round magazine and, when used as a handgun, is carried in a wooden holster. This curious choice of material for a holster is essential: for long-range employment the holster is clipped to the pistol butt and this provides a stock which is held against the shoulder so the user can lay down devastating fire over a considerable distance. With a little luck and a lot of skill it could decimate the crew aboard a patrol-boat. Praying that he wouldn't have to attempt that grim execution so close in to the coast, Petrie waited while the thunder of the MAS boat's engines grew louder and two fishing craft drifted towards them. At a word from Petrie, Johnson swung the wheel, slipped them between the fishing boats and inside the fleet. Something hard clanged down on their gunwale. Petrie gripped the weapon under his coat tightly as he stared at the boat-hook fastened to their side, then at the man holding it less than five feet away. The Sicilian's voice was throaty and urgent and he spoke in Italian. 'The catch is good tonight?' he asked.

'The catch is bad for July—enemy submarines disturb the waters,' Petrie replied, completing the password.

'I am Guido. Say nothing when the patrol-boat comes . . .'

Some signal must have been passed which Petrie didn't see—because without warning they were surrounded with fishing craft, lost inside a chaos of vessels as two men aboard Guido's boat manhandled a fishing net across the gap. Johnson, his engine stopped, grasped the net without hesitation and Petrie helped him to haul it into their boat. Chugging slowly, the MAS boat was now unceremoniously nosing its way in among the craft until its hull loomed above Petrie's boat and the commander appeared on deck with a loudhailer. The fishermen were muttering angrily at the intrusion as Petrie slipped his hand inside his coat again. This didn't look too promising: the machine-gun aboard the MAS boat was manned and other men on the deck above were armed with rifles. What the hell had made the commander suspicious? The Italian raised the loudhailer, bawled down through the instrument. 'Have you seen any sign of a British torpedo-boat tonight?'

'No! Only the other MAS boat!' Guido shouted back 'You are fouling our nets!'

'And you are too far out! Palermo does not permit fishing so far from the shore at present.'

44

'We go where the fish are! You want to eat in your mess, don't you?' Guido replied insolently.

'I shall report your conduct to harbour control!' the Italian commander snapped.

The MAS boat reversed out of the fishing fleet, turned to the west and sped out to sea as Petrie relaxed a little. So Guido had come out beyond the permitted limits to meet them; well, that was a little co-operation from Scelba he appreciated. He turned as the engine fired in the Sicilian's boat and Guido made a beckoning gesture shoreward. They were going in to Palermo at once, so soon they would face the next dangerous hurdle—the passage inside the heavily-defended harbour. It wasn't a prospect he looked forward to as Johnson started their engine and followed the Sicilian craft into the night.

For some reason the craft Vosper had seen heading for the shore was waiting a short distance away, but when Guido's boat moved south the lead vessel began moving again and behind them a group of boats followed in a huddle. There was some kind of plan here, Petrie felt sure, a plan which had doubtless originated in the devious brain of Vito Scelba. The Sicilians were chanting again, the sound of their doleful voices floating over a sea like black oil, a sea now as calm as a village pond, and Johnson found it hard to credit that only a short time ago they had been fighting for their lives in the storm. Petrie sat in the bows of the craft as the jetty wall came closer, a long high mole extending eastwards, and soon they were close enough for him to make out a gun position protected by sandbags, the helmeted silhouettes of the gunners, a marching sentry with rifle sloped. It looked as though they were going to get through.

Following Guido's example, Johnson reduced speed drastically so that they barely drifted forward under the lee of the jetty looming high above them. He was gazing hard at the Sicilian standing in his own vessel a few yards ahead; if trouble was coming they'd have a few seconds' warning from Guido's reaction. Petrie left the bows, came to stand beside Johnson. To enter Palermo harbour they had to sail past the jetty until they reached the entrance where a second shorter mole, farther in, projected out from the east, almost overlapping the outer jetty wall. It was very quiet as the vessels slid forward under the stone rampart. The engines chugged dully, water slapped against the stone Petrie could have reached out and touched, and the chanting had stopped abruptly. In front of them Guido was standing very stiffly, as though expecting something he didn't look forward to. 'Trouble with that chap,' Petrie whispered, 'is he hasn't learned to relax.'

'Relax! At a time like this . . .' Words failed Johnson who was gripping the wheel tightly, his body like drawn elastic as a faint creaking sound travelled over the water. The boom was being swung open to admit the fishing fleet inside Palermo harbour. As they passed the tip of the outer jetty Petrie glanced up and saw the long barrel of an ack-ack gun poked skywards above his head, then the end of the wall glided past and he saw inside the harbour, saw the ancient rooftops, the shadowed wharves below them. The tug which had swung open the boom was puffing smoke into the moonlight sky and they were turning to starboard, drifting in behind Guido and the craft just beyond him. To Johnson it all seemed a shade too easy, and he had reached the state where he dare not relax unless that should be the signal for disaster. The spotlight flashed on seconds later, a glaring light which lit up the entrance like day. Petrie swore inwardly, took a firm grip on the Mauser.

The spotlight was stationed at the tip of the inner mole, its beam projected downwards so every vessel would have to pass through its searching glow. And I'll bet these boys can count, Petrie thought grimly, count the same number of boats in as they let out. And we're one over. Probably they could even identify the occupants of the craft caught in that hideous glare they were drifting towards. The boat ahead of Guido was hardly moving as Petrie grasped the manoeuvre: the lead craft was waiting for Guido and their own vessel to come up behind them so they could move through the spotlight in a huddle. Glancing to the stern he saw other craft almost on top of them. Johnson also understood what was being attempted. 'Shall I speed up a little?' he asked.

'Maintain present speed,' Petrie murmured automatically: an increase in speed would draw attention to them. He looked quickly round the familiar anchorage, searching for warships, for troops on the dock-side, but the place seemed as quiet as he remembered it. As Johnson turned the wheel a fraction to take them alongside the *mafiosi* craft ahead Petrie murmured again. 'There's a machine-gun behind that lamp. If it opens up, swing hard to port and I'll deal with the spotlight . . .' They were creeping forward when two boats behind them speeded up, passed them to starboard, swung in ahead of Guido and into the spotlight flare. The men on board were clearly illuminated in the glare, Petrie noted grimly. Then they passed beyond it and something happened which only Scelba could have planned. The two boats collided with a heavy thud, there was a chorus of Sicilian oaths, a burst of angry shouting as though a fight had broken out.

The man behind the beam reacted instinctively, swivelled the light to his left to see what was going on, and while the spotlight centred on the collision Guido and Johnson drilled past the end of the mole with a huddle of other vessels close behind them. Realizing suddenly that he was missing the rest of the fleet, the Italian swivelled his beam back again. For seconds only it lingered on Petrie's boat and then switched to the craft behind, leaving them lit only by the glow of their own lamp. And I'll bet, Petrie told himself, that one of the fishing craft has been beached somewhere farther along the coast, so they'll count the same number in as they checked out. Scelba wouldn't forget a little detail like that. 'We're there,' he told Johnson as they cruised over the water in Guido's wake towards a deserted wharf. Johnson grunted; they were still inside the heavily-guarded harbour area. As they approached the wharf scum was thick on the surface and spars of wood floated in the discoloured water. There was a smell of stale oil in the night, a smell which mingled with the odour of rank fish. Guessing the American's reservations, Petrie explained a little further. 'I know this wharf, Ed. There's a subterranean passage underneath it which leads outside the harbour area.'

A heavy thud warned them that Guido had reached the wharf and then Johnson cut the engine

48

and let the natural motion take them forward until they thumped into the Sicilian's craft. They had arrived inside Sicily. The enemy had no hint of their presence. And within an hour they should have reached the underground headquarters of the mafia. Then, Petrie thought grimly, his battle with Vito Scelba would begin.

CHAPTER FOUR

Friday. 9 July—Before Dawn

Don Vito Scelba, the key man in the operation, the only man in Sicily in Petrie's view who could outwit the massive Italian-German forces, who could—if he would—take a sabotage team the breadth of the island and inside the fortress-like defences of Messina, knew within five minutes that the two Allied agents had landed at Palermo. The phone message from his *mafioso* stationed in a house overlooking the harbour was brief and cryptic. 'The grain has been delivered.'

'Thank you, Nicolo. Stay where you are.'

Scelba replaced the receiver, knowing that Nicolo would immediately leave the building as instructed. There must be no risk of anyone connected with this operation being seized by the *carabinieri*—and the *carabinieri* were tapping half the phones inside Palermo, these days in their frantic efforts to hunt down the mafia underground. Cupping his hand, he lit a dark cigar and stood motionless in the vast unfurnished room; until three days ago the *palazzo* which was his new

49

temporary headquarters had been the home of the Gonzagos, one of the wealthest families in Sicily. But now like so many others of their class they were gone, fleeing to the Italian mainland away from the endless assault of the Allied air forces.

Scelba was not as alone in the vast chandeliered chamber as it appeared; crouched low behind each of the tall windows overlooking an inner courtyard, *mafiosi* watched the darkness with shotguns in their hands; short, swarthy-faced men armed with the most diabolical weapons available on the island—*lupara*. The word had three meanings—denoting the ammunition, the gun, the way of death. Even in Sicily it was strictly illegal to dice up lead, to feed it inside cartridges, to load the horrible cartridges into a gun—but this was the staple ammunition of the mafia underground. In Sicily many died of the dreaded *lupara* sickness, a disease for which there was no known cure. The motionless figures by the windows of the unlit room waited while Scelba waited, lost in thought. This could be the most decisive moment in his long career, the turning-point he had waited for so many long, bitter years. Petrie had come back.

Signor Scelba knew more about the military record of Major James Petrie, DSO, than the wartime soldier would ever have suspected; he knew that Petrie was normally sent in to destroy vital objectives, that his recent eight-week stay on the island had been unusual inasmuch as he had simply acted as liaison officer between AFHQ and the mafia, and he had guessed correctly that the return of Petrie was for quite a different purpose. For one thing there had been the urgent radioed request for a car—with a full petrol tank. That suggested a long journey from Palermo and two possible destinations and objectives—the naval guns of Syracuse or the train-ferry, *Cariddi*, at Messina. His network of *mafiosi* agents spread throughout the island kept Vito Scelba well informed and he had heard of the near-desperate attempts of the Allies to sink the sole surviving train-ferry plying the Messina straits. Yes, it was probably one of these two cities Petrie would be heading for—Syracuse or Messina. And the AFHQ message, signed by Petrie himself, had further asked that he should be personally present when the two men from Tunis arrived. It was an interesting situation which might be capable of enormous exploitation.

Barely literate, a shepherd boy in his youth, Scelba had hoisted, bludgeoned and schemed his way up the mafia ladder until at twenty-five he became a *capo*, a chief of the hideous organization which 'protected' the poor of Sicily while they exploited them. As steward to a great landowner he had controlled the labour supply, tightening his grip over the people who worked for his employer. For those who cooperated with the mafia there was protection when they were in trouble; for the few who rejected his advances another kind of payment was meted out—a knife in the back in a dark alley, a draught of poison in a man's wine, or a shotgun blast in the face as he was walking home one night. Then Mussolini had seized power, and because fascism couldn't tolerate any other source of power, things had gradually changed for the mafia. In the late nineteen-thirties Moro had come to the island with his incorruptible policemen, a force specially picked to deal with the Sicilian scourge.

And Scelba had gone underground.

Scelba, who had no education, was a man of vision. He foresaw an Allied victory—because without that the fascist police would remain and there would be no future for the mafia—and in an Allied victory he saw a tremendous opportunity. For a re-birth of mafia power. For Vito Scelba. For a renewal of the mafia links with Naples and Marseilles—and with New York. Vito Scelba had a dream, a dream of a vast international system powerful enough to fight governments, even whole countries by organizing crime on a global scale; although the word 'crime' never entered his calculations. For Scelba everything was a matter of business. Strange to think that the one man who might help him to achieve his ambition was an Allied soldier who thoroughly mistrusted him. Scelba smiled grimly at the thought as he smoked his cigar behind his cupped hand. He would have to go down into the cellars soon but it was claustrophobic below and there was still time.

He checked his watch. A little after eleven. Petrie, he calculated, would arrive at midnight. Stubbing out the cigar under his boot, he picked it up again and slipped it into his pocket; there must be no trace left of their presence in this room. Before he went downstairs he looked about him curiously at the dimly-seen frescoed ceiling, at the gilt mirrors which lined the walls, at the expensive marble floor. Its luxury meant nothing to him. In his personal habits he was a simple man who needed only a roof to sleep under. Issuing a sharp order in Sicilian he went through the door which led towards the entrance to the cellars to wait for Petrie. The mafia boss who controlled the Palermo underground was already—preparing his ambush—the ambush for the post-war world.

*   *   *

'He's inside there? Are you sure?'

Petrie gripped Guido's arm, half-dragged him into a dark doorway off the deserted street while Johnson took up a position in front of them. They had come from the harbour area by an indirect route, threading their way through the network of alleys which honeycombed the Albergheria district, and twice they had almost run into large *carabinieri* patrols, while in the distance they heard constantly the rumble of Army vehicles. They were now on the fringe of the Albergheria and Petrie was staring at a *palazzo*, one of the great homes of Palermo. Behind stone walls elegant staircases curved upwards, reached a terrace, then curved up to a second terrace. The top of the main *palazzo* wall was decorated with statues, vague silhouettes which Petrie had momentarily mistaken for sentries looking down at them. 'Guido,' he said sharply. 'Scelba can't be inside there.' The Sicilian looked frightened at the open mention of the name, then protested.

'He is, *signore*. This is the Villa Gonzago—the family left for Naples a few days ago and the villa is empty. Quickly, we must not stay here! This way, *signore*!'

Guido was impatient to get away from the street and Petrie didn't blame him as they followed the Sicilian across a paved yard, through a gateway in a second stone wall which took them to the rear of the *palazzo*. It was pitch-dark now and they hadn't yet adjusted their night vision as Guido fumbled in his pocket and walked more slowly over a cobbled area so they could keep up with him. Reaching the wall of the *palazzo*, he thrust a key into a small wooden door, turned it, pushed the door inward. A torch flashed from the interior and by its light Petrie saw the ugly barrel of a shotgun aimed at Guido's throat. There was a brief exchange in Sicilian, a language so different from Italian that Petrie caught only a word here and there, then they were ushered inside a long passage. The Sicilian with the shotgun took the key from Guido, re-locked and bolted the door by the light the second *mafioso* was holding, and then led the way down the passage to the head of a flight of steps leading below.

*　　*　　*

'Welcome again to Palermo, Major Petrie!'

'There's a lot of activity outside, Signor Scelba,' Petrie said quickly as they shook hands. 'What's happening?'

They were thirty feet under the city, in the catacomb-like atmosphere of a large wine cellar lit by oil-lamps suspended from vaulted arches. There was a pungent aroma of sour wine in Petrie's nostrils, a feeling of damp and coolness on his cheek as the mafia chief courteously guided him to a plain wooden table in the centre of the cellar. 'You have come at a dangerous time,' Scelba warned him. 'General Bergoni is conducting a night exercise and there is a curfew throughout the city—but that is only a pretext. Later there will be a military sweep through one district. Houses will be

54

searched from top to bottom, people will be dragged out in the middle of the night. They are still looking for us, you see.'

'Which district?'

'San Pietro,' so I am informed.'

'Not the Albergheria?' Petrie persisted.

'No—unless they change their minds at the last moment as a security precaution.' Scelba regarded his guest with some amusement and Petrie suspected that once again the *capo* was emphasizing how much he risked by collaborating with the Allies. 'We will have some wine in a moment,' Scelba went on. 'As you can imagine, supplies are plentiful here . . .' Johnson was introduced by Petrie and then he took his place at the table while the other two men continued talking. The American had never met the mafia boss on his previous visit because Scelba rarely showed himself to Allied agents, but for the moment Johnson was studying the other occupants of the cellar who hardly attracted him as drinking companions. The five Sicilians sitting on the stones round the edges of the cellar were only half-visible in the glow from the oil-lamps, which was probably just as well. From what he could see Johnson summed them up as the scum of Palermo, grim-faced men in peasant clothes like his own, men who had been carefully picked to guard the mafia chief in his hideout, so it was more than likely that each man had already committed several murders by some foul means or other. They sat silently in the shadows, shotguns rested in their laps, and one individual who appeared to have lost an eye whiled away the time by picking at his teeth with the point of a broad-bladed knife. In his pre-war days along the Mexican border the American had encountered some unsavoury characters, but they were saints compared with this mob.

'Your health—and success to your enterprise, Captain Johnson,' Scelba toasted.

'Your own health!' The American raised the glass poured for him and drank cautiously. Scelba had sat down at the head of the table and for the first time Johnson could see him clearly. In his late fifties, the Palermo *capo* was an impressive figure even though dressed in shirt-sleeves and braces, a strong-featured Sicilian with a heavy jaw and eyes difficult to see behind a pair of tinted tortoiseshell glasses. Broad shouldered, the mafia chief was heavily built, but when he had received them standing up he was half a foot shorter than Petrie. Wiping sweat surreptitiously from his forehead with the back of his hand, Johnson was struck by the *capo*'s impassive manner, by the impression he gave of being in complete control of a dangerous situation as he sat with hands clasped on the bare table and a cigar between his thick lips. The tinted glasses made his eyes almost invisible and the American had the uncomfortable feeling that behind the lenses the eyes were assessing him, looking for weak points. Petrie put down his glass, glanced significantly at the *mafiosi* spread round the cellar walls. 'We haven't time to waste and I want to talk.'

Scelba spoke quickly in Sicilian, the men clambered to their feet, left the cellar by a second staircase which ran up behind where the *capo* was sitting. He waited until the thud of a closing door reached them and then looked at Petrie inquiringly. 'It is something very important that

56

brings you back to Sicily so soon?' he asked softly.

'What makes you think that?'

'Because of the vehicle your wireless message requested.'

'The car is ready for us?' Petrie asked the question to avoid answering the *capo*'s inquiry, to learn as much as he could before Scelba began his devious bargaining session.

'No, there has been an accident.'

'Good God! The arrangement was that you would have transport waiting for us. And with a full petrol tank.'

'The arrangement?' Scelba settled himself back in his chair and spoke with the cigar in his mouth. 'There has been no arrangement yet! Your message requested a vehicle and I simply acknowledged receipt of that message. And a full petrol tank also?' There was a hint of irony in the Sicilians tone which irritated Johnson, but Petrie seemed insensitive to the *capo*'s manner as their host continued. 'Has your military command not heard that there is severe petrol rationing here?'

'Get it on the black market then,' Petrie told him brusquely. 'We know who controls that in Palermo.'

Johnson intervened, feeling that Petrie was going too far. 'We really do need to leave Palermo at the earliest possible moment,' he explained. The Sicilian turned to him, as though suddenly aware that he was still there, and a mocking note crept into his voice.

'Captain Johnson a vehicle was ready for you up to five hours ago, then the *carabinieri* raided the garage where it was waiting and confiscated it for their own use.'

'So you've found another for us,' Petrie assumed

with deliberate confidence.

'You have great faith in me—considering the difficulties we work under here,' Scelba observed. 'I hope that AFHQ realize that we take our lives in our hands every hour we collaborate with you, that the authorities are intensifying their efforts to hunt us down, that our families are always at risk . . .'

Something in the Sicilian's tone alerted Petrie. 'How is Signora Scelba?' he inquired.

'She is no longer in Palermo. I have sent her away to Catania together with my son.' Scelba paused, emphasizing how critical the situation had become, but the information interested Petrie: had the Sicilian already guessed the service they might ask him to perform, sending away his family to ensure their safety during his absence? The next words were more encouraging. 'My own car will be at your disposal . . .'

'Now?'

'As soon as it has been repaired. Men are working through the night to get it ready . . .'

'Through the night? When the devil will it be ready?' Petrie demanded. 'We planned to leave Palermo within the next hour.'

'Impossible! It will not be ready until dawn. It will wait for us at a crossroads in the country outside the city—driving through Palermo at the moment is too risky.'

'Dawn is too late, far too late . . .'

'You will manage, Major Petrie! You will have to, I fear, because the car will not be ready earlier. You are going a long distance?'

'Why do you assume that?'

'Because of the full petrol tank you asked for.' Scelba spread his hands apologetically. 'And I have

58

distressing news, I regret to say. Your wireless operator, Sergeant Fielding, was killed earlier this morning while trying to escape the *carabinieri* on his way to the transmitter.' Scelba saw the alarm in Johnson's face and understood it. 'He was wearing peasant clothes like yourselves and he carried nothing which would identify him.'

Petrie lit a cigarette while he assessed the situation. The news was not good. With poor Fielding gone he would have to plant the explosive charges inside the belly of the train-ferry himself, which left them one man short. And the delay in their departure until dawn was little short of catastrophic with the midnight deadline, which would give them only nineteen hours to drive from Palermo to Messina, to penetrate the waterfront defences and get on board the target. It meant that Scelba simply had to come with them, to get them there in record time. He decided to dispense with the verbal skirmishing and dive straight in. 'Signor Scelba, we're here to hit a major target in Messina. I want you to drive us there yourself—or at least act as guide. We're going by the inland route—via Scopana.'

'Impossible!' Scelba appeared astounded. 'Messina is at the other end of the island! The inland route is very difficult. I might just be able to provide one of my men as a guide . . .'

'No!' Petrie rapped his empty glass on the table. 'Not one of your men—you! You are the only man in Sicily I can rely on to get us through.'

'It is impossible,' Scelba repeated. 'I must remain here to perfect the organization for when you make the big landing.'

'You've done that already.' Petrie's tone was

equally uncompromising. 'AFHQ think the greatest service you can render us now is to take us to Messina—we have to be inside the docks before midnight tomorrow.'

Scelba grunted with unconcealed sarcasm. 'That is the most heavily-defended area on the island.' He prodded his cigar at Petrie. 'And the Germans are there in force—you cannot bluff them. To get you inside the docks is not possible . . .'

'Not for a man who controls the waterfront mafia?' Petrie inquired quietly.

'You ask me to risk my life . . .'

'You've been doing that ever since you started gathering information on troop movements for us.'

'But not with a mad risk like this one! It is hundreds of kilometres to Messina by the inland route. Every kilometre could be our last, every corner a deathtrap . . .'

'But you'll come with us?'

'No!' Scelba paused. looked at Petrie over the end of his cigar. 'Even if you promised to make me prefect of Palermo province after the Allies have landed.'

There it was; the bargaining counter was on the table. Petrie carefully said nothing as the Sicilian refilled their glasses. They had come to grips and the mafia boss had shown them a glimpse of his ace card: appoint him prefect and he would—reluctantly—take them to Messina. After a hell of a lot of haggling. Since AFHQ would never stand for it, the problem was to persuade him to settle for the lesser post of mayor of Palermo city. And despite what Petrie had asserted at the Tunis conference he couldn't be sure that the *capo* would agree. 'There's no question of my people offering you a prefecture,' he said brutally. 'If that's what you want, forget it.'

'Then you must forget your operation.'

'I'll get there without you, for Christ's sake!' Petrie blazed with assumed temper. 'Just give us the car and the petrol and we'll make it on our own.'

'Not by midnight! You do not know the way . . .'

'I have a map,' Petrie snapped. 'We came prepared for the chance that you'd be bloody-minded.'

'He has a map!' Scelba's broad shoulders shook with merriment. His knuckled hand tapped the table genially. 'You should try it on your own! Try to find the track they call a road in that country. You will be lost within two hours . . .' He stopped speaking and stared with the cigar in his mouth as Petrie pushed his chair back slowly from the table prior to standing up as he gazed grimly at the *capo*.

'When I get back to AFHQ I take it I'm to report that you refused to cooperate with us?'

'Perhaps you should say "if I get back",' Scelba observed ominously.

'I'm to report your absolute refusal to help us?' Petrie repeated.

'You can hardly do that if I supply the car and the petrol.'

'We need you as well—you've admitted that yourself. As far as I can see, you've just lost any hope you had of getting an official position in the Allied administration of Sicily.'

Johnson winced inwardly at the assertion. From his previous experience with the mafia along the Mexican border he knew that the organization placed a high value on what they termed 'respect'

61

when negotiating; so far Petrie had not shown the slightest consideration for this attribute; and Johnson was now wondering what their chances were of leaving the wine cellar alive. Scelba regarded them thoughtfully over his cigar, showing not the least trace of resentment at what had just been said. 'It is always possible that the Germans will throw you back into the sea,' he said with a faint sneer. 'Where am I then?'

'Nowhere!' Petrie didn't mince his words. 'The *carabinieri* are already intensifying their search for you—if we lose, you're dead, Scelba. If we win, you're on top of the world. From where I sit I can't see you have any choice—but that's for you to decide.'

'You make it sound good, but you have nothing specific to offer me.'

'I didn't say that!'

'Didn't you?' Scelba leaned his elbows on the table and his near-opaque glasses gave him a sinister look. They were close to the crunch now, Petrie realized, close to the point where he must make his firm offer, but it was important to get the timing right, to convince the Sicilian that he could not bid them up higher. Beyond the oil-lamp glow alcoves led off from the cellar, alcoves where other *mafiosi* could be hiding in case the *capo* decided to terminate the whole business with a blast from their shotguns. It was an unlikely outcome, but the mafia was completely unpredictable and Petrie felt he was sitting on a stick of gelignite.

'You are prepared to make a definite offer?' the *capo* asked after a long wait.

'Yes.'

'If I send someone else, someone very reliable . . .'

'No! In that case, forget it. And we'll attempt it on our own.'

'You are blackmailing me,' the Sicilian said softly. 'I have supplied vital information about troop movements on which you have based your invasion plans . . .'

'Other agents have supplied valuable data from other parts of the island.'

'I was under the impression that I was more than an agent . . .'

'That depends on how you react now.'

'You are a difficult man, Major Petrie. I can see why they sent you to Sicily . . .'

'They knew I had to deal with you!' Petrie smiled for the first time since he had entered the cellar and a wisp of a smile appeared on the *capo*'s facc.

'I hear no offer yet,' he commented.

'You would be appointed mayor of Palermo the moment the Allies gain control of western Sicily.'

'That is nothing . . .'

Petrie exploded. 'You know damned well, Scelba, that it's a great deal! It gives you the top position of power in your homc city. It gives you control of Palermo . . .'

'I am Palermo already.'

'Then drive us out of the city instead of sneaking your car to some obscure crossroads!'

Scelba stared hard at Petrie who again showed amusement; this was the moment for friendliness, for easing the tension out of the atmosphere, because pride is precious to the mafia, and Petrie sensed that he mustn't drive the old ruffian too far. Instead, he kept up the momentum of his attack in a different way. 'You've got what you've been after ever since we first came here,' he went on. 'You played for high stakes—and you've won. I'm damned if I'd have given you the job, Vito, however badly we needed you.'

'Ah! A reluctant emissary!' The *capo* allowed a little of his own rough humour to show. 'You have, of course, offered very little, but because of my fellow feeling for the Allies, I will accept . . .'

'It's conditional on your taking us to Messina.'

'That I shall attempt to do.' Scelba became brisk and businesslike. 'We must leave here two hours before dawn to get to the crossroads by then. But first, you must eat. There will only be pasta and wine, but it fills the stomach . . .'

The food was brought by a peasant woman from another cellar and Petrie, schooled by long experience of interrupted meals, ate quickly, whereas Johnson took his time, possibly because he found the return of Scelba's *mafiosi* to join them didn't increase his appetite. The American was developing a shut-in feeling cooped up inside the cellars far below Palermo, a sensation of being caught in a trap, and the dark, evil faces round the table did nothing to raise his spirits as he ate stolidly at the pasta which wasn't properly cooked. He was only halfway through his meal when Carlo, Scelba's nephew, burst in on them with his urgent warning.

*   *   *

He came running into the cellar, a large, hungry-looking peasant whom Petrie instantly mistrusted, followed by the men who had earlier admitted the two soldiers. He began talking without ceremony, and Scelba frowned as the words tumbled out between gasps for breath. '*Signore*, the *carabinieri* are coming—hundreds of them. They have tanks and armoured cars and they have surrounded the Albergheria, They are searching everywhere . . .'

'When did the operation start?' the *capo* demanded calmly.

'Over an hour ago.'

'You took all that time to get here?' The mafia boss drank from his glass and something in his manner told Petrie that he intensely disliked his nephew. It was nothing obvious; outwardly Scelba retained his normal air of impassive self-control, and the dangerous news Carlo brought appeared not to have disturbed him at all, but during his earlier eight-week stay on the island Petrie had come to know the *capo* well, and now he even wondered whether the *capo* believed Carlo.

'It was difficult, Don Scelba,' the nephew rattled on. 'I was almost caught myself—there are so many of them. Never before have I seen this number of troops inside the city. They have thrown an iron ring round the Albergheria—no one can escape . . .'

'Then we shall not try. We will wait here until they have passed over our heads.'

Petrie had the impression that the reply hadn't satisfied the new arrival. Twisting his cap in his hands, Carlo hesitated as he darted another glance in the direction of the two strangers sitting close to Scelba. Petrie was watching Carlo closely, wondering why he was in such a nervous state. And his nervousness was infecting the other men in the cellar—several *mafiosi* were looking at Scelba as though hoping for an order to evacuate the place.

If we're not careful, Petrie thought grimly, this nasty piece of work is going to start a panic. Standing more erect, the nephew began speaking again. 'They are searching everywhere. They will be here within half an hour, perhaps even sooner. They have sent men inside Count Lucillo's palace so they are bound to come here . . .'

'Calm yourself, my friend,' Scelba told him. 'It is most unusual to see you in this state.' He considered for a moment, staring at his nephew through his dark lenses as the man shifted his feet uncomfortably. 'In fact, I do not remember ever seeing you like this before. Is there something else worrying you, Carlo?' he inquired softly.

'What else could there be, *signore*?'

'That is what I am asking you.'

'I am frightened for your safety, Don Scelba. If you stay, I am sure they will find you . . .'

'So you brought your own friends to protect me?' In the passage which led back to the rear of the *palazzo* something stirred and Petrie stiffened as he noticed two things at once: Scelba's right hand was lolled over the edge of the table and below it in his lap rested a large revolver which had not been there earlier; and in the passage several new figures had appeared, Sicilians who carried guns. The situation was more serious than he had realized. Putting his hand over his mouth he whispered to Johnson, 'Under the table, Ed, if anything breaks . . .' The nephew screwed up his cap tighter.

'They came with me to make sure I reached you . . .'

'I find your concern for my welfare most touching. Are you staying with us, Carlo?' Scelba

66

inquired pleasantly.

'I must go to my house. My wife . . . you understand?'

'Of course, Carlo. It was good of you to come and warn me.' Scelba was at his most amiable as he stood up to shake hands, slipping the revolver on to the chair, repeating that he would remain in the cellar until the alarm was over. Carlo cast another glance at the strangers, refused Scelba's offer of a glass of wine, and went back hurriedly down the passage with his men. The *mafiosi* still in the cellar relaxed, lowered the weapons they had casually turned in the direction of the passage, looked to Scelba for instructions.

'This nephew of yours,' Petrie asked quickly, 'he's a member of the organization?'

'Of course!' Scelba was imperturbable as he finished his wine. 'Now, we will leave at once for the crossroads! With this military sweep in progress we shall have to move more carefully. You are ready?' He was staring at Johnson's half-eaten pasta.

'Not very hungry tonight for some reason,' the American told him lightly. 'I'm ready.'

'We get out through the cellars?' Petrie inquired as he stood up and watched Scelba pocket his revolver without comment.

'No, the *carabinieri* will search them. But do not worry—we are going out over the rooftops of Palermo. We shall be at the crossroads by dawn.'

CHAPTER FIVE

Friday. 5 AM–9.30 AM

The crossroads was rutted and gouged where carts had changed direction, a junction where roads little more than mule tracks dropped steeply between stone walls to the intersection and then sheered up again from the bowl buried among barren hill slopes. Petrie flashed his torch on an ancient signpost which leaned at a drunken angle. Southeast to Petralia and Scopana, the direction they were to have taken; northwest to Palermo, from where they had come; northeast to Cefalù, west of the point where Lawson had made his abortive landing; and southwest to Sciacca on the southern coast. What the devil had happened to Scelba's car? He switched off the torch and stood listening with his head on one side as Scelba came down the verge behind them. He heard only the enormous silence of early morning; no dawn birdsong, because in the wilderness of the Sicilian interior nothing grows so there is nothing to keep the creatures of the air alive. It was almost too quiet.

'The local cab service must be on strike,' Johnson commented.

'It must be here somewhere,' Scelba growled as he stared into the half-light with the revolver in his hand. He's not showing it, but he's bothered, Petrie thought. The car should have been where he could see it. A dozen yards above them was a wide gap in the stone wall they had passed on their way down

68

to the crossroads. It was the only possible place where the vehicle could have been hidden and Petrie told them he was going back to have another look at that gap. Scelba followed closely at his heels and now, as they walked on the road, their boots scuffed up dust from its appalling surface. Petrie approached the gap cautiously, the Mauser in his hand as he peered round the end of the wall. The dark silhouette of a small car, a Fiat, was parked close to the inner side of the wall a short distance away, and so far as Petrie could see it was empty. 'Take care,' Scelba whispered in his ear. 'One of my men should be waiting with it . . .'

'There's no one there.'

'Then be very careful!'

Twenty yards beyond the gap a hill slope climbed steeply up from a shadowed gash which Petrie guessed was a ravine. There was no sign of life anywhere but he wasn't relying on eyesight in this treacherous light to detect the presence of someone else, someone who might be waiting for them, using the parked car as bait. Motioning to the Sicilian to keep perfectly still, he listened again. There was something wrong here: he sensed it. 'Wait here,' he whispered and started moving along the inner side of the wall, crouched low to make as small a target as possible. He was walking on tufts of grass, shrivelled-up vegetation which had been burned to a whiskery texture by the sun of many weeks, and he was careful not to make a sound as he crept closer to the apparently empty vehicle.

Reaching the Fiat, he squeezed himself into the space between wall and car, peered in at the back and front. Empty. On the surface everything appeared to be fine: they had their transport and now all they had to do was to get inside, start the engine, back it out of the field and take the road for Scopana. Obvious. A shade too damned obvious. He went back the way he had come, found Scelba crouched behind the wall with the revolver held in front of him. 'Your car's a grey Fiat? Well, that's it, but the chap who was supposed to wait hasn't. Could he have taken fright, run off before we got here? It's not a very cheerful place to hang around.'

'Pietro would wait! There is something peculiar here.'

'You could be right, so we'd better find out what it is.'

With Scelba he searched quickly in the vicinity of the car and found nothing. Even in Sicily it was cold at this hour and the chill penetrated Petrie's coat as they went on searching and came close to the shadowed gash. The ravine was about ten yards wide and deeper than he had expected, at one point a sheer drop to a depth of close on thirty feet to a dried-up riverbed below. Moving along the brink of the drop, Petrie stopped frequently to stare into its depths while distant peaks became clearer, sharp-edged with rugged summits as the dawn spread. The growing light also penetrated the ravine and Petrie had returned to the point where it dropped away vertically when he stopped, grasping Scelba's arm. 'Do you see that dark heap at the bottom? It could be a man.'

'We should leave soon,' Scelba warned. 'There has been a lot of army traffic recently along this road from Palermo to Cefalù.'

'Your last report mentioned it, but I don't like mysteries. We can get down into the defile a bit farther on here.'

They scrambled down a zig-zag path which might have worried a goat, but despite his heavy build the mafia boss again showed great agility, propelling himself from boulder to boulder like a man half his age. Earlier Petrie had been surprised at the *capo*'s athletic ability when he had led them over the crumbling rooftops of Palermo, an obstacle course which only a man with unusual reflexes could have managed. They reached the base of the defile together. At the bottom Petrie, still fearing a trap, hauled out the Mauser before he began walking along the ravine. He paused as he reached a corner of rock where the river turned, listened again, then went forward a few paces and stopped. Spread over a boulder lay the body of a man in peasant clothes, staring sightless at the sky. It was hardly surprising: no one could survive a fall from such a height, smashing straight down on to solid rock. Petrie stood aside to give the *capo* a better view; Scelba bent down with pursed lips, then glanced up. 'Yes, this is Pietro, the man who brought the car. He knew this area so he should not have fallen . . .' Bending down beside Scelba, Petrie levered the body gently over so it lay on its face. The haft of a broad-bladed knife protruded from the back just below the left shoulder.

'That's why he fell,' Petrie said softly. 'Or else he was pushed over the edge afterwards. Is your nephew, Carlo, handy with a knife?'

'Carlo?' Scelba looked sharply at Petrie. 'Why do you think of him?'

'Because I spent eight weeks over here and got to know something of Sicilian ways. How old is that son of yours you sent away to Catania?'

71

'Seventeen. But I do not see . . .'

'I do—and I think you do as well. Carlo looked about twenty-four, I reckon. And I also saw him arrive in that cellar with a bunch of his own bully-boys. I think, Scelba, he hoped to find you alone, and in that case there'd have been an accident—and you'd have been the accident. When he saw you were well guarded he tried to scare you out into the streets where you'd run slap into a *carabinieri* patrol. I think this is a typical mafia situation—Carlo thinks he's ready to take over your position, and he's lying to eliminate you. Personally, knowing you, I feel sorry for him. What are you waiting for, Scelba,' Petrie asked shrewdly, 'the right opportunity to eliminate him?'

'I may talk about this later.' The *capo* stood up, stared at the sky which was now a pearl-grey colour. 'But I think the time has come to leave here quickly.'

They went back along the silent ravine, climbed the zig-zag, and when they reached the top it was broad daylight. Johnson stood up from behind the wall as they arrived and when Petrie told him what they had found he gave a noiseless whistle. Hoisting the sack over his shoulder, he followed Petrie to the car while Scelba stayed by the gap to keep an eye on the road. 'So someone bumped off the guard but left the car conveniently parked for us to drive off in,' the American speculated. 'It doesn't make too much sense when you remember they could easily have tipped the Fiat into the ravine as well.'

'Which happens to be the same thought that occurred to me. I wouldn't start that engine if I were you, Ed.'

While Johnson dumped the sack in the back of the vehicle, Petrie examined the bonnet carefully for tell-tale wires, for any evidence of a booby-trap. Finding nothing, he dropped to the ground and wriggled his way under the chassis where he examined the underparts of the Fiat with the aid of his torch. He had no time to waste on checking; they were already four vital hours behind schedule; and Brigadier Dawnay would undoubtedly have been foaming at the mouth could he have seen what was happening. But it was this kind of precaution which kept Petrie alive over the past three years and he wasn't changing his habits now. Crawling out from under the car, he shook his head at Johnson's unspoken question, went back to the bonnet, took hold of the handle and turned it slowly.

Checking for booby-traps was always a nerve-wracking business: the constant fear was that some joker had come up with something new, had hit on some fresh technique for blowing you sky-high, a technique you would only discover when the charge detonated. Lifting the bonnet cautiously he almost laughed; not that it was very funny. They had used the oldest trick in the book—a stick of gelignite was wired up to the ignition system. It would still have killed everyone inside the car had they started it without checking. 'Ed, get me a pair of pliers out of that toolkit under the driver's seat—then go and fetch Scelba. He's going to talk before we leave here.'

Johnson took a quick look at the obscene cylinder before he went back to find the *capo*. 'Cosy neighbours they have in these parts,' he commented. Petrie cut the connecting wires carefully, lifted out the stick and placed it in a gully some distance from the vehicle. The gelignite showed signs of 'sweating', which meant it was in an unstable condition. He pointed to it as Scelba walked across to him slowly and then looked down through his tinted glasses. 'A birthday present from Carlo? Or is there someone else who can't wait to see you six feet under? It's your car, remember, that was wired so it would go up like a bomb the moment the ignition fired.'

'Carlo, I regret,' the *capo* explained quietly, 'is collaborating with the *carabinieri*. He does not realize that I know this and I have permitted him to live because a known traitor can be useful—you can feed to him what you wish the enemy to know . . .'

He stopped talking as Petrie, grim-faced, strode quickly back to the Fiat. The old bastard was lying in his teeth, he wouldn't let an outsider hear of any domestic dispute; it was all part of the mafia code, omertà, the code of strict silence the Honoured Society preserved towards the outside world no matter what vendetta they might conduct among themselves. As he got behind the wheel Scelba clambered in beside him, as calm as if they were setting off for a peacetime drive in the country. At least the old villain didn't scare easily, Petrie thought, as he started the car and backed it towards the gap in the wall, but he would have liked to know how many men Carlo could muster in an emergency. Not that there was much danger of further trouble from that quarter; for one thing, when they'd passed the crossroads there were three alternative routes the Fiat could have taken. He stopped to let Johnson get in at the back, then drove down towards the crossroads.

Early morning mist was beginning to fade as the sun, still invisible behind the mountains, climbed higher and the lower flanks of rugged summits came into view through a gap in the hills. Petrie drove over the crossroads, changed gear, started up a steep, winding hill between high stone walls which would eventually lead them to Scopana. Blast the mafia! They were positively medieval; even close relatives were prepared to knife one another in the back in their greed for power. In the back of the car Johnson sat with his revolver in his lap and the sack of explosives on the seat next to him while he stared out of the window on his left. Climbing sharply, they were coming to another gap in a wall, a place where stones without mortar or sealing of any kind had collapsed inwards, and the American hoped that this would give him a view across country. As they passed the gap he twisted his head, had a glimpse of the lonely crossroads a long way down, then stiffened as he saw a peasant on horseback staring up from behind the wall which bordered the road to Cefalù. It was only a glimpse but he had time to see the mounted peasant turn away, start riding off at speed as the car went on uphill.

'We've been spotted,' he shouted. 'There was a peasant on horseback near the crossroads. I think he was watching for us—he started riding off like hell towards Cefalù!'

'That's helpful,' Petrie commented. He glanced at Scelba. 'Now they know which way we're going so you'd better talk—if you want to stay alive.'

'I think we must prepare ourselves for trouble,' the *capo* informed them calmly. 'Carlo has a few friends and somewhere ahead they may try to

75

ambush us.' He took his revolver from his coat pocket and laid it in his ample lap. 'He wishes to kill me, of course, but since you are with me he will have to try and kill you also. It looks as though I may have to attend to my little domestic squabble before I get back to Palermo!

'How many friends?' Petrie asked tersely.

'A few . . .' Scelba made a vague gesture with the cigar he had extracted from his case. 'Do you mind if I smoke, gentlemen?' Petrie said nothing as they came close to the crest of the long hill; he was recalling something the *capo* had said earlier about the journey across Sicily. *Every kilometre could be our last, every corner a death-trap . . .*

*   *   *

The sun had climbed well clear of the horizon as they came over the hill and beyond the crest the road forked—left to Scopana, right to Sciacca on the southern coast. Petrie took the left fork and the bright orb of the ascending sun caught him briefly in the eyes. The sun was an old enemy he respected and feared. In Crete, in the Greek islands, above all in the Libyan desert during his early infantry days he had come to know the sun as the deadliest enemy of all. Another day had started, another fifteen hours when the sun would slowly wheel higher, scorching the tortured landscape with its burning rays, drying up the already parched earth a little more until, with no moisture left, the baked ground began to crack open under the pitiless glare as it was cracking open on the hill slope ahead of them.

'If we run into a *carabinieri* patrol, Scelba,' Petrie

began, 'do you think they'll recognize you?'

'After we have driven half an hour, I do not think so. We move away from Palermo province into a new military zone.'

'If we do run into one you'd better do the talking. How are you going to explain us?'

'It is simple.' Scelba waved his cigar. 'I am taking you to my cousin's place in Scopana for you to do a job. What papers are you carrying?'

'They show we're from Taranto in Italy—that will get over any difficulty about our not speaking Sicilian. The identity papers were produced by an expert and they'll pass inspection, so you don't have to worry about that. And we're stone-masons—the sack on the back seat contains our tools.'

'Let us hope they do not ask to look inside the sack! As stone-masons you are perfect. Since the bombing there has been a great demand for your profession over here.'

'That's why we chose it. This damned road isn't getting any better.'

'This is nothing,' Scelba assured him genially. 'Farther on it becomes really bad. You must both realize that we have a very long journey ahead of us . . .'

They drove on across a vast tableland hemmed in by distant hills like frozen waves, and gradually it became warmer and the warmth started to fill the interior of the car. Scelba was the only man who had foreseen the necessity for divesting himself of his jacket and soon the other two men were in their shirtsleeves as the air inside the vehicle became stuffier and the sun wheeled higher. It was still not hot, but unlike North Africa the atmosphere here

77

was humid and Petrie, his hands gripping the wheel tightly, found he was licking his lips. From a brief motion of Scelba's head he realized that the *capo* had seen him and understood that the first ill-effects were beginning to show. They were in the heart of the tableland now. Ahead the land was scrub and rock and burnt-out moorland, a desolation which looked completely waterless. The track began turning and twisting among huge boulders, some of them almost crag-sized, so that Petrie was perpetually swinging the wheel this way and that when he wasn't struggling to extricate the vehicle from some deep rut.

But above all else it was the dust which made their lives a misery, and dust was an insoluble problem. It lay so densely upon the evil road—and they were compelled to move at such a low speed—that the front wheels churned up clouds of the grey powder and plastered a film over Petrie's windscreen, gradually obliterating his view so that his first intimation that a deep rut lay ahead was liable to be when his wheels met it. Half a mile away a fresh cloud of dust was rising as a group of horsemen galloped over the tableland in an easterly direction, the way they were going. The *capo* dropped his hand on the butt of his revolver as Petrie called out, 'See them Ed?'

'There's another lot to the right,' Johnson replied bleakly.

To the south, again about half a mile away, more horsemen were racing forward on a parallel course with the other group, sending up great clouds of dust as they thundered eastward at far higher speed than Petrie could drive as he crawled round the boulders. The threat was obvious and unnerving:

78

Petrie had no doubt that the horsemen were Carlo's friends, that they were riding ahead to organize an attack on the Fiat, that the attack could only be a matter of time, and it could be significant that they were coming to the end of the tableland. Less than half a mile ahead the ground was rising, climbing up past a series of fantastic crags which loomed enormously in the gathering heat haze, and beyond the crags huge yellowish cliffs stood against the glowing sky. The trap would be sprung somewhere there amid the wilderness. 'Ed, get the waterbottle out of the sack—we're rationing ourselves to one mouthful apiece. Those horsemen are Carlo's, I take it, Scelba?'

'It seems likely.' Scelba had taken off his glasses to wipe them with a soiled handkerchief. 'I am sure you will find a way of dealing with the problem.'

'A few, you said!' Johnson snapped from the back of the car. 'I counted nearly twenty of them!'

'You have that automatic German gun with you, Major Petrie,' Scelba observed as he replaced his glasses. 'Those men will be armed only with shotguns, revolvers and knives.'

Petrie looked at him. 'So a little matter of being outnumbered by seven to one needn't worry us at all? Is there some particular place ahead where they're likely to wait for us?'

'I think there is, yes. When we come near those cliffs the road will climb, then drop inside a gorge. The far end of the gorge is where I would set a trap if I were in their shoes.'

'How long is that gorge?'

'Less than two kilometres.'

'About a mile. Any way round it?'

'No.

Lovely, Petrie thought, just lovely. He'd come prepared to elude Italians and Germans and now the first enemy they had to confront head-on was a pack of dissident *mafiosi*. And there was irony in the situation: Scelba was supposed to help them, but now they were going to have to help Scelba if they wanted to escape with their lives and get the job done. He took the bottle Johnson handed him drank a mouthful, passed it to Scelba. The water tasted stale, like mineral water gone flat. Through the growing heat, the drifting dust, he drove closer to the crags, and in a quarter of an hour the yellowish cliffs loomed above them as the track began to climb, leaving the boulders as it ascended the rocky slope. Through the open window the dust enveloped the interior, filming the seats, coating the backs of moist hands, clinging to sweat-stained faces. Johnson could even taste dust and his mouth was parched and gritty as he stared anxiously at the cliff-top. He saw the big horseman a few seconds later, the figure of a large Sicilian wearing a peasant cap and perched motionless on his horse at the cliff edge. 'Jim, there's someone up there!'

'It is Carlo,' Scelba said quietly. 'All right, Carlo, do not get impatient. We are coming.'

*   *   *

As they drove down into the gorge the cliff walls on both sides closed round them, shutting out the sun's glare as they moved into the shadow. Mounted Sicilians, armed with rifles or shotguns, lined both cliff-tops as they rode slowly along the rim over a hundred feet above where the Fiat was crawling among the rocks. With their straw hats and their weapons they looked like bandits, and there was something eroding to the nerves the way they rode on, deliberately keeping pace with the car, eight men on the northern cliff, over a dozen on the other. 'Carlo has a lot of friends,' Petrie observed.

'They are all up there.' The *capo*'s tone was contemptuous. 'I have more men than that along the Messina waterfront.'

'Glad to hear it. We'll be needing them later.'

'Nice to hear there's going to be a "later",' Johnson said with mock pessimism, but inwardly he wondered as he stared up at the slow-moving files. 'Why the hell are they drifting on like a funeral procession?'

'It is Carlo's way of showing that an execution is planned,' Scelba explained. 'He is paying me his respects.' He lifted the revolver in his lap. 'If he comes close enough, I will pay him mine.'

They drove on and on as the gorge, no more than two hundred yards wide, curved one way and then the other through the shadows while above them the files of horsemen plodded forward at an even pace like an escort. The crisis, Petrie was convinced, would come near the end of the defile where, according to the map, the cliffs sloped downwards and the assault could be launched from both sides. For the moment they could only crawl on through the endless gorge, but now Petrie was staring ahead through the windscreen, watching for the wedge of sky between the rock walls which would warn him they were approaching the exit. He checked the milometer. They had travelled over a kilometre since entering the gorge, over two-thirds of a mile, so they were getting close to it. As

81

he turned the wheel he saw the file of horsemen on the southern cliff still plodding forward and evenly spaced out, but some of them were missing, must have ridden on ahead. He thrust his head out of the window, looked up at the northern face. Some missing there, too. 'Ed, in a minute I'm going to pull up and get out—you take over the wheel. I'm going ahead on foot to see what they've cooked up for us. We've got to know what they're planning before it happens.'

'They'll see you . . .'

'Maybe not.' Petrie pulled up, left the engine running. 'Ed, give me the Mauser—I'll leave you the Glisenti revolver. Some of those horsemen have disappeared, and I think I can persuade the rest of them to perform the same vanishing trick. When I've left the car I want you to drive on at the same speed. Ready?'

Stepping out of the car, he aimed the Mauser at the cliff-top, heard a distant cry, and the horsemen vanished. When he swung round to stare up at the southern face that was also deserted. As Johnson jumped in behind the wheel Petrie ran towards the northern cliff, and when he was close to the rock wall he began running along underneath it. In the middle of the gorge Johnson was driving the Fiat at minimum speed, threading his way among the rocks, and Petrie was counting on the sound of the Fiat's engine to deceive the *mafiosi* into thinking that everyone was still inside the vehicle. He tried to run faster, hugging the cliff wall, but it was difficult ground to cross; spurts of rock protruded from the cliff-face, shoals of loose stones littered the precipice base.

Jesus! Ed was out-distancing him and probably

didn't even know it, blinded by the dust. Scrambling over another rock spur, Petrie heard the gears change and the Fiat began backing over the way it had come. Johnson's manoeuvre worked; when he changed gear again and moved forward Petrie was ahead of him, still under the lee of the cliff, his heart pumping madly, the agony of a stitch cramping his side, but well in front of the vehicle. And he could see round the curve now, could see where the cliff walls lost height rapidly, sloping down on both sides in great ramps, converging in towards each other so that close to the exit the gorge became a funnel less than a hundred yards wide. The exit was scarcely four hundred yards away, a triangle of hard blue sky extending upwards from its apex between the cliff slopes. He saw the smoke seconds later, smelt the acrid aroma of something foul burning and then the smoke was drifting across the exit as he reached a point where a large buttress of rock sloped down the cliff and extended halfway across the gorge, forming a bottleneck where the track passed through. He ran up the nearside of the buttress, and from its crest he had a view of what lay beyond the bottleneck where the smoke was spreading rapidly.

The oily black smokescreen now spread right across the track beyond the bottleneck, but from his elevated position Petrie could see behind the smoke where the track ran straight, ran out of the gorge into hill country. A hundred yards beyond the neck formed by the buttress, scattered close to the track on either side, were more of the boulders, mammoth-sized masses of rock, and behind them he could see men moving on foot with their horses tethered in a cluster close under the southern slope. Then the smoke spread farther and hid everything. It was a clever stratagem: the car would have to stop when it came to the smoke; the occupants would get out of the vehicle to see what was happening; then they would be picked off by concealed *mafiosi*. Except that now he knew what was planned the tactic might be turned against them. Jumping from the buttress Petrie met the Fiat only yards away from the bottleneck as Johnson pulled up and leaned out of the window. 'Jim, what's happening . . .'

'Get in the rear seat! I'm taking over the wheel—I've seen how we can get through . . .' He scrambled into the seat the American had vacated, went on talking breathlessly as he handed the Mauser over his shoulder. 'They've set up a trap ahead of us . . . they're burning something to fog the road, hoping it will stop us. It's not going to— we're going straight through them—but we've got to watch that smoke. Ed, give me that bottle of Chianti . . .' He had his handkerchief folded when the bottle came over his shoulder, soaked the cloth liberally, then tied the improvised mask over his face with only the eyes showing. 'Both of you do the same,' he mumbled. 'That smoke could choke us and we need the windows down for shooting. Are you ready for what's coming, Scelba?'

To show how ready he was, the mafia boss took a handful of ammunition out of his coat on the floor and dropped it in his lap. 'Which side of the road are they?' he asked quietly.

'Both sides. You concentrate on the right—Ed, you take the left with the Mauser . . .'

'With this I take both sides,' the American answered as he hauled out spare mags from the

84

sack and spread them on the seat beside him. He had already fixed his own mask and passed the bottle to Scelba. 'There's nothing in the way of the car?' he inquired.

'There's everything in the way—boulders the size of houses, but the track runs straight and I think I can drive between them . . .'

'Through the smoke?'

'That just makes it a shade harder.' Petrie glanced to make sure Scelba had fixed his mask. 'We're going through. Now!'

The Fiat crawled past the bottleneck as though its driver were uncertain whether to proceed, and since there was no one in sight the waiting *mafiosi* could only guess at what was happening by the sound of the car's engine. The black rolling screen of smoke came closer as the vehicle crept forward and now the dense cloud filled the width of the gorge and curled at the edges where it came up against the cliff walls. A hundred yards . . . Seventy-five yards . . . Petrie rammed down his foot, the engine revolutions quickened and the Fiat built up speed as it roared forward. In his mind's eye Petrie was trying to visualize the boulders, to imagine a dead straight course which would take them hurtling down the track with clearance on both sides. He pressed his foot down farther and they went into the smoke.

The attack began instantly. A Sicilian, his face covered with cloth, appeared close to Scelba's window with a shotgun elevated. Scelba fired, emptied half the chambers as the man vanished, fired again at a shadow, fired blind until his gun was empty, reloaded swiftly, then shot a third soot-smeared *mafioso*. The car swept on through the black fog as Petrie gripped the wheel with both hands and Johnson emptied a magazine out of his own window. The smoke was inside the Fiat now, dung-laden, paraffin-tinged fumes which eddied in front of Petrie's eyes as he hunched well down and kept the wheel fixed in the same position, praying that he was holding to a straight course. If he smashed into one of those massive boulders which were nowhere to be seen because there was no vision, the car, travelling at this speed, would concertina. His eyes were already feeling the ill-effects of the turgid fumes as he drove on, elbows dug into his sides, back braced, shoulders stiffened as he fought to keep the wheel in exactly the same position despite the fact that they were speeding over uneven ground which pushed and tugged at the racing tyres as though determined to throw them off course. And it was a long stretch through the boulder avenue; it needed only a slight veering off course for them to angle away and rush headlong into a rock. Any second Petrie expected to see an ominous solid shape looming up in front of his bonnet and the confusion was appalling enough to distract any man with the bursts from the Mauser rattling in his ears mingled with the sharp reports from Scelba's revolver, the high-pitched beat of the engine, the shouts from the *mafiosi* outside.

Scelba was continuing an astonishingly high rate of fire, emptying his gun, reloading, firing again as men appeared in the fog and vanished. The nerve-shattering jumble of noise was increased by the frantic efforts of the *mafiosi* to stop the car as they fired shotgun blasts blindly, and they didn't always miss: behind Johnson, crouched low on the rear

86

seat as he fired alternately through one window and then the other, the Fiat was open to the world where a shotgun blast had shattered the rear window, scattering glass all over him, and the roof was riddled with bullet-holes. But so far Petrie's gamble was working and outside in the gorge the *mafiosi* had been taken horribly by surprise. Expecting easy victims, they were now faced with a car moving at frightening speed as a fusillade of bullets poured from it, catching any man who came in close. Once, Johnson was emptying his gun when he saw a Sicilian less than a foot from the running-board, a fat peasant lifting a rifle as the Mauser burst laced his throat. The peasant jerked horribly, half-jerked his hand towards his neck, then fell backwards as the Fiat rushed past. And now, as though perversely adding to the hellish chaos of sound, Petrie started pressing the horn non-stop so its blaring shriek cut through the other sounds as he pressed it, released it, and immediately pressed it again as they passed the position where he estimated the horses had been tethered.

Inside the car the smell, the choking fumes, were getting worse as Petrie rammed his foot down even farther knowing that they couldn't go on like this much longer without swerving fatally. Then something happened which made him lose speed as rapidly as he dared: a boulder showed to the left. He lost more speed, and changed direction a fraction, straightened up again when he calculated he was back on course, and for the first time a Sicilian reached them. Revolver in hand, a tall, lean-faced man jumped on the running-board on Scelba's side. Carlo. Scelba shot him twice in the face deliberately, then he was gone as Petrie increased speed and pressed the horn continuously. The mafia boss had just solved his little domestic problem. A figure came out of the smoke, the front mudguard struck him a pounding blow, and Petrie wondered when the hell they were going to emerge from the black pall. Behind him Johnson fired a long burst at a muddle of staggering figures and then without warning they had broken through the ambush and saw riderless horses stampeding in all directions as Petrie tore the mask from his face, threw it out of the window and accelerated up the road leading into the foothills. He glanced at his watch. 9.30 AM. Less than fifteen hours to reach Messina and they were not yet halfway across the island.

*   *   *

In northern Calabria on the mainland of Italy it was also 9.30 AM, was also very warm, but the mountain peaks were lost inside the heavy cloud bank which had persisted through the night. Thank God, thought General Rheinhardt, mindful of the Allied air forces. Perched on a mound overlooking the river, he held a field telephone in his hand while he watched—the spans of an emergency bridge being thrown over a watercourse. It was a damned nuisance, but they'd be moving again soon. He looked behind him where a column of German tanks stretched along the road while the crews sat eating on the verge, then stiffened as Kesselring came on the line.

'What's wrong?' The field-marshal's tone was sharp.

'A bridge down. Allied saboteurs must have

attached timebombs to it. We were lucky—it blew five minutes before the lead vehicles reached it.'

'How much delay?'

'Two hours from now, maybe less, we'll be across it.'

'I want the 29th Panzer on the straits shore by nine this evening.'

'That would be pushing it, sir.'

'By nine this evening. Not one minute later!' Kesselring rang off. Rheinhardt decided he would be there by nine.

CHAPTER SIX

Friday. 9.30 AM–12.30 PM

Two hours later the wheeling sun was still glaring down on the car, slowly roasting its occupants as they drove along a high ridge crest with an immense view out over Sicily on all sides, and the sight of the terrible landscape which surrounded them had brought a hush inside the Fiat. It was as though long ago this part of the world had been convulsed by a titanic upheaval, a catastrophe which had driven up bizarre mountains whose peaks had been bent as they forced their way upwards—while in other areas the earth had collapsed, leaving behind gaping chasms which plunged down from grim yellow-stone bluffs. Wherever Petrie looked there was some rocky horror—a precipice, a landslip, a sterile pinnacle— and he thought he had never seen a wilder region in all his wanderings as a mining engineer. A whole army, dying from thirst, could be swallowed up here and who would ever find them? Driving with one hand on the wheel, he swatted irritably at a persistent fly and then, as they drove past the putrefying carcase of a mule, a swarm of flies invaded the car and they all began swatting the pests.

'Isn't it time we wet our beaks?' Scelba suggested. [A common mafia phrase meaning the quenching of thirst and implying friendship. At least of a temporary nature.]

'Later. We had a drink an hour ago,' Petrie reminded him.

'How far have we come?' Johnson asked hoarsely.

Petrie glanced at the dashboard, made a quick calculation, but it was Scelba who answered first. 'We have travelled eighty kilometres from Palermo. I think I should warn you that the road between here and Scopana gets worse . . .'

'Any more encouraging comments?' the American interjected.

Scelba twisted his bulk round in his seat and stared at Johnson through his tortoiseshell glasses. 'I think it best that you should know what faces us. It is not even warm yet and today will be very hot—from midday onwards it will become like an inferno. You see, Sicily is unique in Europe. The sun shines down, the iron-hard ground and the rocks absorb the heat, then they release it so . . .'

'Very interesting!' Johnson snapped. 'But if you could defer the geography lesson until next week when I have an ice-cold beer in my hand . . .' He stopped speaking; a vision of that glass of ice-cold beer was vivid in his mind and he cursed Scelba for putting it there. The *capo* shrugged, turned to face the front as Petrie repeated his answer.

'About eighty kilometres it is, Ed. And we'll stop after a while and have a drink.' The brief conversation had reminded him that they were still a long distance from the rendezvous at Scopana with Gambari, the Italian agent who operated from inside Messina and whom he had never met, and Messina itself was over two hundred kilometres away. There were less than thirteen hours left in which to reach the straits city, and with every hour that passed they were falling farther behind schedule because they could only crawl along this diabolical track the Sicilians called a road. It was the delay in leaving Palermo which had upset everything, the mischance of a *carabiniere* patrol finding the first vehicle and confiscating it. Beyond Scopana, Petrie thought, we'll have to take a chance and strike up north for the direct coastal highway to make up for lost time. Beyond Scopana . . . But how many hours yet before they reached the rendezvous with Gambari?

Scelba stirred restlessly in his seat. 'If you wish to reach Messina before midnight we must hurry . . .'

'Along this track—in this heat!' Johnson exploded. Scelba regarded him passively through his tortoiseshell glasses, then turned to Petrie and explained. A long way ahead after they left the ridge the road forked south to make a detour round a cliff as it headed for Petralia and Scopana beyond. But at this point there was also a track which led off to the north to a small village called Puccio, and from this village a main road ran direct to Scopana.

'It would save many miles if we could take that

91

more direct route,' he pointed out.

Petrie pulled a crumpled cloth map from his pocket with one hand, a map of Sicily printed on silk, and spread it over his lap. There was something in what Scelba was suggesting: a main road came down from the coast, ran close to Puccio, continued on direct to Scopana, bypassing Petralia. 'This track leading off where the road forks,' he said, 'you really think the Fiat could use it?' Johnson peered over Petrie's shoulder and inwardly shuddered: the so-called second-class road they were moving along was indicated by a continuous line, but the link-track broke down into a series of separate dashes. What the hell that might indicate in Sicily he scarcely dared contemplate.

'I have only been across it by mule,' Scelba conceded, 'but a driver like yourself might manage it.'

'We'll decide when we reach it,' Petrie replied.

They drove on a long distance over the burning ridge and the only sounds were the soporific throb of the engine, the irksome drone of the flies, the slap of hand against irritated skin and the creak of overheated leather when someone tried shifting into a less uncomfortable position; beyond the ridge the air became heavier with haze and shimmer and the brutal landscape danced gently where the heat was building up. They ate without stopping and without appetite, ate tasteless salami and cheese and dried raisins, and tried to wash it down with the remains of the Chianti because the brandy bottle had been smashed by a bullet during the attack in the gorge. At the end of the meal Petrie rationed them to two mouthfuls of water each and to his surprise Scelba swallowed only a single mouthful, handing back the bottle when he was told to take more. 'It is enough,' he explained. 'I am used to this climate and we may need that water badly later.' Petrie stared at him in surprise, remembering his earlier plea for a drink; the Sicilian had only made the suggestion because he thought his companions needed it. Not that the mafia boss was noted for his compassion—he was simply determined that they should get through to the straits city to make sure that one day he became mayor of Palermo. I was right about Scelba, Petrie thought grimly: he is the man to get us through, blast his eyes!

The first warning sign of danger ahead came within five minutes of finishing their meal. The ridge was narrowing, poising the track on little more than a knife edge with a sheer drop of hundreds of feet on either side, when Johnson screwed up his eyes and peered towards the south.' The sun glare was so fierce he had to shade his gaze with his hand to make sure, then he called out urgently. 'Jim, there's someone out there! On horseback.'

Petrie resisted the impulse to take his eyes off the road, swore to himself, stopped the car and left the engine running as he twisted round in his seat. 'Over there—on top of that big rock,' the American said. Petrie couldn't see a damned thing. He climbed out of the car carefully; little more than a foot of level track was available for him to stand on before the ridge plunged into space. The American joined him, pointed over the car's bonnet. Yes, Ed hadn't imagined it: the shimmering silhouette of a horseman was perched on top of a

93

massive crag hanging in the haze. How the hell had he taken a horse up there? Cupping both hands like primitive binoculars, Petrie stared at the horseman perched less than a quarter of a mile away, a man in army uniform. Then he was gone, vanished like a conjuring trick, but there was no doubt that the soldier must have seen the Fiat.

'Who the devil was he?' Johnson inquired as he mopped the back of his moist neck.

'An Italian soldier. And he saw us.'

'Just one of them—out here?'

'That's what worries me—that he won't be on his ownsome.'

The lone horseman had been on the south side of the track, and now Petrie was swivelling his gaze methodically through a three-sixty-degree circle. He saw the wilderness through the dazzle like an endless mirage, a wilderness bereft of water, bereft of trees, bereft of life itself. He was completing the circle, staring in a north-easterly direction where distant peaks wobbled against the sky, when he found them. A file of uniformed figures toiling over another ridge on foot with pack mules which carried cylinders that looked like mortar barrels. He pointed briefly. 'Couple of dozen of them. At least. I'd say they're part of an Italian mountain division.'

'Jesus! And we came through here because there were no troops!'

'Because there were very few troops,' Petrie corrected him. 'That division is on some kind of exercise and the last thing they'll be expecting up here is enemy saboteurs. What the hell is there to sabotage out here?'

You think we'll run into them?'

'It's possible. The trouble is they're on both sides of us. We'll have to try and slip past between them.'

It was a slim hope: Petrie admitted it to himself as he got in behind the wheel. One horseman to the south, footsloggers to the north. All the indications were that the troops were spread out across country and somewhere ahead they were liable to be spread across the track itself. Releasing the brake, he began driving forward very slowly sitting up straight to gain as clear a view as he could of the track immediately ahead. It was climbing now, a steady incline, and as they ascended loose stones disturbed by the wheels went over the edge and disappeared from view. Several times Scelba peered out of the window on his side without enthusiasm as he looked down into a chasm which dropped almost vertically, and behind him Johnson was watching the track ahead where it appeared to narrow even further. As they reached a crest and went over it Petrie braked abruptly. A crude barrier, a pole perched on wooden tripods, barred their way.

'What the hell does that indicate?' he asked irritably. The *capo* said he had no idea, that it could hardly indicate road-mending operations. Johnson lit a cigarette while Petrie got out to investigate; there was something about the barrier he found disturbing. He saw Petrie staring down the brink on the northern side, then grab hold of pole and tripods and send them hurtling over the edge. 'There was some kind of noticeboard which has fallen halfway down,' he remarked as he came back to the car. 'I couldn't read the wording on it so we'll just keep moving . . .'

The disaster struck them a hundred yards

95

beyond. They were bumping along over uneven ground, driving out of one pothole into another, when the explosion came, a muffled roar which echoed across the wilderness as Petrie braked and a shower of debris descended on the bonnet and roof of the Fiat. A cloud of yellowish dust, fog-thick, blinded their view for half a minute as they waited inside the car, tense with the uncertainty of not knowing what had happened. Then the dust settled, drifted away down into the abyss on either side, and the track ahead came into view again. What was left of it. A large portion had been sheered away to the left, dropping wholesale into the abyss, so that now barely half the original surface remained, remained with a sinister jagged edge where the landslip had gone over the edge.

'Christ! What was that?' Johnson called out.

'Land mine!' Petrie wiped dust off his damp hands as he surveyed the track remnant. The track had widened since they had left the barrier point behind, but the section which had survived the explosion was meagre. 'That mountain division must have mined this part of the track,' he said. 'That noticeboard probably carried a warning. This is a difficult one, gentlemen, in case you haven't noticed. We can't turn back and, theoretically, we can't go forward. We can just stay here and fry . . .'

*   *   *

Petrie walked with some care along the remnant of track, placing one foot carefully in front of the other, and as he walked the old, familiar sensation started, the tingling sensation on the soles of his feet which would take the first fearful impact of

96

detonation as a mine exploded under him. To his left the edge was ragged and crumbling, but his eyes were fixed on the ground ahead, searching for any sign of metallic project which would warn him that the next section of track was also laced with mines. Already his legs felt like jelly, his nerves screaming at him to retrace his steps before he was horribly mutilated, if not killed outright, and the sweat streaming down his back had little to do with the sun beating down on him. He walked on for some distance, then turned back and the return journey was no more comfortable. When he climbed into the car his two companions stared at him grimly. 'We'll have to risk it,' he said, reaching for the hand-brake.

'You know that walk of yours didn't prove anything?' Johnson said quietly.

'No sign of any more of them, Ed.'

'But it wasn't anti-personnel mines that shifted that load over the edge,' the American persisted.

'How about piping down and letting me concentrate?'

But Johnson had a point, a possibly lethal point: the weight of a man walking was hardly likely to detonate mines laid to destroy vehicles, mines which could tear the track off a heavy tank or pulverise a light vehicle such as the Fiat as though it had been through a stamping mill. But the only way was forward, forward over the crumbling section of track where mines had already been detonated merely by the vibrations of the approaching car being transmitted through rock. Petrie moved forward as slowly as he dared without stalling the engine, and as they came closer to the landslip area he estimated again the width of

97

surviving track. It appeared to be just wide enough to permit the passage of their four wheels—unless another piece decided to crumble away while they were passing over it. The engine beats were slow as they crawled forward, as Scelba braced himself against the back of his seat, as Johnson sat in the exact centre of the car to help maintain the delicate balance, as Petrie moved the wheel to take them a few inches farther away from the collapsing brink, which took them nearer to the abyss on Scelba's side.

There was, in fact, rather a lot which could go wrong, Petrie was thinking. If they detonated a mine the vehicle would be hurled over the brink, but they would be dead before they left the ridge. Even without a fresh explosion a section of the track, already rendered horribly unstable by the previous detonation, could crumble away. And if they were spared these considerable hazards he could still misjudge the distance by an inch or two, simply driving them over the edge into oblivion. At this point oblivion was about a thousand feet down, he calculated. The engine stalled. It was terribly silent as leather creaked when someone stirred, then they heard the distant hum of aircraft engines. Petrie leaned out of the window, glanced down to see the running-board perched on the edge of the drop, glanced up to see aircraft flying low on a course parallel with the ridge. Beaufighters. Allied aircraft looking for something to shoot up, something which moved.

His hand moved away from the ignition, flopped on his knee while he waited. The aircraft flew on towards the east, vanishing in the haze. 'Our friends,' Petrie said over his shoulder. 'Beaufighters

. . .'

'I'd sooner be up there than down here,' Johnson replied with feeling.

Petrie re-started the engine, began crawling forward again as the track ascended and the car wobbled. Then the right front wheel *dropped*. Petrie stiffened. God, the car was going over . . . The chassis jarred, came to a halt. A deep pothole had stopped them. He reversed carefully, the wheels spun uselessly for a moment, then took them back out of the depression. He prepared to accelerate to take them across the pothole, to accelerate with only inches to spare on either side of the vehicle. The car went forward, dropped into the hole, lurched out and Petrie swung the wheel a fraction as they headed straight for the edge, turning again just in time to avoid taking them over the other brink. Scelba's thumb pressed deep into the unlit cigar he was holding and Johnson stared ahead to where the track was widening again, willing the Fiat to stay on the ridge until they reached that safer area. Then they were moving forward more evenly as the abyss moved away from them, the ridge expanded, and Petrie drove faster, knowing they must have passed beyond the mined zone.

'Those Beaufighters gave me the creeps,' Johnson called out. 'I thought for a moment they'd attack us.'

'More likely than maybe you thought,' Petrie replied. 'I noticed back in the gorge that this Fiat's smeared with dust in a way that makes it look camouflaged. They just didn't see us.'

They drove on a long distance and then Scelba reported that they were almost at the end of the ridge, that soon the track would go down to a lower level and across tableland. 'And there you will be able to drive faster,' he remarked with a wooden expression. Petrie made no reply as he took the car up to a circle of huge boulders where the track ran between them. They drove past the rocks and the track dropped down a long slope into a bowl bisected by a waterless stream. But although water was absent the bowl was not entirely empty: a score or more of Italian mountain troops were halted on either side of the track while they lay on the ground and ate lunch, and behind them stood a mountain-gun, unlimbered and half-concealed under a canvas sheet. Petrie maintained an even speed as he drove down towards them with the sun glaring in his eyes and flashing repeatedly on the windscreen. He held up a hand to cut out the glare and saw several men running up the slope towards him as the sun went on flashing off the glass. At the head of the running men was an NCO who drew his revolver as he ran, waving it furiously at the car as Petrie slowed down and then stopped when he realized that bullets could be coming through the windscreen in a matter of seconds.

'You *bloody* fools!'

The NCO could hardly speak as he pulled up close to the car and aimed his gun at Petrie, then he recovered his breath. 'There are enemy planes about! Don't you realize that flashing windscreen can be seen for miles from the air! You could have killed all my men! By God, I'll have you in prison for the duration. You're under arrest! All of you!'

*   *   *

They stood outside the car in the heat of the sun while the NCO examined their papers. Three Italian soldiers with rifles aimed at them stood close to the sergeant who was clearly not satisfied with their identity documents. As he checked them a second time Scelba glanced towards the troops sprawled on the ground as though searching for a familiar face. The situation was dangerous, Petrie had no illusions on this score: the NCO was so furious that their windscreen reflecting the sun might have attracted the Allied planes he was determined to have them locked up.

'I still find it very strange that you continued along the ridge after the road had collapsed,' the sergeant repeated. 'And you drove past a military barrier—you admitted it. That in itself is an offence.'

'We would have roasted alive had we stayed on the ridge,' Petrie protested.

'Better that you had been blown up by the mines,' the NCO told him savagely.

'I do appreciate your attitude,' the *capo* said stiffly. 'You know my name and I have connections in Messina . . .'

'To hell with your connections! You say I know your name. I wonder! How do I know that these papers are not forged? Tell me that!' He waved the handful of papers under Scelba's nose. 'I do not like the look of any of you—and I do not like the look of your papers!'

'You could be making a bad mistake,' Scelba assured him. 'As a Sicilian I have every right to drive across the island . . .'

'You have not heard the reports then, eh?' the NCO demanded viciously.

'What reports?'

'That British parachutists—saboteurs—were dropped in this area early this morning. I repeat, you are all under arrest until enquiries have been made about your identity! You will be taken by truck later today to Enna and interrogated there by Intelligence . . .'

Scelba dismissed the whole idea with a wave of his hand. 'I have heard this kind of report all over Sicily and it never amounts to anything. We are plagued with spy fever . . .'

'You are under arrest!' the NCO bawled in his face.

'Are there any Sicilians in your division?' Scelba asked.

'Yes, but we will waste no more time talking. Come!'

Petrie glanced at Johnson as they walked down the hill after the enraged sergeant while the three soldiers followed in the rear. It was pointless to argue any further and it was damned bad luck that these reports should be circulating, but they highlighted the extreme state of tension now gripping the island. He looked back as he heard the Fiat's engine start up: a fourth soldier had climbed in behind the wheel and the car was coming down the slope behind them. In his rage the NCO had so far overlooked the simple routine of searching the vehicle, but it was an oversight he was bound to remedy before long. And the sack of explosives was still on the floor in the rear of the vehicle.

As they tramped down into the bowl the troops on the ground stared at them hostilely and one man operated his rifle bolt, but the NCO rapped out an order and the man laid his weapon back on the earth. Clearly the episode of the flashing windscreen had not put them at the top of any popularity poll, Petrie thought. They were marching towards a cave under a large rock overhang where a soldier stood on guard when Scelba halted, staring at a man who had stopped eating as he looked up at the *capo*. One of the soldiers behind him prodded his hip lightly with his bayonet, but Scelba refused to move, glaring back with such ferocity that the soldier paused uncertainly. The *capo* called out to the sergeant who had swung round. 'This man here knows me, Sergeant. He has not seen my papers so ask him who I am—it may stop you making a very serious mistake.'

'We will check your identity at Enna . . .'

'Ask him, please!'

The sergeant hesitated, but there was something in the *capo*'s manner which intimidated him. Petrie held his breath: everything now depended on the NCO's reaction, on the strength of the doubt Scelba had planted in his mind. With an impatient gesture the sergeant spoke to the soldier, who jumped to his feet. 'You know who this man is? You recognize him?

'He is Vito Scelba . . .'

'Who is he?'

'I knew him when I worked on the docks at Messina, Sergeant. He is an important man with shipping interests . . .'

'I am trying to save *you* trouble, Sergeant,' Scelba intervened, changing his tactics. 'You are doing your duty, which I applaud, but in my own way I also help the war effort. Now you have conclusive proof of my identity and I can personally vouch for these two men with me.'

'You are in a hurry . . . ?' The NCO was again uncertain, a man who disliked going back on his own orders, but also a man who feared people with influence. And Scelba had cleverly provided him with a line of retreat. 'Perhaps since we now do have proof of your identity this changes the position . . .'

'I merely wish to continue my urgent journey concerned with dock repairs,' the *capo* explained persuasively. 'And your corporal has considerately brought my car so, with your permission, we should like to drive on at once. . .'

Within two minutes they were driving up out of the bowl with their papers inside their pockets. In the rear seat Johnson sat with his feet planted on either side of the sack of explosives as the Fiat climbed higher, went over a crest, and the military detachment vanished behind them. 'There are many Sicilians in the Army on the island,' Scelba observed, 'but even so we were lucky. They were bringing the car down to have it searched.'

'The same suspicion had crossed my mind,' Petrie replied dryly and then he concentrated on his driving. A long way beyond the burning ridge they saw the great bluffs Scelba had spoken of when he described how a track led off to the village of Puccio. They drove on steadily over the foul road and again they were facing the sun at a certain angle so its rays were flashing off the windscreen. And again Petrie had to raise one hand to shield his eyes against the glare to see where he was going as he weighed up the alternatives. It would save a lot of mileage if they could take the Fiat along that mule track and join the direct route to Scopana.

They were very close to the bluffs when Petrie heard the sound of another engine, a shrilling-pitched whine at high altitude, and there was something about the whine which alerted him. He looked out, jerked his head in fast, stopped the car and switched off the motor.

'Get out! Take cover! Ed, take the sack . . .'

Grabbing his jacket, he leaned over the back seat and hauled the Mauser off the floor as Johnson left the Fiat at speed with his own jacket and the sack. The door on Petrie's side jammed, so he scrambled over the seat Scelba had vacated and ran after the other two men, leaving the road and haring across country towards a straggle of boulders with the scream of the diving aircraft in his ears. Reaching the rocks, he skidded flat on his stomach, wriggled close to a boulder and lifted his head a few inches. The Beaufighter, flying at zero height, its RAF roundel clearly visible, opened up with all its armament—cannon and machine-guns. The noise was deafening. The scream of the engine, the rattle of the machine-guns, the blast of the cannon-shells bursting. Rock fragments showered down on the boulders and Petrie winced at the sound: the fragments had the impetus and instant killing power of shrapnel. The shells ripped along the track, hammered into the Fiat. Bullets riddled the roof, shattered the windscreen as the three men pressed themselves into the earth while the cannonade thundered at their eardrums. Then it was quiet, the engine sound receded rapidly as the Beaufighter climbed, and Petrie dragged himself to his knees. Johnson had a dazed look; Scelba wriggled, raised his head cautiously, stared at the blood on his left hand. 'Keep away from the

105

car,' Petrie warned. 'It's on fire.'

'Bastard!' Johnson was beside himself with fury as he watched the retreating plane. 'You're supposed to be our pal!'

'It was the car,' Petrie reminded him. 'The dust smears made it look camouflaged. They thought they were attacking an enemy vehicle . . .' He stood upright, then frowned as he stared from under his hand at the ascending aircraft. The engine was coughing, cutting out. The silence was total and for a moment the plane hovered in space before it started moving again—downwards. 'What's wrong?' Johnson asked beside him.

'Engine failure.'

'You mean . . .'

'There they go.'

Two more dots appeared in the heated sky, plumed into cones as the parachutes flared and the two-man crew began drifting downwards. Petrie swore briefly and colourfully, then turned to Scelba who was brushing dust off his clothes. 'Scelba! Are those two airmen dropping anywhere near Puccio?' The *capo* shaded his eyes, gazed at the floating parachutes for some time as flames crackled over the Fiat.

'They will come down somewhere near Puccio, yes,' he said.

Petrie swore again. One expressive expletive, and Johnson looked at him in surprise. 'You didn't get steamed up when they blasted our Fiat—so what the hell's wrong now?'

'Those two dangling from their flaming parachutes could be real trouble,' Petrie explained very deliberately. 'Losing the car means we have to hoof it to Puccio because it's the nearest place.' He turned to Scelba. 'Is there a phone wire into the village? Good, that's something at least. The point is, Ed, we'll have to make for Puccio fast and I'll try and contact Gambari in Scopana at the phone number he radioed to Tunis—in the hope that he can drive to the village and collect us.'

'Makes sense . . .'

'But those two parachuting airmen can take away our ace card—secrecy—just as they took our transport. So far the enemy has no idea we're here . . .' He pointed towards the sky. 'But he'll soon know they're about and the *carabinieri* will be combing the countryside to find them.'

'I see. They've buggered us twice over then.'

'It begins to look like it.' Petrie turned to Scelba who was flicking blood from his injured hand. The wound was superficial, but he used an Italian dressing to stop the bleeding as he made his remark. 'You were damned lucky with this, it just grazed you. An inch lower and it would have sliced off your hand neatly at the wrist.' The *capo* stared at him without expression as he mopped his forehead with his other hand.

'I have friends in Puccio,' he said.

'From now on we're going to need all the friends we can muster.' Petrie checked his watch. 12.30 PM. The sun was at its zenith, burning Sicily with its scorching glow, and they were going to have to walk to Puccio under that sun. Behind him there was a dull detonation as the petrol tank went up, and when he swung round a column of dark smoke was rising like a signal, a marker for the enemy to locate their position. 'We'd better get moving,' he snapped. 'The area will be swarming with *carabinieri* shortly.'

CHAPTER SEVEN

Friday. 2 PM–3.30 PM

At two o'clock—ten hours from the deadline—the three men staggered up a hill slope, reached its crest, and looked down on Puccio. The tiny village was about a quarter of a mile below them, a compact circle of grey dwellings on top of a small hill. A church tower rose like a monument from the ragged carpet of shallow roofs and farther down the track a black-garbed priest on a donkey rode away from them as he came close to the village. He was the only living human being in sight.

Temporarily exhausted, they sank on the ground, their eyes fixed on the diminishing figure of the priest because he was a moving object in an otherwise dead world. Beyond the village Sicily was a heat blur, an aching dazzle they preferred not to look at. They had come across country steadily for an hour and a half under the broiling sun, across a rock desert which radiated up the heat so they had received the sun's blessing twice: once when it shone down on their sweat-drenched backs and a second time as it came up at them from the ground's impervious surface. Petrie had led the way along the meagre track and the other two men had followed, plodding mechanically forward, their steps dragging, their legs aching, their backs prickling with the heat trapped under their wet shirts. It was only willpower which had brought them to the hill crest and now they were dangerously close to a state of dehydration, their bodies drained of all moisture, their minds still filled with the endless thudding sensation of boots on rock. It must have been an ordeal because Scelba had thrown away his cigar.

'That must be the road to Scopana!' Johnson said after a few minutes. He was pointing at a pale ribbon running eastward about half a mile beyond Puccio. 'I don't like the look of that village—why don't we cut across to the road and try and hijack some transport?'

'Because there might not be any,' Petrie replied staring at the empty highway. 'I'm going down to the village,' he went on through cracked lips. 'On my own.'

'That's crazy . . .'

'On my own, Ed. Its the only way. That village is pretty deserted and three of us will stand out like a delegation from the League of Nations.'

'There could be *carabinieri* coming to look for those parachutists . . .'

'They could be there already,' Scelba warned. 'We can't see into the square from here.'

'Then one man has a better chance of evading them than three,' Petrie replied. 'You see that small hill over there just this side of the road? I'll meet you on that hilltop one hour from now. If I don't make it, don't wait—try and grab some transport at gunpoint and drive to Scopana. You've memorized Gambari's phone number so you can call him when you get there. It'll be up to you, Ed, to take over and see the job gets done.'

'Supposing you get to that hilltop after we're gone?'

Petrie smiled wearily. 'Then I'll try and grab my own transport and catch you up. Look, Ed, so far

we've done what poor Lawson wasn't able to—
we're well inside Sicily, we've still time to reach
Messina, and no one knows we've arrived. The best
thing is to keep it that way—and if I can get in
touch with Gambari and he can bring transport to
us we're still in business. Hijacking a truck can lead
to complications.'

'This man, Gambari,' Scelba said thoughtfully,
'he is an Italian?'

'Italian-American,' Petrie lied quickly. 'And now
I'm going down there. Who are these friends of
yours in Puccio?'

The *capo* pulled a large signet ring off his finger.
He had to work it off because the finger had
swelled with the heat, and then he handed it to
Petrie. 'Wear that. It may help you because my
friends will recognize it, will know you are
intimately connected with me. Who are my
friends? The grocer, the saddler, the coffin-maker
. . .' He trailed off vaguely and Johnson grinned
sourly to himself. The coffin-maker. Well, that
figured: Scelba, the producer of bodies, and the
undertaker, the man who buried them. A perfect
partnership. He wiped the back of his neck with a
sodden handkerchief as Petrie stood up, handed
him the Mauser and took the Glisenti revolver in
exchange. He couldn't wear his jacket in this heat
to conceal the German gun and in any case it
would have looked strange had he attempted it.

'Watch it, Jim,' Johnson warned. 'That place
might not be as peaceful as it looks.'

'I'll be doing nothing else but that. See you in an
hour.'

Starting down the track with his jacket looped
over his arm, Petrie noticed that Puccio had the

curiously blitzed look peculiar to so many Sicilian villages. Its shamble of decrepit rooftops sliding in all directions gave the impression it had recently been subjected to a severe air raid, though he doubted whether a single bomb had ever fallen on the place. Poverty was the national industry on this benighted island, and if you could arrange it almost anywhere was better to be born rather than in this mafia-ridden hell-hole. As he dropped closer, the village had a closed-in feeling, the atmosphere of a hamlet where you never see anyone but you cannot rid yourself of the certainty that you are being watched.

Had he been approaching Puccio in the darkness, Petrie would still have known he was near a Sicilian village: the smell would have warned him, a smell compounded of animal dung and household refuse, to put it no lower. And the flies came out to meet him. Wearily, he batted at them with his left hand as he walked uphill now, along a dust-covered road while his right hand inside the jacket pocket gripped the revolver. Inside the village the street was of beaten earth, a narrow street with the houses close together and washing festooned along wires which spanned the narrow gap over his head. Climbing higher up the incline, he passed an open doorway where saddles and animal harness lay on a stone floor. The saddler, one of Scelba's friends. But there was no sign of a telephone wire yet, so he went on up the street past the saddler's.

'S-a-a-l-e!'

The salt-seller, a large pannier basket looped over his back, came round a corner as a woman in a black dress appeared on a balcony and lowered a small basket from a rope. She shouted her order in Sicilian and the street vendor dumped his pannier on the ground. As Petrie walked past slowly he scooped up a pinch of salt behind the man's back, slipped it in his mouth and swallowed some water from the bottle he took from his jacket pocket. That should take care of the dehydration problem for a while. Walking even more slowly, he studied the tiny square coming into view at the top of the hill, the heart of Puccio, such as it was. Like the rest of the village, at siesta hour the square was deserted except for some mules tethered in a strip of shade thrown by a wall. The animals turned their heads to watch him with the resignation bred of generations of servitude and their action irked him, anyone watching from behind the shuttered windows overlooking the square had only to follow the mules' stare to see him. The square seemed peaceful enough and Petrie stood gazing at a telephone wire which ran to a small bar on the left-hand side. The grocer's shop was shuttered and closed but the door to the bar was open. Releasing his grip on the revolver butt, he wiped his moist hand on his hip and then took a fresh grip on the weapon as he walked towards the bar entrance. *Mario's*. The faded writing could just be made out above an open window where soiled lace curtains hung motionless in the foetid air.

From inside the entrance to the bar came a clicking sound which echoed sharply in the sun-drenched silence of the tiny *piazza*. The sound stopped, was succeeded by a coarse chuckle and a murmur of voices. Petrie stepped into a tiled passage, walked through the open doorway on his left. The sight of the bottles behind the bar counter, a crude wooden plank partitioning off a deep alcove at the back, made his chronic state of thirst almost a craving. The room was small, low-ceilinged and stuffy despite the open window where he saw the patient mules watching him again. Hadn't the beasts anything better to do with their time? They seemed to be checking his every movement. A dozen bare wooden tables occupied the floor and at several of these Sicilians sat playing some kind of checkers game. Tanned swarthy faces looked up at him from under peaked caps and then went back to their games and their wine. Petrie walked confidently up to the bar, asked the dark-haired young girl behind it for wine. 'Bianco, and a bottle of unopened mineral water.' Long-jawed, the girl had quick intelligent eyes and within seconds they noticed Petrie's right hand on the counter, noticed the distinctive ring Scelba had loaned him.

She hesitated in the act of uncorking a bottle and her eyes met his briefly, then dropped as she poured wine into a glass. Without looking up again she called out sharply, 'Arturo!' One of the men playing checkers stood up, wandered across to the counter, shoved his hands in his trouser pockets as the girl banged the bottle on the counter close to where Petrie's hand still displayed the ring. The peasant showed no reaction as the girl poured a second glass and pushed it towards him. Controlling a rising feeling of impatience, Petrie waited as he lifted his glass. The telephone, an ancient instrument attached to the peeling wall, was close to where he stood, but he wanted to see what was going to happen before he got involved in the endless business of a Sicilian phone call. The

113

peasant, short and squat, with an unpleasant, moon-shaped face, lifted his own glass at the same moment. *'Salute!'* The single word was his only acknowledgement that he had seen the ring and then he went back to his table. Glancing round the room again, Petrie handed the girl a fifty-lire note.

'I'd like a Scopana number,' he said, keeping his voice low as she refilled his glass. 'Keep the change till you know the cost of the call.' He gave her the number he had memorized and waited, sipping a second glass while she revolved the bell-handle and stood with her hand on her hip. Yes, it was going to be a long business. And one of the many things Petrie had learned during his service with the Felucca Boat Squadron was that you don't linger under strange roofs in enemy territory a moment longer than is necessary. For no solid reason the atmosphere inside the bar disturbed him. The click of the checkers, the peasants sitting drinking and placidly waving flies away seemed oddly unreal; but here was the real Sicily, living each day as it had done since time immemorial. Apart from rationing, these villagers probably hardly knew there was a war on. 'Not long now,' the girl assured him in Italian, then switched to her own language as she spoke to the exchange. Not long now could mean an eternity on the island, Petrie reflected grimly.

The spasmodic clicking of the checkers pieces went on a sound which began to irritate Petrie in his keyed-up state. He suppressed the urge to get moving, to get out of this place fast, and when he glanced at the tables again something caught his attention. Arturo was absorbed in his game with three other peasants, apparently no longer aware of Petrie's presence, but at another table a lean, hard-faced Sicilian was staring in his direction. Their eyes met and the peasant's gaze shifted back to his game, but there had been something in his expression which alerted Petrie. Now I look like one of them, he thought calmly, so what attracted Hard-Face's attention to me? It must have been something in Arturo's manner when he stood next to me. Turning his head casually back to the bar, he rechecked an item he had looked for the moment he had entered the place. A second exit. At the back of the alcove a door was half-open. In an emergency he could slip round the end of the counter and make for that door. He swallowed more wine as the girl lifted a dark eyebrow. 'The exchange—pzut!' Revolving the bell-handle ferociously, she lifted a finger. 'Ah! Scopana!' With a nervous smile she handed him the receiver like a blessing. Petrie took a firm grip on the instrument and leaned against the wall so he could watch the room. This was going to be damned tricky.

'I'd like to speak to Signor Gambari please,' he requested in a low voice. 'Urgently.'

'I'm sorry. He is not here. Who is that?'

It was a man's voice which had answered, a powerful, controlled voice, and it had given Petrie the worst possible news. One of the peasants at Arturo's table got up and left the bar while Petrie wondered whether there had been a brief hesitation before the man in Scopana had replied.

'Who is that?' the voice repeated sharply.

Petrie took a deep breath. He'd have to risk it and give the identification phrase. 'I've brought the consignment of oranges from Palermo.' There was a distinct hesitation this time before the man at the other end replied.

'The price cannot be high in season. How many oranges?'

Petrie kept the relief out of his voice. The voice had given the pre-arranged reply so he was talking to Gambari. 'Ninety kilos, *signore*. I am afraid there may be a little difficulty getting the consignment to Scopana.'

'Where is it now?'

'In Puccio. That's a village . . .'

'I know the place! I could drive there and collect them at once. The problem is transport, I take it?' Gambari's voice was quick and competent and Petrie felt a surge of relief as he replied.

'Yes, we haven't any. But you'd better pick up the three of us outside the village . . .'

'On the Scopana road?' Gambari inquired.

'Not too far away from here.'

'I will meet you in one hour, maybe sooner. My car is a grey Mercedes, licence number ML4820. I will be travelling alone and I will meet you at the Cefalù fork. Coming from Puccio, the left-hand turning goes to Cefalù, the one straight ahead to Scopana. Understand?'

'Yes. And thanks. How far out . . .'

'The fork is about one kilometre east of Puccio.' The voice became more casual. 'You are late with the delivery, *signore*.'

Cautious Signor Gambari, Petrie thought. Yes, they were damned late: they had planned to arrive in Scopana at ten in the morning. 'Over four hours late, I fear,' he said.

'When I arrive at the fork I will stop there and wait for you . . .'

The phone went dead. No wasted salutations, just a terminal click at the other end. Petrie was

116

handing back the instrument to the girl when three men came into the bar and sat down at the table nearest the door. One of them was the peasant who had left Arturo's table, another of them wore an apron smeared with white powder. The grocer. Scelba's friends were assembling to see the man who wore the mafia boss's ring. Accepting his change, Petrie started walking towards the exit and then stopped. A roar of truck and motorcycle engines shattered the quiet. There was a squeal of brakes in the *piazza,* a thud of boots, then, as he moved back to the bar to make for the rear exit, *carabinieri* burst into the room with fixed bayonets as a sergeant shouted in Italian for everyone to stay where they were. The girl poured Petrie a drink quickly and he raised it to his lips as he leaned against the counter and waited.

*   *   *

The uniformed troops lined up with their backs against the side wall as they faced the occupants of the bar with their rifles at the ready. The sergeant, seeing Petrie on his own at the bar, shouted and gesticulated. 'You! Sit down at a table! At once!' Petrie slouched over to the empty table next to Arturo and sat down, directly facing the hard-faced Sicilian two tables away. The sergeant, liking the sound of his own voice, bawled out more threatening instructions as to what would happen if anyone moved, then stiffened to attention and saluted as an elegantly-dressed officer walked into the bar. 'This is Captain Soldano,' the sergeant shouted. 'Keep quiet!'

Since no one had spoken, the injunction was a

117

little superfluous. Petrie glanced from under his cap at the hard-faced Sicilian. The peasant appeared to be in a state of indecision; once he almost stood up as though to speak, then he caught Arturo staring at him and changed his mind as Captain Soldano began addressing them in Italian, which meant he was from the mainland.

'Two British spies have been seen near Puccio and they may be hiding in the village. Have any of you seen any strangers arrive here in the past two hours? Anyone you have never seen in Puccio before?'

Soldano looked round the room expectantly, adjusted his cap to a more jaunty angle, his gaze wandering from individual to individual. His eyes rested on the hard-faced Sicilian, paused, then resumed their search. The peasants at the tables stared at each other blankly, shrugged their shoulders, and Petrie noticed that none of them looked in his direction. He was the only man sitting at a table by himself and even though he had been directed there by the sergeant he felt conspicuous. The girl behind the bar polished a glass as she looked at the ceiling, out of the window, at the soldiers, anywhere except at Petrie.

'There might be a reward for their discovery.' Soldano flicked his fingers as though riffling banknotes, and again he waited for a reaction. Petrie cursed inwardly at the double misfortune which had resulted from the Beaufighter's appearance. 'Two British spies . . .' Soldano was undoubtedly referring to the two airmen who must have been seen coming down by parachute. The peasants were repeating their earlier reaction, glancing at each other and shrugging their shoulders. It was a little unnerving: every civilian in the place must know he was a stranger and the only man Petrie was uncertain of now was the hard-faced Sicilian. There had been a significance in the way Soldano's gaze had paused when he saw the man, and Petrie was almost sure the Sicilian was a paid informer, the type of man Scelba had wrongly accused Carlo of being. And he was also pretty sure that the only thing keeping the man's mouth temporarily shut was the presence of Arturo and his *mafioso*. With the armed *carabinieri* only feet away it was a fragile balance of terror and he wondered how long it would last.

'Well,' Soldano announced philosophically, 'obviously no one knows anything of the matter, so we had better make use of the bar.'

It was a popular decision. Soldiers crowded forward to the counter and then stood aside as Soldano himself walked up to the counter and doffed his cap with an exaggerated politeness to the girl who poured him a drink with a blank expression. The tension should have relaxed, but instead it increased under the surface. Sentries were still posted at the door and no one seemed inclined to leave as the girl went on serving drinks to the *carabinieri*. Petrie sat sipping from his own glass, his eyes on the hard-faced peasant who was now standing up prior to moving towards the counter. The manoeuvre was obvious: Soldano had planned it to give the Sicilian a chance to get close to him while he whispered information in his ear. And the information would concern Petrie. Within a few minutes he would be under arrest. Several other peasants were also making their way towards the counter when Arturo whispered something to a man at a table behind him. The peasant stood up, bumped into Hard-Face, said a few words in Sicilian and grabbed the empty glass from his hand. He was on his way to the bar before Hard-Face could object. Reluctantly, the peasant sat down again and Petrie rubbed at his bristled chin to ease away the tension. A reprieve. But not for long, he guessed. A hand nudged him in the back, gestured over his shoulder to the bar where the girl was looking at him as she raised a bottle. What the hell were they up to?

Standing up, he eased his way between chattering soldiers, reaching the bar as Arturo's friend collected two full glasses and headed back for the tables. Soldano, slim and voluble, had turned round and was looking across the room, wondering why the Sicilian was still at his table. Keeping his folded jacket close to his body for fear he might bump someone and they would feel the hardness of the concealed gun, Petrie edged in towards the end of the counter where the girl directed him with a nod. This charade wasn't going to last much longer: Soldano was already wandering towards Hard-Face's table. If the mountain wouldn't come to Mahomet . . . Taking the glass from the girl, Petrie leaned against the wall near the phone and watched Arturo's friend handing Hard-Face the filled glass. The peasant was cautious—with a quick movement he took the other man's glass and raised it. *Salute!*

Sweat gathered on Petrie's back as he watched Soldano chatting to the grocer. It was going to be easy: the Italian had already spoken to several peasants, so when he stopped for a word with Hard-Face there would be no public display that he

120

was an informer. The peasant who had brought back the grocer stood up, leaned over to pull at Hard-Face's sleeve, and the Sicilian turned nervously as the grocer spoke to him. Only a few words were exchanged but while Hard-Face was turned the other way Arturo emptied a phial into his glass. The sweat started to run down Petrie's back and when he glanced at the girl she jerked her head to indicate the door behind her. It only needed a violent distraction now, perhaps when Hard-Face swallowed his knock-out drops.

'You are still going out with Maria?' the girl asked him brightly. Perhaps she thought it was too long since he had spoken to anyone, that it might soon be noticed.

'Of course!' Petrie drank more wine, watching Hard-Face. 'She is the loveliest girl in Puccio.'

'And you will be getting married—to Maria?'

'I suppose so.' Hard-Face was getting impatient or nervous. He had stood up, was edging his way towards Soldano with the glass in his hand. 'It's a little early to think of marriage,' Petrie replied.

'That's what you say about all of them!' the girl pouted. 'I don't think you are an honourable man at all.' She was polishing the same glass again and again, twisting the cloth tightly while she carefully didn't look in Arturo's direction. And it wasn't going to work, Hard-Face wasn't going to drink until he had spoken to Soldano. With the untouched glass in his hand he came out behind the tables to where Soldano was standing ten feet away from Petrie while he chatted with one of the peasants. A burly soldier with his rifle looped over his shoulder stood next to Petrie, lingering over his drink. A good try, Arturo, Petrie thought grimly, but it isn't going to come off. And he couldn't expect any help from the *mafiosi* if it came to a shooting match with all these *carabinieri* present. He asked the girl for brandy quickly, took the glass, held it ready to throw in the eyes of the soldier next to him as Hard-Face reached Soldano.

The Italian officer turned with his own glass in his hand as though to exchange a pleasantry with the new arrival. He raised his glass. *'Salute!'* Hard-Face automatically lifted his own glass, drank heavily from it. Then he was spluttering, screaming at the top of his voice, a scream which swiftly faded to a horrible gurgle as he clutched at his throat, lurched into Soldano, stumbled past him and crashed down on his back close to the bar. He lay still and his lips were purplish, had a burnt-out look. There was a moment's hush and then pandemonium broke out as the peasants stood up, started shouting, moving about. *'Dottore! Dottore!'* The grocer rushed to the door, pushed past the stunned sentries as the soldiers began shouting, trying to restore order as the confusion grew worse while the burly soldiers and Soldano bent over the Sicilian's lifeless body. Petrie slipped round the end of the counter, saw no one was looking in his direction, walked quickly past the girl and through the doorway at the back. Closing the door, he shut out the babble of sound, hurried along a narrow passage which was stone-paved and littered with straw. At the far end he opened another door slowly, saw sunlight on cobblestones, felt the heat on his face. He went out into a walled yard, shut the door behind him, ran to the end wall and scrambled over it. Beyond the village wall it was open country, a naked hill-side running down to a dried-up stream-bed, and in the distance he could see the rounded hilltop where he had told Johnson and Scelba to wait for him for one hour.

He ran awkwardly down the hill slope at first because his muscles were taut with tension, but gradually he limbered up and moved faster, and when he first looked back the rooftops of Puccio were half a mile behind him and there was no one in sight. He kept on running, anxious to get under cover before any *carabinieri* appeared, and as he ran he couldn't force out of his mind the vivid picture of a Sicilian lying on his back with burnt-out lips. It wasn't knock-out drops Arturo had fed to the informer, it was prussic acid, hideous liquid which would have reduced the informer's innards to nothing in seconds. And the organization had been flawless. If this was what the mafia was capable of when it was outlawed, battered underground by the fascist police, what on earth would it be like if the monster was ever released from its cave?

*   *   *

The Wehrmacht armoured column was vanishing in a cloud of dust, disappearing westwards in the direction of Puccio as a grey Mercedes raced towards the Cefalù fork from the east. A hundred feet above the fork on a mound Petrie crouched with Scelba inside a shepherd's hut which was four stone walls open to the sky with an entrance at the back. The unsealed stones were loose and between gaps he had a clear view down to the road below, to the countryside beyond where precipices towered a mile back from the highway, and along the

123

secondary road which forked off beneath them towards Cefalù and the sea. Now that the German column had rolled past it was an ideal meeting place, Petrie was thinking—lonely, unobserved, except for the hilltop shelter where he waited with the *capo*. He took a tighter grip on the Schnellfeur as the car came closer and he tried to read the number plate, but the Mercedes was moving too fast, obviously wasn't stopping. 'This can't be Gambari,' he murmured to Scelba.

'Then he is late,' the *capo* observed, and there was something in his tone which suggested he was only too ready to criticize this Italian who worked for the Allies.

'He'll get here in due course. Gambari is very tough and very reliable—and while we're on the subject, Scelba, I don't want any trouble between you two. We're all on the same job, remember.'

'Trouble is our life,' the mafia boss replied cryptically.

Hunched down behind the wall, Petrie switched his gaze to another hole, and his disappointment was considerable as the car sped on. Passing the fork, it reduced speed, braked savagely, half-skidded on the edge of a chasm then reversed rapidly as the sole occupant, the driver, twisted round in his seat to watch where he was going. Stopping at the junction, the driver leaned out, peered round, then settled back in his seat as he opened a map and studied it. The licence number was ML4820.

'You know this man, Gambari?' Scelba asked.

'Never met him in my life.'

'Then we had better be very careful.' Squatted on his haunches, the Sicilian checked his revolver,

124

used the soiled handkerchief to wipe sweat off his forehead in case it ran into his eyes at the wrong moment. From his elevated position Petrie was looking straight down into the vehicle, was able to see that it was empty except for the driver, a bald-headed man wearing a dark business suit. Was this really Gambari? The car carried the correct number plate and there was only one man inside the vehicle, but the driver had given a most convincing performance of not knowing the district well, of being unsure where he was headed for. Or had he carried out a little charade in case the wrong people were waiting somewhere near the fork? 'We'll go down and have a look at him,' Petrie said. 'Keep well behind me and don't let him see you're armed.'

Returning the Mauser to the holster attached to his side, Petrie wriggled his way into his jacket, fastened it, and crawled out of the rear entrance. As he started scrambling down the steep slope towards the road below the driver reacted at once. Getting out of the car, he cupped his hands to stare upwards and then turned and opened the rear door for them. The easy acceptance alarmed Petrie: this man was careless—he had expected three people and only two men were coming down the slope. If he was as sloppy as this he could be sloppy about other things, about his departure from Scopana, for example. With growing anger, with the sun burning his back, Petrie stopped and looked along the road the way the driver had come, but it was still empty as far as the eye could see. He started scrambling down again, grabbing at boulders to keep his balance, then stopped. The driver had swung round, but this time his hands were no longer

125

empty as he shouted the command in Italian. 'Stay exactly where you are—both of you!' The weapon aimed at them was a German machine-pistol.

'We hoped you could give us a lift,' Petrie called out quickly.

'Both of you—get your hands up! You in the front—come down by yourself!'

With his hands at shoulder level, Petrie edged his feet down the final section while Scelba halted higher up. The driver of the Mercedes was about five feet tall and broad across the chest; in his early forties, his smooth-skinned forehead was high and the wings of dark hair above each ear did not give him an angelic look. But there was vitality and intelligence—and a hint of ruthlessness—in his slightly curved nose and the quick-moving eyes which were heavy-lidded. A patch of dark moustache was neatly trimmed and his suit was well-pressed and expensive. It made Petrie feel like a tramp simply to look at him. The man smiled faintly as he aimed the machine-pistol point-blank at Petrie's chest.

'You have brought the consignment of oranges from Palermo?' he asked softly, repeating the recognition phrase.

'Yes, but the price cannot be high in season . . .'

'I am Angelo Gambari . . .'

'James Petrie . . .' He started to lower his hands but the gun muzzle jabbed at him and he lifted them again as Gambari went on speaking.

'Major Petrie, I have one problem, one doubt. I was expecting three people. Where is the other man?'

'Right behind you.' Petrie had raised his voice. 'And I'd be pretty careful if I were you, Angelo—

126

he's been covering you ever since you arrived.'

From behind a boulder on the far side of the road Johnson stood up with his revolver levelled at the Italian's back. Gambari looked quickly over his shoulder, smiled again, then laid the machine-pistol on the Mercedes's running-board. 'So, you take precautions also? That is encouraging.' Mopping his bald head with a silk handkerchief, he stared up the hill slope where Scelba still waited with his hands hoisted. 'And that, I fear, will be Don Vito Scelba. I hope you don't regret using that mafia bastard on this operation.'

'We'd never have got here without him,' Petrie said tersely, then he introduced Johnson and waved for the *capo* to come down to the road. 'And we'll need him again to get us inside the docks at Messina,' he reminded Gambari.

'So long as you don't expect me to shake hands with him—and I want a private word with you.'

The shaking of hands proved to be no social problem. Scelba arrived on the road and when Petrie introduced him to Gambari he merely nodded and started cleaning his glasses. They had never met, these two, Petrie thought, and already they were showing by their attitudes that they hated each other's guts. Scelba undoubtedly feared that some of the credit he hoped to gain in the eyes of AFHQ might be diverted to Gambari; as for Gambari himself, Petrie had been warned by Parridge back in Tunis that the Italian had detested the mafia for years. So he'd better have a quick word with the man from Messina, let him get it off his chest. 'We're bloody short of time,' he warned Gambari as he accompanied him across a rough patch of ground between the highway and the road to Cefalù. Johnson and Scelba were climbing into the back of the Mercedes where the American had deposited the sack of explosives as Petrie halted in the open a dozen yards from the car. The Italian dropped the machine-pistol into a gulley at his feet. 'It might look strange if I was holding that if a car comes past,' he remarked. 'You had better hear about the disaster first.'

'What disaster?'

'We have lost all means of communicating with Africa: my transmitter—and agents—were seized by the Germans eight hours ago. You have brought your own?'

'No! I was relying on yours. What the hell happened?'

'I don't know. I was always careful to have people watching the approaches to the house for enemy detector vans when we were transmitting. I am wondering whether they are using some new method.' Cambari offered his pack of cigarettes. 'What worries me now is the fact that you have brought Scelba with you.'

'We need him.'

'I have a cousin who is a *mafioso*,' the Italian said vehemently, 'and I conceal my detestation of him because he is useful—but I know what scum these *mafioso* are . . .'

'We need Scelba,' Petrie repeated curtly.

'It is dangerous to use this mafia boss,' Angelo protested again. 'I have even heard that the Allies may offer him an official position when they occupy Sicily! That would be madness. Once in power he would . . .'

'Angelo!' Petrie's voice was ominously quiet. 'My job is to sink that bloody train-ferry. If it stays

128

afloat it could cost thousands of lives by bringing in heavy reinforcements at the wrong moment. The only reason we've got as far as this is because Scelba was with us—and I'm convinced we're going to need him again to get us inside the Messina docks. I don't like the idea of using the mafia any more than you do, but Scelba is essential to the operation and he's coming with us, by God! From now on you'll live, breathe and think of only one thing—*sinking the* Cariddi! Do I make myself quite clear?'

'I am under your orders,' the Italian replied quietly. 'Do not walk towards the car yet—it will look suspicious. We will wait until this vehicle has passed us.'

'It's a Volkswagen.'

'I know. That is why I advised caution,' Angelo replied.

The Volkswagen continued towards them at speed as Angelo extracted a road map from his hip pocket, opened it out and pretended to study it. They had been standing in the full blaze of the afternoon sun and Petrie was feeling horribly fatigued as he watched the racing vehicle out of the corner of his eye while he looked at the map. The Italian's deeply-tanned forehead was coated with moisture, but otherwise he appeared unaffected by the high temperature as he glanced down at the machine-pistol lying in the gulley. The Volkswagen slowed down and Petrie guessed the thought running through Angelo's mind. 'If it stops,' he warned him, 'we don't want any trouble—our job is to get through without anyone knowing we've arrived.'

'That rather depends on the enemy, doesn't it?'

Angelo inquired blandly. 'And this car is stopping. So please leave all the talking to me. The Germans have a contempt for peasants!'

Petrie glanced at his watch. Nearly 3.30 PM. Less than nine hours left to reach Messina and now another delay was coming up. The Volkswagen lost more speed, dawdled forward as a man in the front passenger seat peered out of the window, then it pulled up close behind the parked Mercedes. Petrie felt his heart thumping a little faster. Angelo had miscalculated badly. Two Germans in black uniform sat inside the car and the man sitting by the driver was an officer. Opening the door, he paused to say something over his shoulder to the driver, then he climbed out, stretched himself to his full height, hooked his thumbs inside his belt and stared at Angelo and Petrie. The SS had arrived.

CHAPTER EIGHT

Friday. 3.30 PM–7.30 PM

The SS officer was tall and wide-shouldered and immaculately uniformed. His face and hands were almost white, which told Petrie that he could only have arrived on the island within the past few days, that he must recently have been stationed north of the Alps. But he was also an alert tactician: he had hardly got out of the car when the SS driver stepped out with a machine-pistol in his hands, a weapon identical to the gun Angelo had dropped into the gulley. He leaned casually against the bonnet with the weapon's muzzle aimed towards

130

the rear of the parked Mercedes where Johnson and Scelba were still sitting with their backs to him. And the officer's holster flap was unbuttoned as he stood with one hand knuckled on his hip close to the butt of his pistol. 'What is your name?' he called out to Angelo in Italian.

'Who wants to know?' Angelo demanded.

The German stared for a moment, then reached a hand towards his trouser pocket. Taking out a pack of cigarettes he extracted one, placed it between his thin lips, returned the packet to his pocket. And then the pistol was in his fist, aimed at a point midway between the two men. A couple of deft squeezes and he'll have killed us both, Petrie thought grimly. The hand movement had been expert, as swift a manoeuvre as he had seen. 'Lieutenant Hauptmann of the Wehrmacht would like to know,' the SS officer replied softly. 'And you have exactly ten seconds in which to reply . . .'

'I am Angelo Gambari,' the Italian told him calmly. 'You are, of course, a stranger to Sicily . . .'

'Is this your car?' the German rasped.

Angelo was looking down at his map again as Hauptmann asked the question and he took his time before he raised his head and stared as though surprised that the SS officer was still there. He gazed back at the man steadily with an unpleasant expression which made Hauptmann turn his pistol a fraction so it was aimed point-blank at his adversary. For God's sake, watch it, Angelo, Petrie prayed, this young bastard is probably from Russia where they shoot first and inquire about your identity afterwards. He drew no comfort from Angelo's reply. 'Why?' the Italian inquired. Hauptmann had some difficulty maintaining his

131

self-control. He looked over his shoulder where he could see Johnson staring at him through the rear window of the Mercedes while Scelba only showed the back of his thin neck. Then he turned his attention again to Angelo.

'I asked you a question.'

'And I asked you one!'

There was something compelling, almost arrogant in the Italian's supreme self-confidence as he held the opened map and stared at Hauptmann as though he were interrogating a hostile witness in the box. The tension rose under the blazing sun, was close to breaking point as the German weighed up the opponent who was almost a foot shorter than himself, and Petrie knew they were only a whisker away from the squeeze of that white hand. What the hell was Angelo playing at?

'It is a German car,' Hauptmann pointed out.

'How observant of you . . .' Angelo's tone was mocking and without warning he had switched to speaking in fluent German. The surprise, the shadow of a doubt showed in Hauptmann's taut face.

'You speak German?' he interjected sharply.

'Again, how observant of you!' Angelo continued speaking in the officer's native language. 'Perhaps you have further observed that it carries Italian number plates?' Angelo let his map fall and it landed on top of the machine-pistol concealed in the gulley. He stooped as though to pick it up, changed his mind, and left it where it was for the moment. Petrie had no doubt that when the Italian next stooped to retrieve the map he would come up with the weapon in his hands. It wouldn't work, of course—Hauptmann could fire twice, kill two men

132

before Angelo would be able to aim the machine-pistol. Then the driver would kill Johnson and Scelba before they were able to get out of the car. Angelo, who had spent over six months as a spy behind the enemy lines, had gone over the edge, had reached that shredded state of nerves when a man takes suicidal risks.

'What about the number plates?' Hauptmann demanded.

'Amazing as it may seem,' Angelo continued in German, 'we Italians do occasionally bend our national pride and buy another country's car. You should be pleased,' he went on, 'when I bought that car Germany needed the money!'

Hauptmann's white face showed a trace of colour as he began moving towards Petrie and Angelo. If he comes much closer, Petrie thought, he was bound to see the machine-pistol which was only half-concealed by the map. Angelo stared suddenly at the Mercedes and his quick· glance worried the SS officer; swinging round, he looked at the vehicle where the two men sat placidly in the rear seat. 'What are you staring at?' he rapped out in German.

'A lizard,' Angelo explained innocently. 'It ran under the car—rather a rare variety. But you were saying?'

The brief diversion had worked: the German remained where he was as he studied Petrie carefully before he returned his attention to Angelo. 'I would remind you that this is wartime, that Sicily is a theatre of war. And two British spies are known to be in this area. Where are the car's papers?'

'They are in the pocket of the Mercedes . . .'

Hauptmann turned his head to issue an order to the driver but Angelo stopped him. 'Wait a minute! I could show you the papers to prove my ownership but I have no intention of doing so. You have no authority! Furthermore . . .'

'No authority!' Hauptmann's rage was visible now and in the tenseness of the moment Petrie's fatigue vanished as the hand under his jacket touched the butt of the Mauser. He found himself noticing minute details: the slight flaring of Hauptmann's thin nostrils which quivered almost like a nervous horse's, the braced body of the German driver preparing to use his weapon, a red spot which could have been wine or blood on Hauptmann's collar-patch. 'Tell those two men in the Mercedes to get out and cover them with your weapon,' the German called out to his driver. 'Make them lie down on the ground and then search the car . . .'

Petrie calculated whether he could withdraw the Mauser from its holster and shoot the officer in time, then decided it was impossible as Hauptmann faced them again with his pistol levelled while the driver went to the Mercedes and spoke in German. The sack of explosives would be discovered within a minute: Ed had dumped it on the floor at his feet. Angelo spread out his hands regretfully as he spoke. 'Neither of those two men understands a word of German—and if your driver molests either of them I shall report the assault to General Guzzoni . . .' He waited as Hauptmann shouted a face-saving order.

'Hans! Leave them alone! They don't understand German.'

'That is better,' Angelo continued quietly. 'I fear

that if I have to report your conduct you will be sent back to Russia within twenty-four hours . . .'

'You insolent swine!' Hauptmann levelled his pistol, aimed it direct at Angelo's chest, but the Italian still held his hands apart in a gesture of defencelessness as the German went on speaking. 'You realize you are threatening an officer of the Wehrmacht . . .'

'Merely warning him. The report would go via General Hubner.'

'You know him?'

'You asked my name—but you failed to ask me my profession. I am a lawyer and my services have more than once been called on by your own people. General Hubner is one of my clients—I have been handling a little legal matter concerning billeting for him and we have come to know each other quite well.' A change was coming over Hauptmann's attitude, a look of frustration and a hint of doubt in his expression as to whom this man Gambari, might be. Changing his target, he glared at Petrie.

'You! What have you got in your hand?' he demanded in Italian.

'This!' Petrie withdrew the hand which was holding a pack of cigarettes. He let a foolish smile drift over his face. 'You would like a smoke, sir?' An Italian car passed along the highway at speed, followed by another. Neither of them seemed inclined to linger when they saw the German uniforms. Angelo addressed Petrie as though talking to a village idiot.

'Pietro! The officer doesn't smoke cigarettes made of dung! Keep quiet and let me deal with this!'

'Why does a man in your position travel with peasants?' Hauptmann inquired contemptuously.

'Because I need workers to help repair my offices in Messina which have been bombed by the bloody British!' Angelo snapped. 'You have only just arrived here so you know nothing of the situation and you are making blunder after blunder! The heavy bombing has made workers scarce in Messina, so we have to come to the country for them and pay outrageous wages.' His voice became vehement. 'Because you are new here you know nothing! Otherwise you would have seen nothing strange in an Italian owning a German car. And now I am going to remind you of the directive issued by Enna GHQ,' he stormed. 'The directive that the Wehrmacht must cooperate with their Italian allies in the most diplomatic manner! I do not think that holding me up at gunpoint qualifies for diplomatic manners ...'

Hauptmann lowered the gun as he spoke, but he still held the weapon by his side. 'It seemed strange that in the heat of the day you should stand waiting in the sun. May I ask why you are waiting here?'

'To find my damned way, of course! What the devil do you think I was studying the map for? I am lost and there is no signpost.'

'You are going where?'

'To Scopana.'

'I have just come from there.' The German's manner was stiff and watchful but less aggressive. 'It is in that direction. I still insist that when spies have been reported in the area we are entitled to check everyone.'

'There are ways of checking,' Angelo snapped. He stooped quickly, picked up his map and strode

136

towards the Mercedes telling Petrie in Italian to hurry up. As they went towards the vehicle Petrie watched the German out of the corner of his eye. Hauptmann was still standing in the same position and he had only to walk a few yards farther to see the German gun lying in the gulley. Angelo got in behind the wheel with an impatient gesture as Petrie joined him in the front passenger seat. Closing the door, he picked up a toolkit which he placed in Petrie's lap. 'May need that,' he said briefly as he waited while a truckload of Italian troops sped past them towards Puccio. Petrie opened the toolkit flap, closed it: inside lay three German stick-grenades. 'They're still waiting there,' he murmured to the Italian as Angelo turned the Mercedes in the road until it faced the Scopana direction. 'The driver has got back into the Volkswagen . . .'

'Let us hope they drive over a precipice,' Angelo growled as he accelerated. 'Do not look back,' he warned the men in the rear of the vehicle.

Petrie glanced at his watch as Angelo built up speed and they began to move across a barren plain. It was 3.45 PM. Eight hours to the midnight deadline. 'Keep her moving,' he urged as another Italian truck sped past in the opposite direction. 'And this road's getting busy.'

'It is abnormal,' the Italian told him 'Usually there is no traffic for miles in wartime along here. Those two cars which passed us while we were with Hauptmann both carried officers. Something is happening.'

'And something is happening behind us,' Johnson warned. 'Our friends are still with us.'

Petrie swung round in his seat, saw in the

distance some way behind them a Volkswagen driving at speed. He shielded his eyes against the sun glare but still couldn't distinguish the occupants of the vehicle. 'Are you sure it's Hauptmann?' he asked.

'Positive. I saw them turning in the road. They're coming after us.'

*   *   *

They were a dozen miles east of the Cefalù fork driving through country which was utterly flat, devoid of any human habitation, a land of dust which spread away on both sides of the endless road like an ochre sea. 'This,' Angelo informed them, 'is the dust bowl.' He glanced in the rear-view mirror. 'Once there were farms and fields here but the Sicilians are bad farmers—they plant no trees and the sun does the rest. Now this is nature's cemetery where the bones of old mules are bleached by the sun. They are still behind us, you know. What does Hauptmann intend, I wonder?'

'He couldn't be sure at the Cefalù fork,' Petrie said grimly. 'Your bluff was powerful enough to worry him, but he's an intelligent bastard. He's new here so he decided to tread warily, to give himself a little more time. My guess is he's still suspicious so he's going to wait until we meet up with more of the Wehrmacht and then he'll pounce again—or maybe he'll just go on following us to see where we lead him.'

'Either would be a disaster,' Angelo observed thoughtfully as he shielded his eyes against sun glare from an oncoming vehicle. 'Christ, this road is busy today!' Another Italian truck flashed past

138

them and then the road ahead was empty. 'I suppose he could keep on our tail all the way to Scopana?'

'He came from there,' Petrie pointed out, 'so his headquarters may be in the village. And he'll have more senior officers to back him up there.'

'We slow down, let him catch us up,' Scelba suggested from the back. 'Then we shoot Hauptmann and his driver.'

'No good,' Petrie replied. 'In any case, he's probably too bright for that one. And remember, our job is to get across the island without causing a general alert.'

'We just kill them and leave them,' Scelba persisted.

'What—out here in the open? So the first army vehicle which comes along finds them and raises the alarm? And in any case there's too much damned traffic on this road.'

'But when we reach Scopana Hauptmann is liable to grab us,' Angelo objected. 'And he will have plenty of men there.'

'I know!' Petrie waved a hand out of the window at the desolation. 'Does it go on like this for much longer?' There was nowhere to hide a dead dog, let alone two fully-grown men, and when he looked back the blurred silhouette of the Volkswagen was still in view.

'For many miles,' Angelo replied.

'Reduce speed for a while. It's just possible they'll drive past us. They may simply be returning to Scopana.'

'Want to bet?' Johnson inquired.

The atmosphere inside the car driving through the heat of the afternoon was almost unbearable, but the temperature was temporarily forgotten as Angelo reduced speed and Petrie twisted round in his seat to watch the German vehicle. It was closing the gap fast as he stared through the rear window and he wondered if he had made a mistake, whether the SS men were going to overtake and stop them. He glanced ahead, saw that the road was still empty, then looked back. The Volkswagen had also reduced speed, was moving at the same pace as the Mercedes. 'They're following us all right,' Petrie said tersely, 'so you might as well speed up again. Our friends are coming all the way with us.'

'We are in a trap then,' the Italian observed. 'Because there is nowhere to hide them and because of the traffic we cannot deal with them on the highway, but if we keep driving on sooner or later we will run into more Germans. Then Herr Hauptmann will act.'

'A trap,' Petrie agreed, 'so somehow we have to get out of it. The problem's really damned simple,' he went on as Angelo built up more speed. 'We have to kill those two Germans quietly and without any risk of someone seeing us. But we have to do more than that—afterwards we have to hide two bodies and one car so they can't possibly be discovered for at least eight hours. They have to vanish into thin air. Any bright idea as to how it could be done?'

There was silence inside the car as they drove steadily on over the empty plain, drove on towards Scopana where the SS would be able to call up reinforcements, drove on with the Volkswagen always keeping the same distance between the two vehicles as solitary Italian trucks drove past them in the opposite direction at intervals, warning them that it would be impossible to tackle the enemy as the mileage between their present position and Scopana shrank with every revolution of the speeding wheels.

*   *   *

'There is this derelict farmhouse,' Scelba said quietly, 'and it is far enough from the road for us to do our work without being heard.'

'You're sure it's derelict?' Petrie queried.

'It is in the middle of all this—it has not been used for a generation. The buildings are in a state of collapse and no one ever goes there.'

'How far from the road?'

'A kilometre.'

'The road that leads to it—where does it go on to?'

'Nowhere. The track leads to the farm and stops. There is no way out.'

'No way out?' Angelo intervened. 'You mean you drive down this track into the wilderness and it's a dead end?'

'Yes. It will be a dead end for those Germans when they follow us. Literally.'

'It is too dangerous,' Angelo exploded. 'We would be driving into another trap. Supposing the SS simply wait by the highway until German troops come along? We would be hemmed in—it would be a death-trap . . .'

'The SS officer has clearly only just arrived on the island,' Scelba explained patiently. 'He will have little idea of the geography of this area. You yourself have been on the island a long time and

141

you didn't know of the farmhouse's existence . . .'

'I do not like it,' Angelo flared, his enmity towards the *capo* bubbling to the surface. 'It is too great a risk to take . . .'

'Hold it!' Petrie snapped. 'We're supposed to be fighting the Germans, not each other. How soon do we reach the point where this track turns off, Scelba?'

'Pretty soon. Maybe in five minutes.'

'If the farm's derelict where do we hide the Volkswagen? We need at least eight hours before there's a chance it could be found.'

'There is an old barn where you could hide the vehicle.'

Johnson looked back, saw the Volkswagen still a quarter of a mile behind them. 'I suppose these guys couldn't be on a regular patrol of this road?'

'And if they are?' Scelba inquired.

'Then they'll be expected back at a certain time at their Scopana headquarters. When they don't arrive search parties will come looking for them, and along here there aren't so many places to search. . .'

'Ed's right,' Petrie said. 'Can you see this farm from the highway?'

'Yes,' Scelba replied. 'The country is completely flat for miles around, and since the farm is only one kilometre from the road . . .'

'First place they'll search then, I reckon,' Johnson said dryly. 'My vote goes with Angelo's. It's too damned risky.'

'Except that we're not putting it to any vote,' Petrie pointed out. 'We may be fighting for democracy, but here I take the decisions. Warn me, Scelba, when we get closer.'

142

'When we get closer you will see the place.'

So I've got about three minutes to make up my mind, Petrie thought. Three minutes in which to take a decision which could be fatal either way. Driving to the farm could lead them into a death-trap—if the SS men decided not to follow, to wait by the highway until a truckload of German troops came along. But as Scelba had pointed out, how could Hauptmann know that the track led to nowhere? Unless he had a detailed map of the area. Taking out his own map, Petrie spread it over his lap and checked it carefully, then passed it over his shoulder to Scelba. 'I can't see any track or any farm marked on this—check it for me.' A few moments later Scelba confirmed that the place wasn't shown. 'It is hardly surprising,' the *capo* remarked, 'since the farm has been abandoned for over thirty years. And you can see it now . . .'

The place was a blurred huddle to the south, a silhouette which might have been no more than a pile of stones amid the brown desolation, bleak and uninviting as a decrepit mausoleum. Through the heat dazzle Petrie watched it, watched for any signs of life as Angelo began to slow down and look for the track entrance while he waited for Petrie's decision. It would tell Hauptmann instantly that something was wrong if they turned on to the track, would confirm his suspicions because they would have left the main road to Scopana which Angelo had reported as his destination. How would Hauptmann react: wait cautiously on the highway or chase after them, confident now that he had been right to be suspicious? Petrie recalled the SS officer's attitude at the Cefalù fork and still couldn't be sure. Any decision could only be a

143

guess and two out of the four men in the Mercedes believed it would be a fatal error to turn off the highway. Even at this late moment Petrie was in a neutral state when he saw another truck approaching from the other direction. If this were a German vehicle . . . 'I can see the entrance to the track,' Angelo said. 'Do I turn off or go on?'

'Slow down a little more. I want to see whether this is a Jerry vehicle.'

'That farm is too exposed,' Johnson said.

'We shall never reach Messina if we turn off,' Angelo pleaded.

Scelba said nothing as he stared at the farm. The truck roared towards them, Johnson reported that the Volkswagen had also reduced speed, the entrance to the track came close, a track almost buried under the dust of many years which had drifted over it. The truck sped past them, an Italian vehicle. 'Turn off!' Petrie snapped. 'We're going to chance it . . .'

*   *   *

'Hauptmann's pulled up on the highway! He's not coming after us.' Johnson shouted.

Angelo's lips tightened as he glanced at Petrie who said nothing. They were moving into the dust-bowl and conditions were appalling: the wheels of the Mercedes whipped up drifts of blinding dust which rose in a cloud like a smoke unit laying down a screen. The dust rose to the height of the car, plastered itself over the windscreen, filmed the bonnet, became so dense that the glare of the afternoon sun was blurred as the car bumped over the pot-holed track and shook so violently that the

144

engine stalled. As Angelo tried to re-start it Petrie looked back and could see nothing through the dust, could gain no idea as to whether Hauptmann was still parked on the highway, confident that now he had them trapped. Then the motor fired and they were moving again, following a curve in the track which gave Petrie a clear view back along the fringe of the dust-cloud. Hauptmann was turning off the highway. The Volkswagen vanished inside the dust. They were coming.

'He's grabbed at the bait,' Petrie said tersely. 'Let's get it quite clear what we have to do. I don't want any shots fired—we're too close to that highway. We'll use knives and bare hands and I don't want anyone to get hurt . . .'

'Except the Krauts,' Johnson said quietly.

'Shut up, Ed, and listen! We have to do this job so no one hears us—and none of you is to take any risk that's avoidable. I don't want any heroics on this trip. So remember the driver has a machine-pistol and Hauptmann is quick with his gun— damned quick. I want to take them separately if possible—two of us to each man.'

'That will be difficult,' Scelba interjected. 'The farm is small. . .'

'The whole operation will be bloody difficult, and don't let anyone forget it. Now, I want to get to that farm well ahead of them . . .'

The Mercedes ground forward through the dust, lurching into a pothole, dragging itself out again, and then Petrie caught a glimpse of the buildings— a roof with half its tiles missing which gave it the look of a carcase picked clean of flesh by vultures, a crumbling wall over six feet high which surrounded the farm, the still intact roof of a long barn. Dust

145

fogged the view and then they were coming in close as Johnson took out a knife and Scelba threw his dead cigar out of the open window. No one spoke as they crept through a gateway in the crumbling wall, entered a large yard in front of the farmhouse and saw the squat outline of a stone well in the centre of the yard. The place was more of a ruin than Petrie had anticipated and half the barn's wall had gone, exposing a framed view of the dust-bowl beyond. As a hiding-place for the Mercedes it was useless. 'Drive round to the back of the farmhouse,' he ordered. 'I want the car out of sight.' Angelo drove slowly past the barn and at the back the wall had crumbled into a scatter of stones. Only the farmhouse was still standing. 'This place is no good . . .' the Italian began.

'It will have to do!' Petrie snapped. 'Switch off and take the key with you. You come with me. Ed, you and Scelba get inside the barn . . .'

He ran round to the front of the farmhouse the way the Mercedes had been driven and glanced quickly round the yard. No hiding-places at all except behind the section of wall still standing— which was the first place Hauptmann would expect an ambush. As Angelo joined him Scelba ran into the yard. 'The well . . .' the *capo* began. 'Get to hell out of it back to the barn!' Petrie ordered. As the Sicilian disappeared Petrie ran over to the well, shone his torch down it briefly. A good thirty-foot drop down a cylindrical funnel with no reflection from the bottom. The well was dry as old bones and was useless for concealment because there were no projecting stones. He could hear the Volkswagen's motor now as the vehicle crawled along the evil track closer to the farm. Thank God for one thing: Hauptmann was still coming. 'The farmhouse, Angelo . . .' It was the only place where they could get under cover and he led the way, running light-footed over ancient cobbles half-submerged in dust. The door to the house was intact when he reached it, but when he touched it the structure fell inwards, leaving its rusted hinges and collapsing inside the house. Powder from the rotting wood sprayed the stone-paved floor beyond. He went inside, using his torch as the Volkswagen's motor coughed beyond the wall and then continued on course.

The house smelled of ancient decay and there was no furniture in the darkened interior; only the room walls were still standing and the doors had disappeared. The place was a shell. In a rear room he found the skeleton of a large bird lying on the stones and the back door was still standing; opening it he saw the empty Mercedes parked in the sun and he left the door wide open to keep an eye on the car: if the Germans disabled the vehicle they were finished. And now they could only wait, wait and hope that the Germans came into the darkness of the farmhouse while their sight was still blinded by the sun's glare.

*   *   *

'Stop the car, Hans! I do not like the look of this.'

Hauptmann gave the order as the Volkswagen came close to the entrance in the wall. The driver pulled up, switched off his motor at a further command, and Hauptmann sat up with his head out of the window as he listened carefully. No sound of a car's engine. They must have stopped

147

somewhere close to the farm. He opened the door quietly, stepped out with his pistol in his hand, motioned to Hans to follow him, to slide across the seat and get out of the same door. His eyes checked the wall for any sign of movement. The Italian had lied when he said his destination was Scopana; instead he was cutting across country to join some other road which would take him south instead of east. Or was this place some kind of rendezvous for spies?

'Shall I circle round this side of the wall, sir?' Hans whispered as he took a firmer grip on his machine-pistol.

'No! We stay together, you fool! Keep abreast of me five paces away. We will go up to that wall . . .'

They moved towards the entrance, placing their feet carefully. Hauptmann was suspicious of the blind side of the wall, the obvious place to lay a trap for anyone approaching it, and as they came close to it he picked up a stone and threw it. The stone ricocheted off the well at the moment the German peered round the wall. The cavernous hole in the barn, the empty doorway of the farmhouse gaped at him. 'They're not here, sir,' Hans whispered. For a moment Hauptmann was inclined to agree with him: the farm looked so damned deserted. Then he made a gesture and they began circling the outside of the crumbling wall. When they found that the track ended at the farm, when they saw the abandoned Mercedes, Hauptmann nodded. 'They panicked when they saw we were following them. Check that barn and then come over to the farmhouse—they will be shivering with fright in some corner . . .' Hauptmann examined the car to make sure it was empty, then went inside the house through the open rear door. Once inside he waited to accustom his eyes to the semi-darkness, then explored the downstairs rooms one by one. Empty. Except for a dead bird. But he was careful not to go upstairs alone: once the barn had been checked he could search the upper floor with Hans to back him up. Outside the house he began to have doubts; there had been no sound of anyone's presence since they had arrived, so perhaps they had panicked more than he had realized, were already making their way through the wilderness at the back to the farm. He walked slowly round the side of the house, his shadow preceding him as he made his way back to the Mercedes with his pistol held out in front and his eyes fixed on a window above him.

Pain like a stab of rheumatism caught him in the back as he reached the rear corner. Petrie's gun-barrel smashed down on his right hand, grazed his knuckles brutally as he dropped the weapon and clubbed at his assailant with his left fist. Petrie saw the huge SS officer lurch towards him, felt hands grappling round his back as the German took him in a ferocious grip and tripped him behind the ankles with his boot, then he was falling with the full weight of the German on top of him. A fist clubbed his face for the second time as he took the shock of the fall on his shoulders and clawed for the German's neck. Hauptmann was still struggling with Petrie when Angelo bent over him, hauled out his stiletto knife, penetrated the German's back and rammed it home higher up. Hauptmann went limp but Petrie still had trouble disentangling himself from the body's weight, and when he staggered to his feet Angelo was staring down in

149

surprise. 'He had my knife in his back . . .'

'Men have walked half a mile with a stiletto wound,' Petrie said breathlessly. 'Let's get over to the barn fast!'

When they entered the tottering structure they saw the German driver sprawled on the floor with a knife protruding from the back of his neck. 'We're up here,' Johnson called out. 'I was going to drop on him but Scelba got him first . . .' The two men were perched in a hay-loft reached by a ladder and the American was talking as he clambered down to join them. 'Scelba threw his knife—the range must have been a good fifteen feet but he got him in the neck.'

'He should have aimed for his back,' Petrie commented.

'I think he did, but we were lucky!'

'Haupmann's dead, too,' Petrie went on quickly. 'Now we've got to hide these bodies . . .'

'The well! I tried to tell you earlier,' Scelba explained as he joined them at the bottom of the ladder. 'No one will ever find them there. I will deal with their carcases while you hide the car.'

'In here?' Johnson asked dubiously.

'No, I've got a better idea,' Petrie broke in. 'If search parties come looking for these two they mustn't find them or the car. Ed, the first thing is to drive that Volkswagen into the yard . . .'

Scelba attended to the disposal of the bodies without ceremony, dragging each one by the heels across the cobbles until he could loop the legs over the rim of the well. Hans went down the thirty-foot drop first, and because he was smaller the *capo* had no trouble with him, but Hauptmann proved more obstinate: his broad shoulders stuck in the neck of

150

the well, refusing to budge as Scelba, sweating at his work in the heat of the sun, twisted and shoved at the crumpled form. Swearing at the difficulty, he padded over to the wall, helped himself to a large rock, went back to renew the onslaught. Raising the rock high above his head he hammered it down with great force. The rock struck the obstacle, leaving his hands as obstacle and rock dropped to the bottom of the deep funnel. He spent the next few minutes dropping more rocks into the well until he filled up the base so that anyone peering down would see nothing but stone. And when he had completed his grisly task the Volkswagen itself had disappeared.

The vehicle had been driven by Johnson into the yard and, under Petrie's instructions, parked close to the inside of the leaning wall. Angelo then used a tyre lever from the Mercedes as improvised crowbar, heaving at the instrument until the wall tottered and threw its great bulk with a crash over the vehicle parked beneath it. For ten minutes the four men worked furiously, piling up more rocks over the still exposed portions of the vehicle until it was totally buried under a wall which appeared to have collapsed naturally with the passage of time. 'We have spent too long on this,' the Italian observed as he wiped his filthy hands on a cloth and surveyed the result.

'You're wrong there,' Petrie told him. 'So far the only evidence that we're on the island is this car and those two dead Germans. If they were found an alert would go out over the whole of central Sicily, but somehow I don't think they're going to be found.'

The highway was deserted as they drove back

151

along the track through another dust cloud, but Petrie only allowed himself to feel a sense of relief when they had reached it and were driving east again. As they sped along the road he looked back towards the blurred outline of the abandoned farm; they needed eight hours before the SS men were discovered, but it could be eight years before anyone unearthed the macabre secret of the dust-bowl.

*   *   *

Field-Marshal Kesselring was chewing a grape as he held the telephone in his hand and stared moodily out of the open window where brilliant sunlight lit the courtyard below. The clouds had gone from Naples so Allied reconnaissance machines would be active. The line crackled, he pressed the instrument closer to his ear, and the Luftwaffe base commander at the other end began speaking. 'You are inquiring again about the position of the 29th Panzer Division, sir?'

'Yes! There is some trouble with communications and I cannot reach Rheinhardt. Have any of your planes made contact?'

'Only half an hour ago, sir. One of our fighters saw a column of his tanks just south of Formio . . .'

'The cloud's cleared, you mean?' Kesselring asked anxiously.

'No, sir! It was only by a stroke of luck that my pilot saw them. There was a very brief gap in a heavy cloud bank and then it closed over. I doubt if any enemy planes will see him yet.'

'And the weather forecast for that area is?'

'Continuing heavy cloud until nightfall. Do you

wish me to report if we see Rheinhardt again?'

'Yes, Honneger. Keep in touch. Formio, you said?'

'It is a small village in southern Calabria ...'

'I know it! Goodbye!'

Replacing the receiver, Kesselring walked quickly to a side table and studied the map. Yes, Formio was exactly where he had thought it was, a hell of a long way south. The sabotaged bridge must have been replaced in record time and Klaus Rheinhardt was living up to his reputation as the fastest-moving divisional commander in the Wehrmacht. Surpassing that reputation, in fact: at this rate the 29th Panzer would reach the straits by eight o'clock in the evening. The decision now was whether to send Klaus straight across to Messina as soon as darkness fell.

Kesselring walked slowly round the huge room lost in thought. He was convinced that the next Allied objective was Sicily, whatever those fools at Supreme Headquarters in East Prussia might think, and he was tempted to send the order for the *Cariddi* to cross the straits at once from Messina and wait for Rheinhardt at Giovanni, the mainland port. But that might be dangerous: if the Gestapo saw what was happening they would inform Supreme Headquarters instantly. No, he would wait a few hours longer until Rheinhardt was closer to the straits. Until 7.30 PM.

*   *   *

'The target is still waiting for you at Messina,' Angelo said in answer to Petrie's question. 'All four thousand gross tons of her. As you know, your bombers sank five out of six of our train-ferries, but that was before the seven hundred guns were brought in to defend the straits. Now I think they will never get through.'

'So we will,' Petrie told him. It was an exhilarating feeling to be racing along the highway, speeding across a shimmering plain after the frustration of crawling along in the Fiat, after the back-breaking walk to Puccio. Fortunately there had been no further exchanges between Angelo and Scelba, and in the rear of the Mercedes the mafia boss sat quietly smoking his cigar while Johnson, tired and with nothing to keep him alert, had fallen into a semi-hypnotic trance as the car moved farther and farther east. The monotony of the endless plain also dulled the American's senses, but in the distance the scenery was changing where the big mountains of the Nebrodi loomed in the haze, jagged summits which seemed to float like islands in a vaporous sea.

'Major Petrie!' Scelba stirred and the overheated leather creaked under his bulk as Angelo's expression became wooden and Johnson, on the verge of falling asleep, forced his eyes to open. 'Somewhere along the way, perhaps when we reach Scopana, I have to make a telephone call.'

'No phone calls!' Angelo interjected firmly. 'We must have no more communication with anyone this side of Messina.'

'What about gas,' Johnson called out. 'We haven't enough in the tank to get us to Messina.'

'I know! When Major Petrie called me I left Scopana at once and there was no time for a refill. But that is no problem—I have a supply in Scopana and we fill up when we arrive there.'

154

'Then I can make my call while you attend to the petrol,' Sqelba said equably.

'No phone calls! The *carabinieri* have been known to tap the wires. The call from Puccio was essential–but no more!'

Petrie listened to the argument without intervening: better to let them get a little of the spleen out of their systems so long as they didn't go too far. After a slanging match, the tension between the two men might relax a little. It was a slim hope, and Scelba's next words didn't do anything to reduce the psychological temperature building up. 'I see,' he said ironically, 'you are quite confident that you can get our friends inside the dock area all on your own?'

'Plans have been made.'

'On the basis that only the *carabinieri* will be guarding the gate to the *Cariddi* dock?'

'That is the situation,' Angelo snapped. 'The *Cariddi* is an Italian vessel and the authorities will not allow the Germans to interfere. Commandant Baade tried that once and was told to take a dive into the straits!'

'But the tension is rising now,' Scelba persisted. 'Soon a state of emergency may be proclaimed and then the Germans may reinforce dock security.'

'We shall know that when we get there,' Angelo replied obstinately. 'And now, perhaps, you will use your mouth to smoke that cigar while I concentrate on driving!'

'When we get there may be too late . . .'

'Major Petrie!' Angelo reverted to speaking in English so the *capo* wouldn't understand him. 'I do not think it is wise to let this man make any phone call.'

155

'Maybe we ought to see who he wants to phone and why,' Petrie suggested in Italian. 'Scelba, what had you in mind?'

'Getting you inside the *Cariddi* dock will be a very dangerous operation,' the *capo* began, stressing the enormity of the service he was rendering. 'You are already many hours behind your schedule, so when you arrive everything must be ready. There must be no delay. Is that correct?'

'Agreed,' Petrie said.

'Then it is essential that I phone a man in advance to make the arrangements . . .'

'What arrangements?'

'There are three possible methods which might be used . . .' Scelba trailed off vaguely. 'Only my men inside Messina will know what the present situation is, so I suggest we must leave it to them to decide . . .'

'You tell us nothing!' Angelo growled as he slowed a little to overtake a mule cart.

'Wait a minute!' Petrie's tone was sharp. 'I'll think about this before we get to Scopana, then I'll decide. Once we're inside Messina, Angelo, we can't afford any slip-up, any waste of time.' He let it go at that. It was obvious that Scelba was anxious to obtain all the credit he could out of helping them, but he didn't want to take any risk of losing the *capo*'s cooperation. It was equally obvious that Angelo so mistrusted the mafia boss that he would happily have thrown him out of the moving car if he had his way. To compensate for his frustration, the Italian pressed his foot down farther. The speedometer needle climbed and in the back seat Johnson looked out of the window with wonderment as a stone wall shot past him in a long

156

blur. Petrie dried his hands on the jacket rested in his lap; the way Angelo was driving they'd be wringing wet again within minutes. 'That cousin of yours you mentioned,' he said, phrasing it carefully so that Scelba wouldn't realize he was referring to a *mafioso*, 'he doesn't live in Scopana, does he?'

'Yes. He is the man who is supplying me with the extra petrol. It worries you?' he inquired shrewdly.

'Your cousin has other friends in Scopana?' Petrie asked.

'Yes, a number of them.' Angelo switched to speaking in English. 'The place is a headquarters for the mafia organization in the province. Does it matter?'

'Probably not.'

But it could matter. Petrie was thinking hard, trying to see round the next corner, to foresee the next danger point. It was this characteristic which Colonel Parridge had noticed long ago in Petrie, a characteristic which elevated him above the other officers in the Felucca Boat Squadron—the ability to keep one eye on the present and another on the immediate future. From what Scelba had told him in Palermo, Petrie reflected, the search for the mafia underground was intensifying, and since there was a mafia faction in Scopana the *carabinieri* might well turn their attention to that place. But they needed more petrol which could only be obtained there. Unfolding his silk map, he spread the coloured cloth out over his knees and studied it for a few minutes, then spoke to Angelo.

'What's this little railway which runs through the mountains beyond Scopana?'

'It is single-track, a very old railway even for Sicily.' Angelo frowned, stared through the

157

windscreen at something in the distance. 'It goes through Sala past the big new German transport park I reported to Tunis about recently, then on to Enna where GHQ is.'

'We've bombed it, I imagine?'

'No, it is still functioning. They are using it night and day to shuttle troops from Enna to the Scopana area. I reported this also, but apparently your planes have been too busy to bother with it. This vehicle ahead is a German staff car . . .'

'With a motor-cycle escort.'

The atmosphere of soporific fatigue inside the Mercedes disappeared. Johnson checked his revolver, Petrie reached for the toolkit bag under his seat and extracted a stick-grenade, then passed the Mauser over his shoulder to the American. 'Keep this for the moment, Ed, in case you have to use it through the rear window. Motor-cyclists first, driver of the car next.' He swung round in his seat to emphasize his words. 'But don't forget this—at this stage we want to avoid trouble if we possibly can. Open up only if you have to!'

'Understood!' Johnson removed the magazine, checked the action, pushed the magazine home again. 'Maybe we should let him keep ahead of us?'

'Running out of time, Ed. We've got to maintain maximum speed while we can.' Turning to the front, he stared through the windscreen for a moment. 'Right, Angelo. Overtake!'

The German staff car, moving at speed less than a hundred yards ahead, was flanked by the motorcyclists and between them they occupied the whole highway. One of the cyclists, hearing the powerful car coming up behind them, turned his head, waved the Mercedes back. 'To hell with that!' Petrie snapped. 'Give them the horn.' Angelo reduced speed, pressed the horn continually with an on-off sound. The cyclist turned in his saddle again, pointed at the staff car, then waved them back viciously. 'Keep up the pressure,' Petrie said. 'They're going to have to shift!' Angelo glanced dubiously at Petrie as he kept the horn going, but Petrie ignored the glance. The last thing in the world an Allied sabotage team would be expected to do was to drive up behind an enemy staff car with a blaring horn—and they were late!

The cyclists and the staff car maintained their positions and Angelo kept his hand on the horn as the two vehicles swept along the highway. Petrie's eyes narrowed as the left-hand cyclist rode with one hand while he unfastened his holster flap, but a moment later a hand came out of the car and made an abrupt gesture. I wonder who the devil is inside this car? Petrie wondered, and then the left-hand cyclist, responding to the hand gesture, speeded up, turned in front of the staff car and the hand was waving again, waving them on. Wiping moisture from his forehead, Angelo swung the wheel, began pulling alongside the staff car, and as they drew level he glanced inside the other vehicle. Christ! The back of the car was empty. In the front beside the driver a uniformed German officer saluted them. Angelo returned the compliment automatically as Petrie spoke out of the corner of his mouth. 'What's the matter?'

'That's General Ganzl, German chief-of-staff at Enna! He's the brains behind the defence of Sicily.' The exchange took only seconds, the Mercedes was still level with the staff car, Petrie was gripping the grenade in his lap under his jacket. One quick toss out of the window . . . 'Get ahead!' he said instantly. The Mercedes pulled past the motor-cyclist, surged forward along the deserted highway. In the back Johnson's hand felt fixed to the butt of the Mauser, his whole body rigid with muscular tension. 'We'll never get another chance like that,' he said. Petrie didn't reply: for a split second when Angelo had spoken the name, Ganzl, his finger had tightened over the stick grenade, but for a split second only. They had come to Sicily to sink a train-ferry, not to kill a general. 'Polite sort of chap,' he said as he looked behind and saw the staff car fading into the distance. 'And he must have read the Enna directive about showing courtesy to his allies.'

'We're in a German car,' Angelo reminded him.

'With Italian number plates. And Ganzl is good—he'd notice a little detail like that.'

They drove on a long distance until an army column brought them to a complete halt. They saw it coming, spread out over the full width of the highway, an endless line of tanks and trucks and guns, and they avoided it by Angelo's quick-wittedness. Dropping into a dip in the road, one hill crest away from the oncoming column, he swung the wheel savagely, took them off the highway, down a short slope and on to the dried-up bed of a river. They waited there for a long time, hidden from the column in the lee of the riverbank but fully exposed to the glare of the lowering sun, slowly melting as they sat in silence because no one had the energy to talk in the terrible heat of the late afternoon. Then the roar of the enemy's engines above them faded, Petrie went up to the highway, found it deserted, and within minutes they

160

were driving east again at speed.

*   *   *

They were coming close to Scopana and Petrie was again studying his map as Angelo drove down a long valley with mountain slopes on either side; on the bare slopes tiny villages clung miraculously high up in the evening haze, so remote you wondered how they were ever reached, but Petrie ignored the scenery as he asked his question. 'That single-track railway which brings troops from Enna to Scopana—does the train take soldiers back to Enna?'

'No, it goes back empty.'

'You're sure?'

'Yes. They bring in troops from Enna, leave them, the train goes back empty. I was talking about the railway only a few hours ago with my cousin in Scopana.' The Mercedes sped past two goatherds with their flock trailing along the roadside in the blazing sun. As they overtook the little procession Petrie caught the faint tinkle of the animals' bells.

'So when it goes back towards Sala and Enna only the crew's aboard?'

'Only one man—the engine driver. In wartime he acts as fireman as well.' Angelo glanced at his companion. 'You are very interested in this railway?'

'How often does the train run?' Petrie asked, ignoring the Italian's question.

'About once each hour, I would say. As I told you earlier, it is a shuttle service and they keep it running through the night. There are two trains in

161

use all the time—because the line is single-track the one from this direction waits on a side-loop about halfway to Enna until the other passes it. Why this great interest in the railway when we can get petrol in Scopana and drive all the way to Messina?'

'Just looking ahead,' Petrie replied noncommittally, then he decided to explain a little more. 'For one thing there might be trouble in Scopana if the authorities go looking for your friends. For another, if one of your captured agents cracks under questioning he may tell them about you and this car. Pull up a minute, Angelo, I want to check something.'

When the car had stopped close to a withered tree, Petrie indicated a place on his map with his thumb. 'The petrol we have left would take us about there, wouldn't it?'

'You mean Scopana Halt? The railway terminus? But we have the transport and I still think . . .'

'Answer the question, Angelo! If we can stick with the Mercedes, we probably will. But I've got a feeling we may run out of luck soon.'

'With the petrol we have left, we could just about reach Scopana Halt. You are thinking about the German transport park at Sala?'

'Something like that had crossed my mind,' Petrie admitted as Johnson leaned over between them to study the map.

'You mean hijack a Kraut truck?' the American inquired.

'Look, Ed . . .' Petrie twisted round in his seat to face the two men in the back. 'We're so far behind schedule we may have to risk turning up to the coast road where we can make speed direct for Messina. For the moment, we'll keep moving for Scopana.'

'We shall be there in ten minutes,' Angelo told them as he started the car again. Five minutes later, at Petrie's insistence, they stopped inside a little village called Pollazzo and Scelba made his phone call to Messina from a bar. During the waiting period Angelo drummed his knuckles savagely on the wheel. 'We are wasting precious time,' he complained eventually. 'You should have let me go with him to hear what he said.'

'And show Scelba we don't trust him?'

'I don't! He is the most powerful *mafioso* on the island . . .'

'Which is why I chose him to get us through,' Petrie replied mildly. 'Here he comes . . .' The *capo* climbed into the rear seat beside Johnson, deliberately not looking at the Italian as he told them that he had got through, that everything would be ready when they reached Messina. Angelo grunted, clashed the gears savagely and drove fast out of Pollazzo. The tension rose inside the vehicle as the Mercedes sped towards the end of the long valley and Scopana came into view, a large village perched halfway up a mountain slope, its huddled rooftops blurred in the evening haze. They were very close to their destination when Petrie leaned forward as Angelo reduced speed, his hands gripping the wheel tightly: the tail of a long *carabinieri* column was disappearing up the side-track which led off the highway to Scopana. Petrie reacted without hesitation. 'Drive straight on—for Scopana Halt!'

CHAPTER NINE

Friday. 7.30 PM–8.30 PM

It was dusk, close to darkness, a warm purple-black darkness, and through the gloom the lights of the little train moved like an outsize glow-worm, its engine panting asthmatically as it belched clouds of dirty smoke into the air. They saw it coming from behind a pile of rocks beyond where they had abandoned the Mercedes, from the top of a slope which looked down into a gulch where the line ended, where an engine shed stood at the tip of a short spur track. A train comprising two small passenger coaches and a wagon which it pushed in front. The coaches which were lit up—a staggering breach of security—were crammed with *carabinieri*, and Petrie suspected that the large open metal wagon held more men, but he couldn't be sure in the fading light. The engine was hardly the latest model and the stack was a tall slim funnel; from the slope he caught glimpses of the engine-driver in the glow from the boiler as the train passed under them, then he stiffened as the little train slowed down and stopped close to the spur track with an impressive hiss of steam. 'First snag,' he whispered to Johnson. 'There *is* a fireman this time.' Doors were flung open, uniformed men left the coaches, scrambled down from inside the wagon and formed up with packs on their back as orders were shouted in the near-darkness. Within a few minutes a column of men on foot with their rifles slung was marching off towards a defile.

'That gorge leads through to a camp outside Scopana,' Angelo whispered. 'We'll wait till they've gone and then hope the engine-driver cooperates.'

'And the fireman—you've noticed there are two of them this time?'

'If they won't cooperate I might just be able to manage that little engine monster myself,' Johnson said quietly.

'You're joking, of course?' Petrie queried sharply.

'Not entirely. When I was with the Border Patrol I used to visit my opposite number on the other side in Mexico sometimes. They had a little train which went close to the border and I rode with the engine-driver a few times when we were checking the crossing-points. He showed me how the damned thing worked.' Johnson grinned in the darkness. 'But I never got any certificate for performance!'

They waited behind the rocks with growing anxiety while they listened to the fading steps of the retreating column as it passed inside the defile. Until the column was out of hearing it would be madness to make a move, and Petrie was praying that the train-crew wouldn't start back for Sala before they could emerge from their hiding-place. The fireman had disappeared inside the engine-shed, but the driver was standing below them, mopping his forehead with a handkerchief and then drying off his hands. He had not turned down the boiler and it was clear he was resting briefly before he began the return trip. By the glow from the engine's furnace they could see his every action thirty feet beneath them as he stamped his feet, blew his nose and stretched his arms. 'I'd better go down there and try and grab him,' Johnson suggested. 'He'll be going back any minute, I can feel it.'

'We'll go down together,' Petrie said. 'And whatever happens, no shooting. The sound of a shot would travel miles on an evening like this . . .'

'Better I go down,' Angelo interjected. 'You are dressed like peasants and the driver may not like that. It is lonely here and my clothes should reassure him.'

Scelba spoke abruptly, surprising them all. 'I will go with Gambari. Someone must watch out for the fireman and I speak the language.' Reaching inside his jacket pocket, he extracted a sheathed knife, removed the short-bladed weapon from its covering and tucked it up his sleeve.

'We will go together them' Angelo said.

'What are you going to tell him?' Petrie asked.

'The truth—partly. It always sounds most convincing. I am a lawyer from Messina and my car ran out of petrol in Scopana. So I have walked here in the hope of finding a train to Enna where I have an urgent appointment. Could I borrow your revolver, Captain Johnson? It is smaller than my Luger which I will leave with you. Thank you.'

'We need that train-crew,' Petrie warned them, 'so handle it gently.'

'If we can,' Angelo, replied. 'And I hope none of those soldiers remembers he has left something and comes back for it.'

'We'll cover you from up here. Good luck.'

The Italian shrugged. 'It is only two men.' With Scelba behind him, he made his way along the slope under the cover of more rocks, keeping an eye on the engine-driver below. The Sicilian was

166

smoking a cigarette now as he walked up and down the single track and Angelo guessed that when he had finished his cigarette he would call to the fireman and they would start back for Sala. Coming to a place where the slope was negotiable, they started their descent through the vivid purple dusk, a light so unreal that the hills seemed to glow with banked-up fires. Remembering how far sound travelled at this time of evening, they placed their feet carefully as they went down while cicadas click-clicked in the warm darkness. At track level Scelba tugged at Angelo's sleeve and whispered, 'I will go to the other side of the train to the engine-shed and deal with the fireman.' Angelo nodded as the mafia boss disappeared. Now the tricky part was coming.

Foolishly, the driver had left on the coach lights, presumably switched on by the troops so they could play cards during their wearisome journey. Typical Sicilian carelessness, Angelo thought as he felt the Glisenti revolver in his pocket and walked quietly along the track. He was close to the driver before the man turned, saw him, dropped his cigarette and reached up a hand to climb into the cab. 'Wait a minute,' Angelo called out. The Sicilian paused, thrust his hand inside the cab and brought out a vicious-looking crowbar. Just beyond the glow from the furnace fireflies danced in the darkness as the Italian halted a few feet away from the driver. 'That is not necessary,' he said quickly. 'I need to get to Enna urgently—can you give me a ride? I will pay the fare, of course.' An inflated fare for the driver's pocket, he assumed. But the Sicilian, a stout man with an unpleasant face, shook his head as he took a firmer grip on the crowbar.

'This train has been commandeered by GHQ at Enna for military use only. And this time I stop at Sala.'

'Sala will do,' Angelo said easily. 'From there I can try and get other transport to Enna. It really is most urgent—my car broke down in Scopana and they said I might be lucky if I came here . . .'

'They told you wrong.'

'An empty train and only one passenger. Surely . . .' Angelo pulled out his wallet with his left hand.

'You can keep the money,' the driver said aggressively. 'You cannot ride on this train—it is for military use only. And now I must go.' He turned to climb into the cab and bawled across the footplate towards the engine-shed. 'Enrico!'

It was hopeless. Angelo realized that the man knew he was an Italian and many Sicilians detested the mainlanders. As the driver started to climb into the cab Angelo pulled out the revolver, but the Sicilian saw the action and jumped down, rushing at him with his crowbar. Angelo stepped back, swung the gun and the barrel caught the driver on the jawbone. Staggering, the Sicilian dropped the crowbar, stumbled, fell backwards, and in falling the rear of his capless head struck the footplate savagely. Too late, Angelo heard the scrape of a boot on metal, looked up, saw the fireman looming above him with a shovel upraised to smash down on his head. The fireman gave a horrible gulp, tottered as though uncertain whether to attack, then he crumpled on the platform and the shovel clattered harmlessly beside the track. Behind the collapsed form Scelba knelt down, used both hands to grasp the knife and ease it loose from the dead fireman's back, then he wiped the blade on

168

Enrico's vest and returned it to its sheath. 'The engine-driver?' he asked. 'Is he all right?' Angelo stooped over the body lying by the track, checked the pulse, and shook his head. Standing up in front of the furnace glow he started to beckon to the others to come down but they were already descending the slope. 'I am sorry,' he said as he handed back the Glisenti to Johnson and took the Luger in exchange, 'but we have killed them both. They were stupid enough to rush me.'

'We saw it,' Petrie replied. 'The main thing is you were quiet about it.' He looked at Johnson. 'It's up to you now, Ed. At least the boiler's got steam up, so see what you can do with it. Scelba, could you give Angelo a hand to shift the bodies into that shed while I have a look at this train?' He left Johnson inside the cab, staring cautiously at the controls, and walked alongside the train. The two small coaches were incredibly ancient and had metal-railed observation platforms at either end. Climbing on to the rear platform of the second coach, he pushed open a door and went inside, where he felt horribly exposed by the lighting. But he resisted the impulse to switch off the lights in case they could still be seen by the marching column.

A small central corridor divided off the seats which were two to a side, and in the middle of the first-class coach nearest the engine he found a tiny lavatory compartment. As he went out on to the last observation platform facing the coal tender the train suddenly moved, went forward a few yards, and then jerked to a halt which almost hurled him from the platform. Promising, very promising: Ed was getting his hand in. Jumping down to the track, he went past the cab as the American called out to him, 'What the hell did you expect? Casey Jones?' The wagon in front of the engine was large with high sloping sides, and when he climbed up on to a buffer and looked inside he saw a mess of coal dust and something white which could have been cement powder. It probably explained why some of the troops had been brushing themselves off before they formed up to march away. As he dropped to the ground Angelo, came back from the engine-shed followed by Scelba.

'I thought I heard the engine move,' the Italian called out.

'You did—in the wrong direction.'

Petrie climbed up to the footplate where Johnson was fiddling with the controls as he spoke. 'I hate to stick my neck out, Jim, but I think I might just manage this brute. That's the regulator—the cut-off's here. It seems pretty much like that old Mexican rattletrap I once drove.'

'Probably made by the same firm. Museum Pieces, Inc.' Using the shovel, Petrie dug out a place in the pile of coal spilt over the rear of the cab, secreted the sack of explosives, and piled coal back on top of it. Without the sack they might just as well have stayed at home. The toolkit containing Angelo's stick-grenades lay on the floor where Johnson had left them, and the Italian picked up his personal armoury as Petrie gave his order to the American. 'Ed, I'd like to get moving immediately!' He leaned out of the cab to shout down to the other two. 'Get aboard, gentlemen! The Santa Fé Special is just about to leave. And you have a choice—whichever you're used to. First or third class. Peasants go in the front coach!'

170

As he'd anticipated, conscious of his status, the mafia boss was not offended, but Angelo winked quickly as he looked up at him. 'I can only travel first—I am a professional man.'

The two men hurried aboard the coach behind the engine and then Angelo leaned out over the platform. 'What about the damned lights? We're lit up like a Christmas tree and a fighter plane could see us miles away.'

'Leave 'em on, Angelo, until Ed blows the whistle, then lights out—all of them. The *carabinieri* may have posted a guard above the defile and he might just get suspicious unless the train moves out as it came in. All right?'

'Let us hope so!' A door banged as Angelo went inside the train and Petrie looked at Johnson. 'You do realize we'll have to drive backwards, I take it? Can you do that?' Johnson stared at him without replying as he reached out for the controls. The train jerked backwards—towards Sala—fully ten yards, then stopped with a jarring halt which threw Petrie against the cab's side. Johnson tut-tutted amiably. 'Sorry about that! Just testing the brakes.' The train started moving backwards again and this time the engine didn't stop as it pushed the two coaches ahead of it and hauled the wagon behind. Leaning out of the cab, Petrie felt the warm night air on his face, saw the large shed which was now a temporary mortuary receding in the darkness, leaving behind Palermo, Puccio, Scopana, the whole bloody lot. He checked his watch. Exactly 7.30 PM. Four and a half hours to the deadline and they were only halfway to Messina.

*   *   *

171

At 7.30 PM the decoded signal from Field-Marshal Kesselring's Naples HQ was handed to Colonel Ernest Günther Baade, commandant of the Messina straits military zone. The high-sounding title meant that the German officer controlled all installations in the area with one exception—the *Cariddi* dock. It was this exception which made him frown as he read the signal in his office which overlooked the channel where night was falling as searchlights probed the sky. *Prepare* Cariddi *for instant departure for Giovanni immediately on receipt of next signal. If necessary invoke authority of Enna GHQ for this order. Confirm receipt of this signal. Kesselring.*

*   *   *

The hot glow of the furnace was on Petrie's back as he leaned from the cab and stared ahead. Darkness, the distorted shadows of the illuminated coaches flying over the ground, the chill clarity of the stars in the black vault above was all he could see. Soon the moon would rise but that wouldn't solve the frightening problem which was insoluble. If there was anything in the train's path, if the line had been obstructed by a landslip, their first intimation of the hazard would be when the front coach smashed into the obstacle. Not knowing the track, taking the train blind through the night was fraught with risk, but at least they were moving as every revolution of the wheels took them farther east. The track was uneven, or the coaches badly in need of maintenance—whatever the cause, the train swayed unstably from side to side as Johnson

172

built up the speed, the wheels hammered the track, the couplings rattled and the tall stack belched out furious bursts of smoke which lost itself in the dark. A good mile from the train-shed Petrie told Johnson to blow the whistle. It shrieked shrilly and then the drunken patterns of light sweeping over the earth vanished one by one as the men inside the coaches switched off; now the only light indicating the whereabouts of the racing train was the orange glow from the engine-cab, a glow which reflected off Johnson's face as he kept his balance with one hand and used the other for the controls.

To stay upright on the footplate was becoming a problem as the engine rushed forward, pushing its coaches, heaving at its wagon while the metal floor of the cab shuddered and vibrated under the rising speed and cool night air began streaming into the compartment, so they were alternately roasted by the furnace and chilled by the cold from outside. With a crisp gesture Johnson indicated to the fireman that more coal was needed for the boiler, so Petrie picked up the shovel and started feeding the furnace, an action which involved splaying his legs well apart midway between tender and furnace mouth where he could shovel up supplies and sweep them round into the redness. He went on digging out huge quantities of the dubious-coloured ore, sweeping them into the flames until Johnson, unsure of how much it would take to make the boiler burst, urged him to desist.

'We're not going all the way to Messina on this,' he shouted.

'Pity—I'd like to steam her straight on board the ferry!'

They had been travelling downhill for some

distance but now the track started climbing and the train moved more slowly as they ascended into mountain country with massive slopes closing in on both sides while the engine panted with the effort, sending up wheezing smoke-bursts and shuddering irritably. The moon was visible now, a thin quarter-moon which began to illuminate peaks and saddles and ridges while the valleys and gorges below were lost in dense shadow, and as the track climbed and turned Petrie again leaned out and saw behind the pale curve of rails descending and then, beyond the coaches in front, another high curve disappearing round a mountain slope. Withdrawing his head, he took out the crumpled cloth map and looked at it by the light of the furnace with his feet well straddled. 'There's no station before Sala,' he said, 'and the Jerry transport park is just this side of the town.'

'Convenient.'

'It's about time something was, but they won't have what I'd ideally like.'

'Well we can't just keep going with old Bellow-and-Spit until we run into GHQ at Enna. I thought you were after a Kraut vehicle?'

'Frankly, an Italian truck would be better. The Italians own this island so they can stop anything, and from what I've heard of their relationship with the Wehrmacht they're liable to stop a Jerry truck just to show who's still boss over here. They're less likely to worry about their own transport. Yes,' he summed up, 'Italian would be better, but beggars can't be choosers.'

'And that's what we're beginning to look like.' Johnson had twisted round and was staring into the distance. 'We're coming up to a tunnel.'

174

'Where?' Petrie stuffed the map back into his pocket, hung on to the side of the cab and peered out. The tunnel entrance, no more than a quarter of a mile above them, had a sinister look. A squat archway at the base of an almost vertical wall climbing hundreds of feet, its dark aperture showed no sign of moonlight beyond. Petrie told Johnson to slow down and when the American protested that they were already at half-speed he repeated the order. 'I'm thinking about what could be waiting for us at the other end of the tunnel—there could be a whole mountain division camped alongside the track,' he explained. The train slowed down, the tunnel mouth came closer as the engine chugged backwards at crawling pace. 'When we get near the far end, stop,' Petrie said. 'I'll get down on the track and have a look before we go sailing out.' The track was levelling, the coaches jostling gently as the shadow of the mountain wall fell over them and the tunnel mouth loomed opaquely, more like a slab of dark wall than an entrance. Petrie was leaning well out of the cab as they trundled closer and he saw a head emerge from the coach in front, glance in both directions, then withdraw again. Angelo was wondering why they were moving so slowly. The engine shunted backwards, crawled inside the opening, and darkness enveloped them, a darkness relieved inside the cab by the glow from the furnace.

'We'll have to speed up when we get to the other side,' Johnson said irritably.

It was a long tunnel and it changed direction several times as the slow stamp of the pistons hammered their eardrums and the fumes accumulating under the low tunnel roof settled

175

back into the cab. 'Exit coming up!' Petrie shouted. 'Keep her going until I drop my hand . . .' The train stopped almost without a jerk ten yards from the exit and as Petrie jumped down, hauling the Mauser out of its holster, Angelo appeared on the observation platform holding his Luger. 'Better come with me . . .' Petrie called up to him.

They walked past the darkened coaches and there was no sign of Scelba as Petrie asked about the mafia boss. 'He's on the other side,' Angelo explained. 'We are playing cards and I imagine he is stacking the deck against me for the next game!' Petrie grinned in the dark as his boots crunched over loose stones. An hour ago while they had the Mercedes Angelo had been prepared to ditch Scelba, but now he had the sense to realize that every man counted, especially a man of Scelba's brutal calibre. And it could have something to do with the fact that the mafia boss had saved the Italian's life when they tackled the train-crew. 'You'll end up being pals,' Petrie joked.

'Never with the mafia! But in wartime one must temporarily make use of people.'

'That's what I've been trying to tell you for the past few hours!'

They peered cautiously out of the tunnel and then walked out along the track. There was nothing in sight to indicate that human beings had ever lived here; only a slender thread of road far down the track where it passed over the railway via a level-crossing at least showed that people sometimes travelled through the terrible wilderness. The track dropped a great distance in a long curve almost immediately after leaving the tunnel, disappearing here and there inside a

176

shadowed gulch before it reappeared again farther down, and at the distant bottom it crossed over a trestle bridge spanning a waterless river. From that height the trestle was tiny, no more than a toy bridge, but Petrie estimated that it was quite a long structure, curving in a considerable arc before it reached the far side where the track ascended again.

'We mustn't forget there'll be that other train heading towards us from Enna,' Petrie reminded the Italian. 'Have you any idea where the loop is where we wait until it's passed us?'

'My cousin mentioned that it was this side of Sala,' Angelo said vaguely. 'I wasn't taking too much notice at the time because it didn't seem important.'

'Well, it's damned important now if we're to avoid a head-on collision,' Petrie snapped. 'Didn't he say anything else?'

'Something about a lake . . .' Angelo scraped a thumbnail over his dark-speckled chin where beard growth was showing. 'Yes, I remember now—the loop is next to the lake. There are very few lakes in Sicily so we should see it coming up.'

'You hope! We'd better get back on board now— and Ed will have to push the guts out of old Bellow-and-Spit until we reach that loop.'

The mention of the side-loop, the fear of a collision, had a sobering effect inside the cab as Johnson reacted to Petrie's instructions—although there was nothing sober about the way he began to drive the train. They came out of the tunnel at a sedate pace and then the American began manipulating the controls as they started the great descent. Soon the train was rocking, wobbling from side to side as the wheels revolved faster and faster while the coaches rattled and shook and shuddered under the increasing velocity. The gradient was steep and Petrie suspected that this was one of the many stretches where the regular driver would have taken it cautiously, but time was against them and they were reaching that inevitable stage in an operation he was so familiar with—the stage where you took more and more risks.

Moving to the other side of the cab, Petrie caught a glimpse of the structure, a high wooden trestle, much higher than he had realized earlier, then a flank of mountain shut it off from his view. He made his way along the cab, clinging to its side until he was close enough to the American to be sure he would be heard. 'Ed! I'll warn you later—but when we get near that bridge we'll have to slow down!' Johnson nodded, stared at the controls again as gauges flickered uncertainly. Moving at this speed they'd go straight off the bridge, no doubt about that. The train continued its headlong dash down the mountain, raced inside another gulch, a gulch so deep that again they were shut away from the moonlight and might have been inside a fresh tunnel as the reverberating clangour of the thudding wheels beat at their eardrums and made any kind of speech impossible. Seconds later they plunged out into the moonlight.

The bridge was clearly in view, a huge structure, far larger and longer than he had ever imagined, its straddled supports climbing high above the wide riverbed where rocks the size of small houses littered the watercourse floor, a floor which showed not even the track of a trickle. 'Slow it, Ed!' he shouted at the top of his voice. The bridge

178

came closer and they were still descending too fast when Petrie caught a glimpse of something moving high up in the sky. Jerking his head back, he saw the blip-like silhouettes reflecting moonlight. One of the bombers dropped away from its friends, peeled off like a bird and then started diving steadily. It grew bigger very quickly, became identifiable as an American B17 as it came lower to pinpoint its target—the trestle bridge. Once again they were under attack not from the enemy but from the Allied air forces. Angelo's recent report was being acted on—to destroy the bridge, to stop the enemy troop movements. 'Stop the bloody engine, quick!' Petrie shouted. Johnson paused a fraction of a second, then applied the pressure. The train came to a bone-jarring halt, hauling back the still-moving coaches. Buffers collided, rebounded, collided again, but the train held the track as the first bomb came down.

*   *   *

They had stopped half-inside a gulch with the engine and wagon still protruding into the open as the whistle-shriek of the first bomb ripped at their nerve ends. The detonation was a dull thump, followed by the scream of the B17s motors as it climbed up again over the mountain slope, then for a brief time the only sound was the drone of the bombers high up. 'Get farther inside the gulch,' Petrie ordered and they dropped to the track as Angelo and Scelba appeared on the platform. Petrie led the way between train and rock wall and opposite the second coach he found alcoves cut in the wall where rusty track-laying tools lay on the

179

ground. They pressed themselves into the alcoves and waited. 'If they get the engine they'll get the explosives,' Petrie said grimly.

'Christ! They'll get us too!' Johnson said in fear and indignation.

The comment was pretty valid, Petrie thought. A bomb landing on the engine would project the full force of its terrible blasting power straight down the gulch. The alcoves might save them but he doubted it. Angelo and Scelba shared the next alcove and Petrie could just see the toe of the mafia boss's large boot sticking out beyond the wall. Then the second whistle-shriek came, the horrible sound you never, never get used to no matter how many times you hear it, and as always, the bomb sounded to be heading straight for them, hurtling down to land dead centre inside the gulch. They instinctively stared upwards to where the noise was coming from. Its note grew shriller, hundreds of pounds of high-explosive confined inside its metal casing, falling briefly horizontally as it left the bomb-bay, then plummeting vertically downwards at incredible speed for the target. Muscles tensed, the bomb detonated, nerves jumped, relaxed limply. 'Not this time! It's your pals, this trip,' Petrie informed Johnson. 'B17s. Four of them!'

'Lovely!' Johnson swore colourfully. 'Not a single shot fired at us yet by the enemy. . .'

'Which is the way we planned it.'

'But this is the second time our own air force has come after us. We didn't bloody well plan that, did we!'

'It's the bridge they're after,' Petrie said calmly.

'But they'll have seen us!'

'Yes, they'll have done that. But they shouldn't

180

make us the first priority . . .'

'Shouldn't!' The American was furious at being bombed by his own planes. 'I wish I had your touching faith,' he said savagely.

Johnson squeezed his body deeper inside the alcove as he heard the third bomb coming, pressing himself against the rock like a man trying to merge into it as the hellish sound was repeated. This time the detonation was deafening, a bursting roar which seemed to overwhelm them as a cloud of debris rained down over the coach-tops, and Petrie had to twist a finger inside his ear to clear the deafness. That one had been damned close. 'They're aiming for the train,' Johnson said as he clawed muck out of his hair. But Petrie didn't think so: they'd destroy the bridge first and only then, if they had any eggs left, would they try to lay them on the train. The last bomb had been an overshoot, but the four men were so close to the bridge that they were well within the bombing arc. It wasn't a pleasant thought as more bombs fell and a second plane soared up over the mountain. In all, he counted twenty bomb-bursts, and then a B17 roared over their heads. Petrie saw the five-pointed white star clearly on its fuselage, the plane vanished from sight, and suddenly it was strangely quiet. They listened for several minutes before Petrie eased his way out of the alcove and started walking alongside the track towards the bridge.

It gave them a shock when they saw how close the structure was; less than a hundred yards beyond the gulch the track wound its way out over the trestle. 'It's still standing!' Johnson said in amazement. 'Those buggers couldn't hit the White House if they were standing on it. Thank God!' he added a moment later.

'Wait here!' Petrie said. 'I'm going out over it a little way to see how it feels. Angelo! Get back to the engine-cab and guard it—the explosives are buried under the coal.'

'I'm coming with you,' Johnson said obstinately. 'Then if you get dizzy I can hold your hand.'

Walking along the trestle was a distinctly unnerving experience: the great drop so close on either side, allied with the moonlight, seemed to exert a magnetic pulling power, drawing him to the brink. Petrie looked ahead and that was no improvement: the continuing leftward curve of the trestle was equally unsettling. And he couldn't make up his mind whether or not the trestle trembled slightly as he went farther and farther out over the elevated span. 'I don't like the look of this one,' Johnson said and pointed downwards. A large crater had excavated the riverbed very close to one of the trestle legs, so close that Petrie couldn't understand why there was no apparent damage to the leg itself. It was chilly as he crouched to see more clearly, the chill of the night which drastically lowered the temperature in Sicily even in summer for a few hours, but his hands were moist with sweat as he tried to make up his mind and knew that it was impossible to be sure. Or half-sure. 'Let's get back to the train,' he said.

Scelba met them at the entrance to the gulch and there was a strained look on the *capo*'s face as he asked the question. 'Will it support the train?'

'Can't tell until we've tried it,' Petrie replied non-commmittally.

No one said anything else as they quietly took their places aboard the train, and when they were

182

inside the engine-cab the American wiped his hands carefully before he turned to the controls. 'Dead slow, I take it?' he asked rather unnecessarily. Petrie nodded as he took up his position close to the cab entrance. As though reluctant to proceed out on to the bridge, the engine made a false start, stopping as soon as it had moved a few feet. Johnson swore, took a deep breath to calm himself, then tried again. The train began moving, steamed slowly out of the gulch, each revolution of the wheels a deliberate turn. Gently, they descended the last hundred yards, and Johnson, found himself looking at the firm ground with a pang of nostalgia as the train moved forward and they came close to the bridge. Perched in the cab entrance on the left-hand side where he could follow the span's curve, Petrie saw two heads leaning well out of the windows of the first-class coach as Angelo and Scelba peered out. Then the wheel sound changed, became a hollow echo. They were moving on to the trestle.

The two heads in front of him looked down, drawn by the awesome drop, then Scelba crossed himself quickly. It was the first time Petrie had ever seen the *capo* express fear outwardly, and he found himself experiencing an odd double sensation in his legs: the muscles felt tight and strained but the flesh felt like jelly. He stiffened himself as the hollow rumble went on and the whole train moved on to the trestle. At once the fragile-looking structure began trembling, a tremble which travelled up through the slowly-revolving wheels and into the footplate floor. He looked round quickly, caught Johnson's rigid glance, and looked away. The trembling seemed to increase as they steamed farther out along the span, following the gradual curve until they were approaching the place where Johnson had pointed out the large crater close to one of the legs. This, Petrie was convinced, was a critical moment. If one of the great bomb-blasts had been close enough it could have caused a structural failure which simply needed the weight of the train to expose it. The two heads peering out of the coach were staring fixedly downwards, hypnotized by the tremendous drop as the trembling went on and the train shuffled forward. The tremble might be natural, Petrie told himself firmly; once, before the war, he had crossed a trestle in Switzerland which also shivered as the train passed over it, but the Swiss were rather more highly respected than the Sicilians for engineering expertise.

'How's it . . .' Johnson coughed to kill the croak. 'How's it going?' he called out with exaggerated firmness.

'About a quarter of the way across.' He didn't have to look at Johnson's face to know that he was disappointed, that he'd hoped they'd be much farther along the span than this. The tremble increased as they passed over the place where Petrie estimated they had looked down at the outsize crater, and now the sensation of travelling aboard the train was different from anything Petrie had noticed earlier. Instead of shaking vigorously it was wobbling erratically as though its equilibrium were disturbed by no longer having firm earth under it, and as they moved out towards the middle of the trestle Petrie had a better view of the riverbed. It wasn't a view which enchanted him.

In the moonlight the distorted shadows of the

184

trestle supports leaned ominously, had a crazy tilt as though the bridge were bending slowly under the train's weight prior to a total collapse. Then he saw something which brought instant sweat to his forehead, a moisture so copious that when he ran his hand over it the palm came away running. Midway between the centre of the bridge and the far side a portion of the trestle beyond the track had been sheered away, torn out as though some projectile had struck it. He knew exactly what had caused the gash—the projectile was lying on the riverbed close to the trestle's base. He had counted twenty bombs but there had been twenty-one—maybe twenty-five because if you started a count of falling bombs the fear often muddled you badly. But there had been at least one extra bomb—he was staring at it lying in the moonlight, still virgin in its sinister, cylinder-shaped casing. It could be a dud, but it could be a delayed-action job already close to zero. He licked his lips, turned, caught Johnson staring at him, winked and turned away without saying anything.

The bomb lying below them had fallen closer to the trestle than any of its fellows, and Petrie knew that if it decided to detonate within the next few seconds it would take away at least two of the supports, maybe four, slicing them clear out of existence with its fearful blasting power. Amazingly enough, neither Angelo nor Scelba seemed to have noticed the bomb; they were probably not seeing the riverbed any more, not seeing anything in their numbed minds as the train trundled patiently on while its fluted stack emitted short puffs of smoke. As they came close to the bomb Petrie stared at the obscene object hypnotically. It wasn't likely but it was technically possible: the vibration of the train's wheels might shiver the leg near the bomb. The vibrations might be transmitted through the hard rock surface of the riverbed, they might reach the casing and trigger off the hitherto defective mechanism—if it was a dud. With his elbow rested on the cab edge, Petrie watched the dark sausage-shape pass under him, then he glanced in front and saw two heads turning towards him. They *had* seen the bomb! Only Johnson had travelled in blissful ignorance of what lay under them. The train continued along the trestle, and hours later, so it seemed, the hollow thump of the wheels changed to a more solid sound and they were off the bridge.

Standing up straighter, Petrie had difficulty in moving his elbow, which had stiffened with the tension. Taking a deep breath, he jerked his elbow, a bone creaked and it came loose. 'Build up a head of steam, Ed,' he called out. 'There's a big climb coming up and I want you to eat it. If we don't reach that side-loop before the other train we'll end up mashed.'

*   *   *

The train started the big climb up the mountain and Petrie watched for the lake which would locate the side-loop. It wouldn't be situated on the ascent, but he suspected that soon after they'd gone over the top they'd find it because beyond the summit of the long incline his map indicated a flattish area. The trouble was it didn't show either the loop or the lake. He was bothered about the timing now: they had waited in the gulch for the bombing to stop, a wait which more than compensated for the

186

speed with which they had come down the incline beyond the tunnel. Which meant that if they didn't make up for the delay they were going to meet the train coming from Enna head-on.

The long ascent went on quietly under the moon, across wilds which seemed remote from war, so it was almost possible to believe that the bombing of the trestle must have been a bad dream. And it was getting colder as the evening wore on and they climbed to new altitudes, so chilly that the jackets they wore were hardly sufficient protection against the low temperature; the coats they had left behind in the Mercedes would have come in useful now, Petrie reflected, as he felt the gradient slacken, and the engine move faster. They reached the top, left behind the sheer fall to their right, and because they were moving into flatter country it was difficult to realize they were still at high altitude. The train sped on over a rock-strewn plateau, and here Petrie was taking a calculated risk—their speed was taking them closer to the loop in minimum time, but it also increased the chances that they would fly past the vital point, missing lake and loop in their anxiety to reach them. The rocks gave way to an uncluttered area, an endless pancake of baked mud, and suddenly Petrie spotted the drooping reeds hanging over the mud. God! This was the lake! Evaporated by the sun to a desert. He called out to Johnson, 'Slow down!' Seconds later he saw the switch lever coming towards them. 'Full stop!' He was jumping from the footplate as the American jammed on the brake and as he ran towards the lever he heard a whistle blowing in the distance. The train heading from the other direction was almost on top of them. He heaved at the lever and it wouldn't budge. His hands were slippery, his muscles felt weak, and he heard the whistle again, louder this time, as he took a firmer grip, braced himself, and heaved with all his remaining strength. The lever moved, eased towards him as he went on pulling until it would move no farther.

'Get her moving, Ed!'

But the train was already moving, rattling gently as the engine pushed the wagon and hauled the two coaches off the main track into the safety of the loop. The moment the second coach was off the main line Petrie pushed savagely at the lever and this time it worked at once, shifting the rails back into their original position. He ran along the track with the whistle again in his ears, ran to the front observation platform, dragged himself on board, almost falling inside the coach as he pushed the door shut behind him. Then, gasping for breath, he eased the door open a few inches.

From behind the almost closed door he saw the oncoming train racing into sight round a bend, moving far too fast as it sped towards the loop with smoke belching from its stack. Inside the engine-cab Johnson bent towards the furnace to avoid being seen clearly, but the precaution was hardly necessary as the train with four darkened coaches hurtled past them, its velocity momentarily shaking their own coaches. When he looked out of the cab all he could see was the receding rectangle of the last coach, and then Petrie was running back to the lever to operate it once more. When he climbed back on to the footplate Johnson offered him a cigarette, but Petrie shook his head as he held on to the side for support, his mind numbed by the nearness of their escape. 'Ed, you've got a clear line now,' he said. 'Full speed ahead for that transport park at Sala.'

CHAPTER TEN

Friday. 8.30 PM–9 PM

The coaches jostled each other, a shudder passed through the train, and Johnson brought it to a halt as Petrie had instructed, brought it to a halt over the deserted level-crossing which carried the road leading to the transport park. They had waited for ten precious minutes aboard the train concealed in a nearby gulch, hoping for a lone German truck to drive down from the transport park a quarter of a mile away, but now something else was coming. From the front observation platform Petrie stared at a wrecked Wehrmacht truck with its nose crushed against a boulder close to the track. 'The poor devil must have skidded,' he told Johnson. 'The driver's gone clear through the windscreen. Now—if only this ambulance will keep on coming ...'

The Italian army ambulance was driving down the hill towards the level-crossing at medium speed, the driver doubtless imagining that the train parked at the crossing would move on before he had to stop. The vehicle was still some distance away and the moonlight reflected dully off its white-painted surface. No siren going, Petrie noted, so it wasn't in too much of a hurry to get anywhere. He started giving quick directions, ordering Scelba to hide behind the stationary coaches, sending

189

Angelo to hide behind a crag a little way up the road, telling Johnson to take up position behind the wrecked truck, but the American broke in with a protest. 'There could be casualties inside that ambulance—air raid casualties . . .'

'Ed, if there are, we'll have to let them drive on, but somehow I doubt it—the siren isn't going. If we find they have casualties aboard we'll pretend we're bandits after money and let them through. We certainly look the part.'

'And if there aren't any casualties inside?'

'We grab it!' He shook his head at Johnson's dubious expression. 'Ed, when we were on the train I worked out a simple specification of what we need to get through to Messina. We need a fast-moving vehicle which will take us clear through the checkpoints along that coastal highway.'

'It's against the rules of warfare . . .'

Petrie stiffened. 'So is the sinking of a hospital ship full of wounded troops—and that's what the Germans did in Greece with their Stukas. I know, I saw it happen. And we're only going to use this vehicle as transport to slip through the cordon the Wehrmacht has clamped round Messina. We're using this ambulance as a taxi . . .' He stared at Scelba. 'And unless it's absolutely vital there'll be no shooting . . .'

'They won't even be armed,' Johnson snapped.

'So there'll be no shooting,' Petrie repeated. 'But watch it, Ed. This ambulance may not be as innocent as it seems.'

They waited out of sight and now the ambulance driver was becoming a little less confident that the obstacle blocking his way was going to move; three hundred yards from the crossing he saw the wreck

190

of the army truck, slowed down, turned to drive over the ground towards the vehicle, then turned back on to the road. Petrie watched the change of direction with narrowed eyes as he glanced to his left where Scelba was crouched down behind the train, then towards the truck where Johnson was hidden. The site of the accident had an eerily deserted look, as though something inexplicable had happened between the stationary train and the wrecked vehicle, and he could imagine the bewilderment of the ambulance driver, but his reaction was odd. The ambulance was descending very slowly as its headlights splayed over the coaches, shining through the windows and out of the other side, showing up its emptiness. Twenty yards from the train the vehicle pulled up with its motor still running, which worried Petrie: if the driver swung his wheel, tumed over the ground and drove back the way he had come there could be no question of opening fire. From where he crouched behind the platform he saw that the ambulance had a very large ventilator on the roof close to an aerial. Was there something odd about this vehicle?

The white-coated driver had his head twisted round now while he talked to someone in the back. They had to wait until the driver got out to investigate—if he ever got out. The minutes ticked past and Petrie knew that something was seriously wrong: from his seat the driver would be able to see the condition of the truck and his normal reaction should have been to get out instantly to investigate the accident. The sense of something abnormal grew and Petrie blessed his caution in treating the hold-up as a military operation. Beside him Scelba placed his revolver on the ground, wiped his hand

191

dry quickly on his trouser leg and picked up the weapon again. The Sicilian's face was impassive at this moment of tension, the impassiveness of a professional gunman who had experienced such situations many times before. Petrie stiffened as the ambulance driver opened his door, stepped out and walked cautiously towards the wreckage. As he walked he kept glancing over his shoulder at the apparently abandoned train, and when he reached a point where he could see inside the concertinaed cab he stopped. Again the wrong reaction: from where he stood he could clearly see the truck driver's body slumped over the wheel and an ordinary ambulance man would have run forward instinctively. But the short stocky man wearing the uniform of the Italian Medical Corps seemed more worried about the empty train as he looked back once more at the stationary coaches. Petrie stood up, walked to the end of the platform, stepped across the track with the Mauser aimed as the driver swung round, half-thrust his hand inside his tunic and then withdrew it when he saw the weapon.

'You have no money inside the ambulance?' Petrie rapped out quickly in German.

'Nein . . .' The driver stopped speaking, realizing he had been trapped into replying in German. Petrie was covering the driver with his gun when a rear door of the ambulance opened and a man dressed in civilian clothes, a belted coat, a soft hat, stepped into view with a machine-pistol grasped in both hands. The gun was firing, bullets were spattering on the ground a few feet to Petrie's left, when Scelba fired twice. The civilian collapsed, let his weapon fall as Angelo appeared running down the road, stooped, then pointed the machine-pistol inside the rear of the vehicle without firing. Johnson came up behind the ambulance driver, extracted a Luger pistol from inside his tunic, patted the man's clothes for other concealed weapons, and then spoke to Petrie. 'That's the lot. And this guy is the most lethal medic I've ever come across. What made you suspicious, Jim?'

'It came from the direction of the Jerry transport park—not that that proved anything. But this character certainly wasn't acting normally—and now I think we'll take a quick look at this so-called ambulance. Scelba, keep an eye on this medical gunman for a minute.'

The civilian lay dead in the road at Angelo's feet but Petrie ignored the body as the Italian gestured inside the vehicle with his gun muzzle. A brawny-looking youth was sitting at a small table between the couches, his hands high above his head while he stared at them sullenly. He was dressed in the uniform of the Italian Medical Corps but on the table was a pair of headphones and a rectangular object like a radio transmitter, which was hardly standard ambulance equipment. When Petrie spoke to him in German he shook his head and said he only understood Italian.

'I see,' Petrie went on in German, 'and that instrument in front of you is the latest blood-plasma machine, I suppose? Get out—or get shot!' The German scrambled out of the ambulance, suddenly familiar with the Teutonic tongue, and while Angelo watched him Petrie bent down and pulled out a wallet from the dead civilian's inner breast pocket. The identity card he extracted from the wallet didn't entirely surprise him and he handed it to Johnson without a word. The American stared at the document and then read aloud: 'Oscar Schliemann, Gestapo officer. What the hell's going on here?'

'Something AFHQ will be interested to hear about. Let's have a closer look at this latest version of an ambulance.' Stooping to clear the roof, he climbed inside, followed by Johnson. Against one wall, where it could easily be reached by a man sitting at the table, was a small control panel. The ambulance's motor was still running as he fiddled with switches and then Johnson stared upwards as they heard a noise of whirring machinery above them. A large metal box was attached to the underside of the roof and the whining came from inside the box. Glancing up, Petrie pushed past the American and was stepping down out of the ambulance when Angelo reacted violently: reversing the machine-pistol, he struck his prisoner a savage blow on the back of the head with the weapon's butt, and then spoke with undisguised satisfaction as the German collapsed unconscious. 'The bastards!'

'What the devil's got into him?' Johnson demanded as he dropped to the road.

Petrie pointed upwards where the large roof ventilator had now expanded into a metal column supporting two metal wings like radar scanners. 'Diabolical, isn't it?' Petrie remarked pleasantly. 'This is a radio-detector van camouflaged to look like an Italian ambulance. And I'm pretty sure the Italians won't know anything about it. You see the point, don't you?'

'Not yet . . .' Johnson said slowly, but Angelo interrupted with a bitter look on his face.

'I see it only too clearly, Major. This is probably how the Germans detected my own transmitter, Orange One. A man who lived in the area where we hid it told me that the day before the transmitter was captured an Italian ambulance was parked in a yard nearby. Like a fool I thought nothing of it. And I also wonder whether the Italian Army would permit this . . .'

'If they didn't know, they wouldn't have any option, would they?' Petrie commented. 'That thing on the table in there is a listening device. So I don't think we need worry overmuch about using this vehicle as a taxi.'

Going back inside the ambulance, he operated a switch and the machinery hummed again as the detector column was lowered inside the ventilator cap. He used his knife to cut the wires, then hid the headphones and the listening device inside a cupboard; the table he folded and put inside another cupboard. The ambulance had now returned to its normal function with the two leather couches fixed to each wall ready for casualties— and casualties were available. They worked with frantic energy under Petrie's prodding: uniforms were stripped from the two unconscious Germans, a task which made Angelo regret his burst of anger since undressing an inert man is far more difficult than making him strip himself, medical tape found in a drawer was used to bind up the two prisoners; and cottonwool from the same drawer was stuffed into their ears so they wouldn't overhear any conversation if they regained consciousness. These tasks were performed after they had hauled all three Germans inside the ambulance in case they had to make a swift departure, and while they were completing the jobs Johnson was inside the engine-cab, digging away furiously to rescue the sack of explosives Petrie had hidden beneath the coal. When he returned with the sack over his shoulder Petrie and Angelo were struggling into the Medical Corps uniforms. Because they were of a similar build, the driver's outfit was the right size for the Italian, but Petrie had trouble forcing himself inside his own uniform; the tunic was a reasonable fit, the trousers were too short.

'If they made me do this for a living in peacetime I'd join the Army,' Johnson grumbled as he dumped the sack on the ambulance floor. He looked at the body of the Gestapo officer with distaste. 'Do we really need Herr Schliemann? I'm a bit fussy about who I travel with.'

'He stays with us for the moment, Ed,' Petrie snapped as he adjusted his tunic. 'When we've gone the only mystery will be the empty train—the truck obviously crashed and they may think the train-crew ran off in a panic.'

Johnson was regarding Petrie's appearance critically. 'Do ambulance drivers normally carry two days' growth of beard?' he inquired.

'They do in the British Army when they've been working eighteen hours non-stop, and I dare say the Italians have been known to work their drivers into the ground. In any case, it gives us a good excuse for not wanting to linger at any checkpoint—we're hell-bent back for our depot.'

'We dump the offal somewhere on the way?' Scelba asked, indicating the prisoners. 'Preferably with a bullet through their heads. Then they cannot talk.'

It wasn't a popular suggestion, and when Scelba

196

saw the expression on the other men's faces he hastily dropped the subject as Petrie climbed behind the wheel and Angelo joined him in his neat uniform. The petrol tank was full, which was hardly surprising since the vehicle had probably been refilled inside the Wehrmacht transport park. 'I'll drive,' he told the Italian, 'and since you look so damned elegant you'd better be the chap who gets out—if anyone has to.'

'That will be logical,' Angelo agreed. 'You are the driver so you stay behind the wheel.'

'Unless we run into a real accident—in which case people are going to expect both of us to get out.'

Petrie re-started the engine he had switched off earlier. In front of them the little train stood abandoned over the level-crossing, and he had the odd feeling that it might stay there until the invading Allied troops found it—if they ever reached this point. All of which might depend a little on four men inside an Italian ambulance. He checked his watch. 9 PM. Thank God Parridge couldn't see him now: the colonel must be assuming he was already inside Messina. He swung the vehicle through a hundred and eighty degrees, straightened up and headed north. 'Theoretically we're already too late,' he said to Angelo. 'So when we hit the coast we'll go all out.'

*　　　*　　　*

The old duelling scar down the right-hand side of General Klaus Rheinhardt's face showed up clearly as he bent over the oil-lamp inside his tent to check the time. His wristwatch showed 8.30 PM. From the tent opening he could see clear across the moonlit channel of water to the mountains rising above Messina, to where he was going, to Sicily. Beyond the tent and under the olive groves of Calabria the enormous force under his command was already on the move. Two Panzer regiments comprising over three hundred Mark IV tanks; a rifle regiment of three motorized battalions and one motorcycle battalion; an artillery regiment of twenty-four guns; one anti-tank battalion; and an engineers' battalion. From where he sat on his camp-stool Rheinhardt could hear the clank of tanks' tracks moving away over the sun-baked ground, could hear the brusque shouts of NCOs issuing urgent orders. Thank God Kesselring had taken his advice and sent the command, *Move into Sicily at once!*

'What is it, Wengel?'

Colonel Wengel saluted from outside the tent. 'The ammunition train is just arriving at Giovanni, sir.'

'As soon as the ferry arrives from Messina, get it on board. I may travel with it to Sicily myself.'

Wengel saluted, went away, leaving the view through the tent opening clear again. It was this view which interested Rheinhardt because from this point, situated seven hundred feet above the straits, he would be able to see the *Cariddi* leaving Messina harbour on its way to the mainland. The moment he saw the train-ferry he would drive down to Giovanni.

CHAPTER ELEVEN

Friday. 9 PM–10.30 PM

The headlights swept through the night as Petrie pressed his foot down, swept up over a pass and raced down the long slope beyond where the mountains soared up on both sides, majestic in the moonlight, their scarred ridges silvered and shadowed and without any sign of life. For a moment, at the pass's summit, they had caught a distant glimpse of sea like mercury, then they were plunging down the slope and a ridge blotted out the view. For a long way ahead the road was unnaturally straight where it ran between mountains which lay parallel to each other, and the surface was better than any they had encountered so far. It was still not good, would have counted as a lane in any other European country, but it was good enough for Petrie to risk a burst of speed as they tore down the deserted road towards the sea.

Beside him Angelo was sleeping, his chin sunk on his chest. Petrie glanced back through the small window into the interior of the ambulance where Johnson was sitting close to him while Scelba sprawled along the other couch, also fast asleep. They were the only occupants: the two German prisoners and the dead Gestapo officer had been left in a derelict barn close to the road a few miles back. 'Better get some kip in, Ed,' Petrie advised. 'There won't be much chance later.'

'What about yourself? You've been driving non-stop half the day and I could take over the wheel

199

for a while—I may not be in medic's uniform but we're not meeting anything.'

'We will—if you take over the wheel,' Petrie assured him. 'And as you say, you're hardly dressed for the part. In any case, I'm geared up now and I'd sooner stay that way until the job's done.'

'You think we're going to make it? It's getting damned late.'

'We should do—so long as Kesselring hasn't started sending over the 29th Panzer already. And I don't think he will—he'll wait until he gets the report of the airborne lads dropping. Then he'll know.'

'And they'll drop when?'

'If they're coming tonight, my guess would be close to midnight—just before the moon fades. It will be an hour after that before the positive confirmations reach Kesselring.'

'And if we're lucky we'll reach Messina when?'

'A little this side of midnight would be my guess.'

'It's going to be pretty close then?'

'It could be pretty close, Ed,' Petrie agreed.

This sombre thought was occupying Petrie as he drove on down the long slope between tall hedges of prickly pear which reminded Johnson of New Mexico. The American stretched out along his couch, listened to Scelba's snores, and then dropped off himself. Petrie had no inclination to sleep: he had got beyond it, and his nerves were so strung up that he doubted whether he could have slept if he tried. Sometime, after the job was done, he'd collapse, all reserves drained, and he'd probably sleep for thirty-six hours. After the job was done. Angelo woke up a few minutes later and Petrie began questioning him about the train-ferry

200

to refresh his memory.

'. . . she was built in Genoa only eleven years ago,' the Italian went on. 'She has a gross displacement of over four thousand tons and is the largest train-ferry in western Europe still afloat. She measures about three hundred and fifty feet from stern to bows and is powered by three eight-cylinder diesel-electric Burmeister and Wain engines . . .'

'Speed?' Petrie queried.

'She can travel at seventeen knots, although her normal service speed is fifteen-and-a-half.'

'And how long does it take to make the crossing between here and Giovanni on the mainland? That's just in case we can't do the job while she's in harbour.'

'The distance is eighty kilometres. Allowing for leaving and entering harbour, she makes the crossing in twenty-five to thirty minutes.'

'Thirty minutes isn't very long,' Petrie said as he noticed the weather ahead; it looked to be changing, and not for the better. Heavy cloudbanks were coming in from the northwest and a breeze was starting to blow in the previously still night. 'Can we do the job while she's still in harbour?'

'Maybe.' Angelo shrugged his shoulders uncertainly. 'But there are many guards on the dockside and only a few on board while she is crossing the straits.'

'Then it may have to be done while she's at sea—that way she'd go down deep.' He swung the wheel to take the ambulance over an ancient bridge spanning a waterless riverbed, then straightened up as the road continued between the high prickly pear hedges. Silhouetted against the moonlight, the

201

cactus extremities looked like crucified hands reaching up towards the starlit sky. Behind him boots hit the floor heavily as Scelba sat up, stretched, and then rested an elbow on the edge of the window at the back of the driving compartment. His sarcastic question showed that he had been listening to the conversation. 'And when you have finished the job you'll swim for it?' he demanded. 'There is a powerful current in the straits, Signor Gambari.'

'That has been taken care of,' Angelo snapped. 'One of my men—who is totally reliable—will take out his boat if the ferry sails with us on board. If necessary, he will keep pace with the ferry and then pick us up when we go overboard.'

'We'd have to have some means of signalling him,' Petrie pointed out.

'There is a Very pistol at my flat.'

'And this boat takes us where?'

'Down the straits towards Malta. We shall be very lucky if we manage it—the channel is infested with German E-boats.'

A match scraped behind them as Scelba lit a fresh cigar. He puffed to get it going and asked his next question casually.

'What colour will your signal light be?'

'Green.' Angelo twisted round in his seat to stare at the mafia boss. 'Why do you want to know a detail like that?'

'Because I also have made arrangements to see that the three of you get away safely after you have done the job,' Scelba explained blandly. 'At least, Giacomo is making arrangements for me . . .'

'Who is Giacomo?' Petrie interjected.

'The man I have instructed to prepare the way

for you.'

'We may not need him,' Angelo said curtly. 'I have organized a complete plan—for getting inside the dock, for sinking the ferry and for getting away afterwards . . .'

'I'd still like to hear Scelba's plan, too,' Petrie intervened again. 'It gives us something to fall back on, Angelo, if anything has happened to your chap. Once a spy-ring's penetrated, they sometimes scoop in the lot.'

'That is true,' the Italian admitted. 'You mean, Scelba, that you could get us off the ferry even in mid-channel?'

'Certainly! By using a similar method to your own. Giacomo is preparing a special vessel in case it should be needed—a swordfish boat.'

'What's that?' Petrie asked.

'The swordfish fishermen in the straits are my friends,' Scelba began. 'They use a peculiar type of vessel for their work and one of these is being adapted so it can travel at speed. One of the latest German outboard motors is being attached to it . . .'

'Where did you get that?'

'The Messina docks are packed with German equipment brought over from the mainland—largely by the *Cariddi*. Most of the men who work on the waterfront are my friends—so you see . . .' the mafia boss shrugged expressively. 'When the time comes I will ask Giacomo himself to take out the swordfish boat and he will carry a lamp at his masthead to identify himself in the darkness—a red lamp. Incidentally, the man in the swordfish boat who will try to take you to Malta, Giacomo, is deaf and dumb. I hope later that you will return him safely?'

'In one piece if possible,' Petrie said shortly. Deaf and dumb? The caution of the Sicilian was diabolical: it meant that there could be no question of interrogating Giacomo later to gain information about the mafia. This bastard doesn't miss a trick, he thought with reluctant admiration. 'There's one problem you haven't covered, Angelo,' he said. 'To do a real job on that train-ferry I need to get inside the engine-room and I think one of our signals mentioned this. Can it be managed?'

'It is difficult but perhaps not impossible. To obtain detailed information about the *Cariddi* I have crossed and re-crossed the straits eight times within the past three weeks . . .'

'Hasn't that aroused suspicion?' Petrie asked sharply.

'Not at all! I am a lawyer. I have clients in Messina and clients on the mainland, so I tell them. Even in wartime people never stop fighting each other legally! During the crossings I made friends with the chief engineer, a dubious character called Volpe.'

'Dubious?' Petrie queried.

'Very! He is a great womanizer and loves to talk about his conquests—and Angelo Gambari can be a very good listener!' He grinned sardonically. 'Volpe has two passions in life—his women and his engines. Also he is very partial to good brandy, and by means I need not go into I have acquired several bottles of French cognac.'

'He lets you go down into the engine-room?'

'He lets my bottle go down—and since I hold on to it he lets me down, too, during the crossing!' Angelo rubbed his head as though stimulating a thought. 'Ah, I have it! A way to get the two of you

204

down with me. You have wished all your lives to become engineers like Volpe, your families were too poor to pay for your training, but you are still fascinated by machinery. The larger the audience, the more Volpe loves to talk.'

They crossed another bridge, sped up a steep hill, then slowed down as they came to a series of bends. So far they had not met another vehicle on the road which passed through some of the wildest country in Sicily, and soon they would be joined by the road Petrie had originally intended coming along direct from Scopana. It was a route he had chosen carefully after studying the reports from the aerial reconnaissance people which showed it was little used by traffic, probably because east and west of it there were more direct routes across the island. 'And how did you intend to get us into the *Cariddi* dock?' he asked.

'We walk through with the other peasants.'

'Walk through? Just like that? With the place ringed with troops?' Petrie stared at him critically.

Angelo showed annoyance and threw out a hand to emphasize his point. 'You do not understand the situation here! For years the ferries have been used like buses by people wishing to cross the straits— each time I crossed the ship carried ordinary people who work all their lives in the fields. They have to buy a ticket and they have identity papers, of course—but you have these.'

'And the Germans let them get away with this?'

'They have no option!' Angelo was becoming heated at Petrie's failure to grasp his explanation. 'The *Cariddi* is an *Italian ship*. Obviously you have no idea of the Italian feeling against German methods. It may seem strange to you, but this is the way Sicilians live and it will take more than the Germans to make them change their ways.'

'All right Angelo,' Petrie said soothingly. 'I've got it. We go on board with the other peasants and all we have to worry about is the *carabinieri*.' They passed a signposted road turning off to their left which read *Scopana–Petralia*, and this was the way Petrie had planned to come when he was plotting out a route back at the Tunis base, so from now on he knew where he was going. At this point they were more than three-quarters of the way through the Nebrodi mountains and they had still met nothing on the moonlit road except a few mule carts, but Petrie was under no illusion that it would continue like this. Soon they would turn on to the strategic coastal highway linking Palermo with Messina, and soon they would meet the checkpoints—and the Germans.

He glanced over his shoulder as Johnson sat up, yawned and winked at him. All his three companions were showing grave signs of fatigue; short of sleep and food, their whiskered faces gaunt and haggard, they looked like men going on leave after a rough time in the front line. The trouble was the rough time lay ahead of them and they were going to arrive in Messina with most of their reserves drained away. It didn't exactly add up to a formula for success. 'I could do with a drink,' the American suggested tentatively. Petrie nodded and they shared what was left of the bottle of mineral water he had bought in Puccio. Later, he caught Angelo glancing at him and from the Italian's expression he guessed that his own physical and mental state was being assessed. And I'm damned sure I don't look any better than the others, he thought grimly. Johnson had taken Scelba's place at the small window, gulping in air to help waken himself up. 'Looks like a storm coming up,' he remarked.

'It can happen without warning at this time of year,' Angelo told him. 'One moment the sea is calm, the next moment you wonder whether you will survive.'

'How much can the *Cariddi* transport in a single crossing?' the American inquired.

'A complete express train—ten coaches and the engine—or twenty-five large freight wagons. In one crossing it can carry fourteen hundred passengers.'

'Fourteen hundred?' Johnson whistled noiselessly. Double the number to allow for cramming troops aboard and that gave a figure of approximately three thousand troops per crossing. It would take only a few crossings to transport an entire division from the mainland to Sicily. No wonder AFHQ was in such a sweat about this huge train-ferry.

The ambulance sped on through the night and the mountains slid behind them as they drew closer and closer to the coast. The gathering storm arrived suddenly, one moment they were driving through a cool, calm night and then the breeze became a wind and they heard its howl above the motor-throb, heard the thump of its force against the vehicle's side while they saw the clouds massing overhead until the moon went out and they were driving into a forty-mile-an-hour gale. The landscape was transformed as shafts of moonlight reappeared, showing a cloud ceiling low and fast-moving as the wind strength increased and blew up scurries of dust which they saw eddying in the headlight beams. Through a break in the prickly pear hedge Johnson caught a glimpse of sheep hurrying for shelter followed by a man on horseback. If they're coming tonight, the American thought bleakly, the airborne boys will be in trouble, to say nothing of the landing-craft wallowing in the rising seas.

As they approached the critical highway the atmosphere inside the ambulance changed and the tension grew. They sat up straighter, checked their weapons unnecessarily, spent more time peering ahead where the headlights would show the first sign that they had reached the highway. Petrie himself sat up a little straighter and now he drove more slowly as he watched for any sign that would tell him they were close to the sea. Even without sight of the coast he knew they were coming near because the freshening gale battering the vehicle's sides carried a tang of salt air as it came blasting in from the Tyrrhenian Sea, and when he pulled up, turned off the engine and leaned out of the window the salt tang was strong. He stayed in this position for several minutes, listening for sounds of traffic on the nearby highway. The wind was cold, chilling his skin, but he welcomed the sensation after the heat of the day and the only sounds he heard were the hissing of pampas grasses, the whine of the wind and a surging noise which was the beat of heavy seas on the shore.

'Looks like we still have the world to ourselves,' Johnson said quietly.

'Maybe.' Petrie sounded doubtful. 'But we can expect trouble soon—this highway is a main communications route.'

                          *   *   *

'I protest!' Field-Marshal Kesselring burst out,
unable to control his fury any longer. 'To hold back
the 29th Panzer Division now would be a strategic
blunder of the first order!' He gripped the
telephone as though it were Colonel-General Jodl's
neck as that august officer asked him to hold the
line a minute.

The clock on his desk under the lamp registered
9.15 PM. The call from Supreme Headquarters in
East Prussia could hardly have come through at a
more awkward moment. The signal he was about to
send to Colonel Baade in Messina ordering the
Cariddi to cross the straits was on his desk, and
Rheinhardt was at Giovanni with his division
waiting to board the train-ferry. But he had been
wise not to bring the vessel across sooner,
Kesselring was thinking—that would really have
taken some explaining now that Supreme HQ had
grasped what was happening. It was, of course, the
Gestapo who had tapped his line and relayed the
information to the other end of Europe. Jodl came
back on the line, his voice as thin and precise and
emotionless as always. 'Rheinhardt must be kept
where he is in southern Italy until we are sure
where the enemy blow will fall . . .'

'It will fall on Sicily! Strickland always takes it
step by step—and the next step is Sicily, *then* Italy!
If we can smash them this time it will take them six
months to reorganize another attempt. . .'

'We know all this.' Jodl's tone remained even.
'That is why we must first be sure where they are
landing. . .'

'When you are sure in war it is too late!'

Kesselring shouted, not caring any more. '*We* . . .' Jodl kept saying. The little man with the moustache was standing at the officer's elbow, probably even listening in on an extension, but the swine would never come to the phone himself. Kesselring took a deep breath. He was not going to give in this time. 'Before I accept that order I wish to speak to the Führer!'

'Wait a minute . . . there is a lot of noise at this end.' So the little man was there! But Jodl would never admit that he was no more than a messenger boy, passing on someone else's lunatic orders. While he waited, Kesselring's agile brain planned the next move. This time he mustn't fail. Rheinhardt was going to Sicily, whatever the madmen in East Prussia wanted. He heard Jodl cough on the phone, a sound he knew well: it meant that the colonel-general was embarrassed. 'Kesselring, the Führer is not available at the moment. And the order must stand. The *Cariddi* is still at Messina, I trust?'

'Yes. You mean that under no circumstances is Rheinhardt to cross the straits?' Kesselring inquired craftily. 'Even if we have positive reports of airborne landings?'

There was another long pause. Stick that in your vegetarian soup and choke on it, Kesselring thought. He had them over a barrel now—the length of the pause showed that. Jodl coughed again when he came back on the line. 'If there are confirmed reports of *sea*borne landings in Sicily, then Rheinhardt can cross, but only then. You understand?'

'Positive reports of airborne landings . . .' Kesselring deliberately gabbled the words.

'*Sea*borne!' Jodl's tone was sharp. '*Seaborne*, I said. You have understood me now, I hope?'

'Perfectly!' Kesselring was careful not to repeat the word himself. 'There was a lot of noise at this end,' he added maliciously, then he terminated the call. There was all the difference in the world between airborne and seaborne landings: the first enemy attack would be the airdrop, possibly just before midnight while the moon was still up. The seaborne landings would come hours later, so at least his manoeuvre meant he could send Rheinhardt across several hours earlier. If his guess was correct and reports of airborne drops came through near midnight the *Cariddi* could sail at once. He used the phone to order coffee as he began altering his signal to Messina. It was going to be a long night.

*   *   *

It was quite dark as Petrie re-started the engine and drove on slowly, knowing that their exit on to the coast road must be a critical moment. Turning a bend, he speeded up a little along a straight stretch and mounted a rise, then immediately reduced speed again. As the ambulance crested the brow of the hill it took the full force of the gale against its windscreen and the view opened out dramatically, spreading away in three directions as the moon came through the low-flying clouds and Petrie felt the wind-pressure tugging at his wheel. To the east the highway was a pale strip running in harness with the single-track railway from Palermo to Messina, but within a few hundred yards it disappeared temporarily behind a ridge and then reappeared in the direction of Milazzo. To the west it ran a long distance towards Palermo. Ahead of them to the north lay the open sea, a dark undulation of heaving waves surging shoreward, rolling in to crash on the deserted beach below with a heavy boom and a burst of surf. Their fears of army convoys, of tanks and troops, were only fears; there was no one, nothing in sight. And the raging sea was equally lonely and unused.

'We must be born lucky.'

Johnson said the words half to himself and then he noticed that Petrie was crouched over the wheel as the ambulance crawled downhill to where the side road joined the highway. What the devil was he worrying about now? At walking pace the ambulance came up to the intersection and Petrie was staring to his right, towards the portion of the highway concealed from view by the ridge. A level-crossing led over the rail track and down on to the main road; beyond that the beach ran out to a headland projecting into the sea with a fringe of shingle following its base. No wire on the beach to indicate minefields; only fishing-boats which were drawn up well back from the surf line.

Petrie drove on to the crossing, bumped over the track, came down on to the highway, was starting to turn his wheel when he saw the bottom of the shallow hill which had been concealed by the ridge. He took it in like a flash from a camera—the piled-up trucks, three or four of them which had been travelling too fast and too close together, the blocked road, the ambulance with its rear doors open ... Then he drove straight across the highway down on to the beach and headed for the strip of shingle between cape and sea with the howl of the wind and the crash of the breakers echoing in his ears. Angelo stared at him but it was Johnson who spoke first. 'What the hell are you doing, Jim?'

'Heading away from trouble! There's an accident a few hundred yards down the highway—road's blocked and there's one ambulance there already. What chance do you think we'd have had of driving past that—in another ambulance? They were Jerry trucks, too.'

'We're waiting here?' Johnson sounded unhappy, became speechless in sheer disbelief as Petrie continued driving along the beach under the headland while to their left the sea surged in as though to overwhelm them.

'We're not waiting anywhere,' Petrie said tightly. 'There's no time left for waiting. We're now on the route I always expected to take—so I studied the aerial photos of this part of the coast before we left. I remember this headland—it goes out about half a mile and then goes back in again to hit the highway well beyond that truck smash . . .'

'You're not driving round this headland,' Johnson protested.

'That's exactly what I am going to do. The aerial photos showed a continuous strip of beach going the whole way round, so now, gentlemen, say your prayers and hope I have read the photos correctly.'

The ambulance drove on. The storm was rising and the sea was rising with it as huge waves gathered up the waters and jostled in towards the cape with a dizzying motion. The strip of beach between headland and waterline was narrow, hardly wider than the girth of the ambulance, and in places large waves rolled in ahead of them and threw themselves close to the headland's base.

213

Driving over the shingle was difficult: the wheels were inclined to slither among the unstable pebbles and the right front mudguard was moving along within a foot of the rock wall. If we arrive at a place where the sea comes right in, where we can't move forward any farther, Johnson was thinking, he'll never get us back to the highway. It was a thought which had not escaped Petrie, but now the time was so short that every risk had to be taken, because if they didn't reach Messina in time, if German reinforcements moved across the straits, they might as well never have come and all the risks taken so far would mean nothing. He was quite single-minded about what he was doing, determined to take the ambulance round the cape if it were humanly possible, but there was another hazard which aerial photos taken on a calm day would never show—the extent to which the sea came in when driven by the fury of a forty-mile-an-hour gale.

On the photographs the beach area had looked very narrow as it came up to the tip of the headland, and he suspected he might be driving with two wheels in the water for part of the way. The question he carefully hadn't raised in the minds of his passengers was whether at some point when he was driving through water the beach might not shelve suddenly, go down heaven knew how many fathoms. He drove on as the beach slowly narrowed; on his right the vertical rock wall was gleaming in the moonlight, its surface damp where windblown surf and spray had splashed it, while to his left where he looked straight out of the ambulance the sea was a turmoil of waves which seemed to be getting bigger, massive waves with

214

leaping crests which rolled in as high as his head, broke, then sent a spume-discoloured carpet of water flooding in under the vehicle. The noise was nerve rattling, a growing surge as millions of gallons of water swept in on the headland which barred their progress. Something slapped him lightly on the cheek and then ran down it. The surf was coming in much closer.

'Ed, keep an eye on the highway through the rear window, will you?'

This was an added anxiety—that some other vehicle would come along the highway from the west and see him apparently trying to commit suicide. But the highway had been deserted for a long distance when he drove over the level-crossing, so if he could only keep going they might make it. Frowning, he started the wipers to clear spray off the windscreen: in the distance the sea appeared to be surging right in to the cliff base, submerging the beach completely, but it could be an optical illusion in the bad light. He heard Scelba clear his throat, looked quickly at Angelo who had lit a cigarette and was watching the incoming sea with screwed up eyes as though estimating their chances of survival. Behind him Johnson's measured voice spoke quietly: 'Jim, I'd better get out and walk ahead of you. It may slow you down but we ought to know what's facing us before it's too late. And Scelba can keep an eye on the highway.'

'Agreed, Ed. And watch that shingle near the waterline—it may shelve suddenly.'

The American went out by the rear door and the wind took hold of him at once, nearly blew him into the cliff face. As he squeezed his way between the

215

vehicle and the rock wall his feet were slithering over the wet treacherous shingle, and when he stumbled his way ahead of the ambulance the storm seemed to be worsening, buffeting his body as he struggled to retain his balance while the wind shrieked, the mighty waves roller-coastered towards him, spray doused his clothes and face, and above the surge of the sea and the hiss of the surf he heard from the direction of the headland's tip a more disturbing sound, the growling boom of rollers crashing against rock as though trying to shift the cape itself. Head down, he walked, slipped, forced himself forward, looking up frequently to see where the beach apparently narrowed even further. Soon Johnson was walking knee-deep in frothing surf as he deliberately moved along the edge of the sea, determined to make sure there was leeway for the passage of the vehicle, knowing that in places Petrie would be compelled to drive with his outer wheels in the water.

As he drew closer to the tip of the headland the character of the cape began to change; the cliff face receded deep into wide gulches which penetrated the rock, gulches of sand instead of shingle, gulches which were culs-de-sac and which always ended at a rock face. The boom from the headland tip was growing louder, developing into a low roar he heard above the wind's howl and the purr of the ambulance following twenty yards to his rear. Could this crazy gamble succeed, he kept asking himself over and over again. The moon was still out, shining down through a break in the ragged clouds scudding overhead, and by its light he could see great combers dashing themselves to pieces against immense rocks, hurling spray high in the

216

air, spray which the wind blew back into the cliff face. He paused to wipe spray off his own face, looked back at the oncoming vehicle and saw the headlights blur as wind-blown surf fogged them. They would never get past the tip of the headland; he was sure of it. Petrie must have made some mistake in reading the aerial photo, in assuming the beach strip ran right round the headland. It seemed unlikely anyway; with a cape like this the beach always vanished when you reached its extremity. Waving his hand sideways to warn the ambulance to keep closer to the rock face, he turned and stumbled onwards.

The atmosphere inside the ambulance was claustrophobic and the passengers were developing a trapped feeling as Petrie drove slowly on after the walking American. It was cold, but the occupants were sweating with fear because the vehicle felt horribly unstable as the wheels ground forward over the shifting pebbles, the sea spread under them, scattered the stones with a loose rattle, withdrew and then came in again as the next wave broke and Petrie drove inches away from the cliff-face, holding the wheel tightly to counter the tendency of the ambulance to swerve seaward. He passed another of the sandy gulches and Angelo glanced longingly inside its walled sanctuary; at least in one of these coves they would be sheltered from the elements. Peering ahead, Petrie was trying to see the island, an island very close to the cape's tip as he remembered it from the aerial shot, but now they were coming near the end of the headland there was no island to be seen. Had he misinterpreted a shadow in the picture? In which case his theory of the feasibility of driving round

217

the cape was exploded. He looked out of the open window to his left, the side of his jacket already soaked with spray, blinked when he saw what was coming.

A great roll of grey water was gathering up sea, inflating itself, furling at the mounting crest, sweeping up higher than the roof of the ambulance; it slammed forward, raced in without any sign of breaking as it climbed higher and higher and the crest lurched forward. Petrie stopped the vehicle, began winding up the window frantically as Angelo instinctively shrank against the other door. They were going to be overwhelmed, submerged, and the powerful backwash from such a comber could easily haul them over sideways, capsizing them into the sea. The wave broke, dropped to a third of its height as the water came on, waist-high, a foaming surge which lost more height just before it arrived and struck the ambulance's side. They felt its impact, felt the vehicle wobble, saw water all around them, then it was receding, battling with an incoming wave, colliding with it, sending spray from the collision high above the dancing waters. Petrie tried to start the engine. It failed. A moment later he saw that Johnson had vanished.

*   *   *

Johnson had seen the wave coming, had run inside the last of the gulches which penetrated the cliff face, a broad sandy channel which went in a hundred feet and then disappeared round a corner. The sea came in behind him, spread itself over the grey sand, stopped, went back. Sodden to the thighs, Johnson went back after it, came out of the

218

exit and waved to the ambulance which was now stationary. The sound of the engine starting, failing, reached him, and a new coldness spread through him: the motor was water-logged. The engine started again, failed, repeated the agonizing performance, then the third time it kept ticking over and the ambulance moved forward again as clouds began to blot out the moon and the headlights showed more sharply. Reluctantly, Johnson left the firmness of the sand and went on towards the headland's tip, his boots squelching over the slippery pebbles. Yes, Petrie had been wrong: he could see it positively where a mass of piled rocks like a breakwater were heaped against the cliff wall while their outer bastion took the tremendous shock of the sea. The beach had gone, ended by the huge rocks which blocked their way. He looked back and froze.

The ambulance had reached a point where the shingle strip was very narrow and Petrie was driving with half the depth of the outer wheels under water, but what scared Johnson was the angle of the ambulance—it was tilting sideways, tilting down towards the sea where the beach shelved steeply. It had only to tilt a few degrees farther, to slither a foot or two away from the rock wall, and it would somersault sideways. For long drawn-out seconds the booming of the breakers, the wind's howl, the realization that their way forward was blocked—all these things went out of his mind as he watched the horrible tilt and saw that Petrie was refusing to give up, was still forcing a passage over the treacherous shoal bank while the headlights wobbled alarmingly. The lights came closer, became parallel again as the ambulance resumed an even keel and

219

approached the large gulch Johnson had fled inside when the wave came. Turning round, he walked on hoping desperately that his eyesight had played him a trick, that there would be a continuous way round the headland. He came to the first of the great rocks and spray from the breakers showered over him, drenched him, and now the booming sound was deafening as he held up a hand to stop Petrie and then climbed the slippery face of damp rock to see whether they could continue forward on foot. He had climbed perhaps twenty feet when the view opened up to where he could see beyond the headland tip, could see the familiar shape of an Italian MAS boat coming round from the far side of the cape. Barely a quarter of a mile offshore, caught in the remaining moonlight, it turned to investigate their side of the headland.

He jumped back down the rocks, jumped dangerously from ledge to ledge, and when he hit the beach he nearly lost his footing on the pebbles. Recovering, he waved sideways frantically, waved to the ambulance to drive inside the gulch, but either they couldn't see him properly or they hadn't understood the gesture because they were still driving towards him and in seconds they would have driven past the sanctuary. He ran on, retaining his balance by a miracle, ran a dozen yards and then he stopped and waved again. The ambulance turned, slid behind the rock wall and was gone. Johnson resumed his lurching run, desperately trying to follow the vehicle inside the gulch before the MAS boat came round the rocks. He fell once, toppling to his knees which hammered the pebbles while his hands were scrabbling for balance, and during the few seconds

220

he knelt there, half-winded, a wave broke and poured itself over him, soaking him afresh, so when he hauled himself to his feet and stumbled on he was bedraggled, his cap, jacket and trousers sodden, dripping with water as he staggered to the entrance, felt hard sand under his boots and forced himself into a run.

The ambulance had vanished beyond the curving rock wall, its tyre marks near the entrance obliterated by the water which had just washed over them. He ran forward, chilled, dripping, clammy, expecting at any second to hear the purr of the MAS boat's engine behind him. For some reason it had been playing a powerful light over the cliff's surface and he was scared the beam might come inside the gulch while he was still in sight. Were they checking for landing parties? He had no idea. He reached a point where the wall curved sharply, a point of safety, when Petrie came round the corner, grabbed his arm and pulled him behind the rock. 'You all right, Ed? What's the trouble?' Johnson couldn't get out a reply as he panted for breath and gestured towards the entrance. Petrie peered round the corner cautiously as the MAS boat came into, view, tossing in the heaving sea while a signal lamp flashed from its deck. For one chilling moment Petrie thought it was signalling their discovery to someone on the coast road, when he realized it must be identifying itself to a coastguard station on the headland above them. 'It's all right, Ed,' he said. 'It can't see us and it's moving on . . .'

'MAS boat . . .' Johnson gulped for air. 'Flashing a light over the cliff . . . can't get any farther . . . rocks in the way.'

'Don't worry about it—and stop trying to talk. It was a routine signal—probably to the coastguard station above us. Take it easy, Ed, you saved our bacon there—and now you can get out of those wet things and wrap up in blankets for a while. There are loads of them in one of the cupboards.'

He helped Johnson back to the vehicle which was parked without any lights part way round the cliff. Scelba opened the rear doors, hauled the American inside and nodded to Petrie who went back to the driver's seat. As he settled behind the wheel darkness seeped into the gulch with the fading of the moon. Behind him the American was refusing to change until he had spoken to Petrie again through the dividing window. 'Jim, we can't go any farther round the cape—there are rocks in the way. The beach just gives up.' Angelo twisted round, offered him a cigarette, and by the match flare Johnson saw the Italian smiling, which was hardly the reaction he had expected.

'It's all right, Ed,' Petrie reassured him. 'I was damned sure I saw a small offshore island at the end of this cape in the aerial shot, but there didn't seem to be one. This is the island.' He pointed to his left out of the window. 'What we thought was the end of the cape is the island—it's cut off from the cape by this gulch which goes all the way through and out the other side. The exit links up with the beach and that will take us to the coast road.'

'You're joking,' Johnson said hoarsely.

'I checked it a moment ago. We go a few yards round this curve and we're at the other side of the headland. Well give the MAS boat a few minutes to push off, I'll check the beach and road again, then

222

we can get moving.'

'What about the coastguard station above us?'

'It's well back on the headland, about halfway between here and the road—I remember that now from the photo. We'll drive close in to the cliff as we did when we drove out here and I'm sure they'll never see us.'

They waited a few minutes; Petrie got out to make sure the coast road was still clear, then they were driving through the gulch and turning right out of its exit on to another shingle beach. Here the shore was wider, probably because the cape sheltered this side from the prevailing wind, and the sea close to the beach was calmer as they drove towards the deserted highway still visible in a shaft of moonlight. Reaching the main beach, Petrie pulled up and told the others to wait for him. He had to find the answer to a dangerous question: was the accident they had driven round the cape to avoid in sight? He climbed a sandy slope cautiously, wondering whether he should have risked driving straight on to the highway—if any vehicle came along now the ambulance parked on the beach was going to look pretty odd. Arriving at the verge, he stood up straight. The road to the west was empty, disappearing as it went down into the dip where the accident had occurred. He ran back to the ambulance, climbed in behind the wheel, drove up the slope on to the highway and checked his watch as he turned east. 10.25 PM. Ninety-five minutes to the deadline. He pressed his foot down.

CHAPTER TWELVE

Friday. 10.30 PM–11.30 PM

At eighty miles an hour the ambulance sped through the night along the hard-surface road which bordered the north Sicilian coastline, its headlights spearing through the darkness, the needle climbing up the speedometer, the air pressure whipping past them as the vehicle swayed round a gentle curve, as Scelba dug his fingernails into the leather couch to maintain his balance while Johnson braced his back against the rocking side. They were close to Messina; it was 11 PM; and they had already successfully passed through three different checkpoints. If Petrie kept up this speed of progress they would be inside the straits in fifteen minutes.

'Another checkpoint coming up,' Angelo said stiffly.

'We'll go through it the way we went through the others,' Petrie said confidently.

'One day this isn't going to work,' Johnson bawled through the window.

The red lights in the distance warned them they were racing towards another checkpoint, although as yet the headlight beams hadn't picked out the barrier or the men guarding it. Petrie operated the siren switch and an unearthly banshee-like scream cut through the night, warning the checkpoint control that this ambulance wasn't stopping, that it was coming straight through, so for God's sake get the barrier up before we drive clean through it.

The headlights picked out the barrier, picked out men in *carabinieri* uniform scurrying madly as they moved the pole and got well out of the way. The ambulance streaked past. Angelo had a glimpse of white faces gaping in the night. Then the headlight beams were turned as they negotiated another curve, headlights which showed briefly a dual curve of steel track to their right, an empty meaningless track which might have led anywhere because the trains weren't running any more, while to their left and below them the troubled sea appeared as the moon came out again. The gale was still blowing, the clouds scudded like an urgent fleet through the sky above them, but moving at this speed the Tyrrhenian seemed to be no more than flurried, a jostle of moonlit waves trundling in to empty themselves on remote beaches. They passed inlets and headlands and bays, and often they saw dark shapes out at sea which were more patrol-boats watching for any sign of enemy intrusion while half a mile to the south of them the headlights of Petrie's ambulance sped east in its headlong rush for Messina.

'There are Germans at some of the checkpoints close to the city,'Angelo warned.

'They'll stop an Italian vehicle?' Petrie queried.

'Not often, but I have seen it happen.'

And at present, with the invasion pending, they'll be in a state of nerves, Petrie thought, as he took the ambulance up the road where it began its ascent into the Peloritanie mountains. The sea receded away from them to the north. The rail track moved over a bridge from right to left, headed east along its own separate route where it tunnelled through the mountains to Messina. The

225

highway climbed and climbed and the temperature dropped a little more as, for the first time since they had landed, they passed wooded defiles and saw trees on the ridges. Then, ahead of them they saw more lights. Another checkpoint. Petrie pressed the siren switch, accelerated. 'Be careful!' Angelo warned. In the moonlight the anti-tank gun showed clearly, its barrel aimed point-blank down the road towards them. German uniforms were also visible, about a dozen of them. On the other side of the road an Italian truck and two motor-cycles with riders on their saddles stood in a clearing under trees, and behind them were more Italian troops. And the barrier was down across the road. Petrie's expression tightened as he continued up the hill and then something happened which took everyone by surprise. It began to rain.

'I'm stopping,' Petrie said to warn the others as he lost speed rapidly and then skidded to a stop yards from the guard-pole. There was too much against them—the gun, the motor-cyclists to pursue them even if he'd attempted crashing the barrier. As the engine ticked over quietly the rain sound increased in fury, rattling down on the roof like miniature drills. Through the open side window he saw a German sergeant striding towards him with a machine-pistol pointed at the ambulance. The Wehrmacht NCO was soaked by the time he reached the window and behind him Italian soldiers were running out from under the trees as some natural water catchment began to flood the place where they had stood. 'Ah! You were not going to stop!' Petrie swore inwardly as he heard the German's fluent Italian, but his face wore a puzzled expression as he looked up at the NCO.

'We are on the way to the hospital with a patient. It's an emergency case.'

'That is no reason for not stopping when the pole is down! You see that gun over there?' The German, wiping the drips off his peaked cap, pointed with one hand while he kept his machine-pistol aimed with the other. 'Your patient could have been a dead man—and so could you.' Six foot tall and heavily-built, the NCO was a man in his late twenties, an arrogant bully, a typical product of the Nazi regime. 'Show me your papers,' he barked and the muzzle of the weapon prodded towards Petrie's face. The German was freshly-shaved, had obviously come on duty only recently, and his temper was not improved by the soaking he was receiving. Behind him several Italian soldiers stood at the edge of the road, keeping clear of the deluge of water cascading into the bowl under the trees they had just left, and the nearest man was a sergeant, a short determined-looking individual who was watching the scene curiously. 'Your papers!' the German rapped out again.

Something inside Petrie snapped. They had been on the move almost constantly for over twenty-four hours; they had survived a *mafioso* ambush, the Beaufighter attack, the terrible journey through the wilderness, the searching *carabinieri*, the B17 bombing raid, and now, almost within sight of Messina, they were being blocked by this bullying swine. He opened the door slowly, stepped out into the driving rain in his ill-fitting trousers, closed the door, and faced the German with his hands on his hips. 'You would have opened fire on an Italian ambulance?' he demanded. He had raised his voice deliberately, raised it so it carried above the sound

227

of the rain to the Italians huddled by the roadside. Their sergeant took a step forward and then waited.

'This is a checkpoint!' the German shouted at him. 'You bloody well stop when you see a checkpoint!'

'And my fist bloody well curls when I meet someone like you! You think you've taken over the whole mucking island? You think we count for nothing any more, we Italians?'

The Italian sergeant behind the German came forward a few more steps and then waited again. A subtle but marked change in the atmosphere round the checkpoint was taking place; on one side of the road the Italian infantry with rifles in their hands stared beyond the ambulance to where the Germans on the far side were gathered round the anti-tank gun as they stared back. Then they transferred their gaze to the protagonists in the middle of the highway where the German NCO was looking at Petrie suspiciously. 'What is the matter with your uniform?' he snapped. 'And you haven't shaved for two days. You look like a peasant.'

Petrie waved his hand provocatively at the Wehrmacht uniform, calling out to the Italian soldiers as the rain poured down on him. 'So, because we haven't got a nice new uniform like Herr Bully-Boy we are peasants! Now we know what our charming allies think of us! Peasants! he said. I get blood all over one outfit, borrow another, and I'm improperly dressed! Twenty-two hours on duty without a break,' Petrie ranted on, 'and it's a crime because I haven't shaved! I should be so lucky as Herr General here whose chin is as smooth as a chorus boy's!' Very deliberately he spat close to the German's boot.

Inside the ambulance Angelo stiffened, sure that Petrie had gone too far. The German stiffened also, lost all self-control as he raised his weapon like a club to fell Petrie. The Italian sergeant jumped forward, grasped the weapon, and for several seconds the two NCOs struggled for possession of the gun as the rain beat down on them non-stop. On either side of the road the mood took an ugly turn. Seeing their sergeant struggling with the German, the Italian troops advanced with their rifles at the ready, aimed across the highway towards the group gathered round the anti-tank gun. A Wehrmacht corporal issued a sharp order and all but two men left the gun, spreading out along the roadside. Jesus, Angelo thought, we're going to be caught in a crossfire. It had happened once before near Catania, a fracas between the Italians and the Germans, and the incident had been carefully hushed up with units transferred to opposite ends of the island.

The Italian NCO rammed a boot down hard, scraped the German's instep, and when they broke apart it was the Italian who held the weapon as he carefully pointed the muzzle at the ground and shouted over his shoulder to his own troops: 'Lower those rifles, you fools!' Seeing his men obey the order, he swung round on the German. 'I shall report this incident the moment I go off duty!'

'Your men nearly opened fire on mine!' the German stormed.

'Look at your own men,' the Italian NCO said calmly. He was quite confident: he had done

229

nothing except to prevent an assault on an ambulance driver and he had the offending weapon in his own hands, trailed harmlessly, as the German looked behind him and cursed. The Wehrmacht troops were lined up along the roadside in an obvious state of alert. He shouted an order in German and the men went back to the anti-tank gun, looking anywhere except in the direction of their allies across the highway. 'From now on,' the Italian sergeant continued, '*we* will check any Italian vehicles . . .'

'I shall make my own report,' the German retorted.

'That is your privilege—do not forget to include that you threatened to open fire on an Italian ambulance,' the NCO reminded him.

'That's a damned lie . . .'

'I distinctly heard you tell the driver that he could have been a dead man—and his patient.' The sergeant turned his back on the German to speak to Petrie who had carefully waited in the pouring rain because it established a state of mutual suffering. 'Your patient is seriously ill?' he inquired.

'He will be if I don't get him to Messina General shortly. He's a sergeant who was working on constructing a blockhouse when a concrete mixer fell on him. I think he'll pull through as long as he gets treatment quickly—that's why I was using the siren. And this is the second time in half an hour I've been held up by the *tedeschi* . . .' He deliberately used the Italian term of contempt for their Teutonic allies. 'They'll be the death of my patient if I'm stopped again before I get to Messina.' He glanced meaningfully in the direction of the two motor-cyclists who still sat astride their saddles in the downpour.

'You mean . . . ?' The sergeant hesitated, and Petrie was careful not to push it. 'He is on the danger list?'

'You could say that. He needs an emergency operation and the only place he can have it done is at Messina. There's a surgeon standing by waiting for us now.'

'And you're worried you'll run into someone else like this?' the sergeant inquired in a low voice.

'Sicily is crawling with them.'

The sergeant, who looked not unlike a more benevolent Angelo, hesitated again as the rain thrashed down on to the highway with greater intensity and this new onset of the storm seemed to decide him. 'I will send the motor-cycle patrol with you,' he said quickly. 'They will get you through all the checkpoints without any hold-ups. You will be moving quickly so they should be back here soon . . .'

'Tell them to get us through the last checkpoint and then they can come straight back here. And the chap inside will be grateful—I'll tell him after the op.'

'I hope it is successful.' The sergeant went quickly across to the motor-cyclists as Petrie got back into the ambulance, and when he sat down his clothes squelched. While he waited for the barrier to be raised he used his handkerchief to dry his face and take some of the wet out of his hair. It suddenly seemed very quiet as they listened to the engine ticking over, the rain pattering on the roof and the wipers clicking backwards and forwards. 'The rain is stopping,' Angelo observed, 'and you

231

almost had a real patient in here. Me! State of shock brought on by excessive terror!'

The barrier lifted, one of the motor-cyclists roared past it into the night, and the ambulance followed with the second motor-cyclist alongside. They drove steadily uphill at speed, moving up the Peloritanie slopes, and the escort took them easily through the remaining checkpoints. The cyclist who had gone ahead paved the way for them, ensuring that the barrier was always raised by the time the ambulance arrived, and as it stopped raining the clouds broke and the moon showed through again, illuminating dark tree-covered ridges. They reached the last checkpoint near the final crest; the motor-cyclists turned their machines round, saluted, sped off back the way they had come. Angelo took out a silk handkerchief and dabbed at his moist forehead. They were alone again. Johnson appeared at the window behind them for the first time in a while. 'God, you gave us the shakes there, Jim. We're through?'

'Last checkpoint behind us.'

Petrie said no more as he raced up the hill; his nerves were singing with the delayed action of the experience. While it had been going on he had felt ice-cold, observing every little detail which might be turned to their advantage, and the thing now was not to relax, not to let the sensation of relief affect him in any way—because worse, far worse, was still to come. They saw traffic ahead of them as they came up to the crest; German trucks coming towards them and branching off down a side road to the north, then another military convoy in front of them travelling in the same direction. A motor-cyclist raced past them heading for the west followed by a line of armoured cars. Almost before they realized what was happening they were surrounded by Wehrmacht vehicles travelling in both directions and the night was full of throbbing engines. It looked like a state of emergency.

Petrie could almost feel the tension in the way the Germans drove, shoulders hunched over the wheel, staring fixedly ahead. Christ, he thought, has the invasion already started? The convoys were travelling at high speed, a dangerously high speed for night-time driving, and he was praying there wouldn't be an accident—because if there was, an ambulance would be expected to stop and give a hand. He was sandwiched in the convoy now, a Wehrmacht truck ahead of him and an armoured car following close to his rear. It just needed something to stop without warning and there would be a multiple smash of the kind he had seen when they first emerged on to the highway, but a smash on a far greater scale. They went over the crest with the roar of Wehrmacht engines in their ears and it seemed as though every enemy division in Sicily was on the move.

'The harbour.'

That was all Angelo said as Petrie stared at the view where Messina could be seen far below by the light of the fading moon—the city itself, the sickle-shaped harbour, the silver-grey straits stretching away to north and south with the Calabrian mountains in the distance where the German reinforcements were waiting on the mainland. As they began the descent, hemmed in by the Wehrmacht, an air raid was in progress over the straits; flashes came from both sides of the channel and they heard clearly above the engine sounds the muted thunder of the ack-ack guns like the approach of a fresh storm. They had come through all the way from Palermo, the enemy still had no idea that they had landed, and it was exactly 11.30 PM as they entered the outskirts of Messina.

CHAPTER THIRTEEN

Friday. 11.30 PM–11.55 PM

They drove on down an endless hill, still trapped inside the Welirmacht convoy, and then Messina was closing round them, a city of substantial three-storey buildings. At the bottom of the hill they moved along a wide avenue with the thunder of the straits guns growing louder, hollow detonations with another kind of detonation mingling with the gunfire as bombs came down some distance away. The Allied air forces were pounding the waterfront non-stop. Petrie rubbed a hand over his damp forehead. 'Angelo, I want to get out of this traffic— if there's trouble we're locked in.'

'Prepare to turn right.'

Petrie slowed a little to increase the space between himself and the German truck in front, then signalled and swung right where Angelo indicated. Immediately they were alone, driving down a side street through the darkness with the massive buildings looming on both sides. No lights anywhere. It was late but the complete absence of lights made Petrie wonder whether the bombing had cut the power lines as he touched the accelerator. At Angelo's instruction he turned left and they drove down a broad avenue similar to the one they had just left, but this street was deserted, might never have been inhabited for all the signs of life they saw as they drove on between sombre buildings which reminded Petrie of municipal offices. Scelba, watching from the window, tapped Petrie gently on the shoulder. 'Stop when we get to the next intersection. I must leave you there.'

'You stay with us until we go to the dock!' It was Angelo who replied, his old suspicion flaring up like a festering sore as Petrie slowed down, then stopped. 'We must stay together,' the Italian protested. 'We only have to call at my flat for a few minutes and then we go straight to the dock, so why . . .'

'What's the idea, Scelba?' Petrie inquired as he looked carefully round. There was no one about. On the corner of the intersection was a shuttered café with a closed garage next to it. A pause in the gunfire allowed them to speak quietly and the ticking over of the motor sounded noisy in the novel silence. The *capo* stared impassively at Angelo and then spoke to Petrie.

'There is a car inside that garage. I must drive to the waterfront to warn Giacomo you are coming and to make sure everything is ready. Your flat is near here, Signor Gambari? Good.' He handed a folded street map to Petrie with some markings he had made on it. 'You come to this point on the waterfront—Gambari will know the way and it is only a short distance. I shall wait for you on this corner.'

Petrie took the map, handed it to the Italian. 'How long will it take us to get there, Angelo?'

'In the ambulance?'

'No—on foot. If we stay with this vehicle much longer we'll run out of luck. I can change into my old things at your flat.'

'Five minutes. I am close to the *Cariddi* dock.'

'We should see you about 11.50 then, Scelba,' Petrie said, checking his watch. They were talking in terms of minutes now, but he was careful not to show his impatience as Scelba went out by the rear door and walked quickly to the garage. As he drove forward Angelo told him to turn left; he completed the turn and was driving on when Angelo told him to stop. 'Why here?' Petrie pulled into the kerb as he asked the question. Angelo got out of the ambulance and ran back towards the intersection as Johnson's head appeared in the window. 'Kinda creepy round here. I suppose Angelo couldn't be right about Scelba?'

'No!' Petrie's tone was decisive as he looked at his watch a second time. 'He's forgetting that Scelba has come all the way across Sicily with us, so he's certainly not going to doublecross us now. What Angelo doesn't know is that we've promised the *capo* he'll be mayor of Palermo . . .'

'Why'd you let Angelo go check then—when we're so short of time?'

'Just to make absolutely sure . . .'

The sound of a car's engine came from behind them, crossed the intersection, then faded away as Angelo ran back to the ambulance and jumped inside as the vehicle began moving. 'Right down this next side street,' the Italian said breathlessly, 'then straight down almost to the bottom. I thought it was funny,' he said apologetically, 'but Scelba had the key to the garage door in his hand when he left us and it seemed a little too neat.'

236

'He's just well organized,' Petrie replied as he swung down inside a street so narrow that the sides of the ambulance almost scraped the walls. The familiar stench of rotting garbage drifted in through the window and the street ahead was a pitch-black canyon. 'He just came out and drove off, I take it?'

'Yes, he didn't waste a second. I also thought it funny that he had a car waiting for him,' he added, still reluctant to let go of his eternal suspicion of the mafia boss.

'He controls the waterfront labour,' Petrie pointed out, 'so he probably comes here fairly frequently.' He turned right at the Italian's instruction, and then left, which brought them out into the same wide avenue where they had dropped Scelba, but much lower down. 'I am keeping off the main streets as far as possible,' Angelo explained. He looked out of the window at the sound of distant gunfire and somewhere overhead he thought he could hear the drone of bombers. Behind them boots hit the floor and when Petrie glanced back he saw Johnson peer through the rear window and come back quickly to the front of the vehicle. 'Trouble, I think'. A German scout-car's following us and it's keeping the same speed.'

'How many men inside it? Can you see?'

'Not clearly, but there could be four of them.'

'Angelo, how close are we to your flat?' Petric asked quickly.

'We're almost there.'

Petrie swore. At the very last moment they'd been spotted. He adjusted his rear-view mirror and picked up the hooded headlights of the scout-car. He was coming up to an intersection and he had to

237

find out whether this was simply a coincidence, which it might be if the car was patrolling Messina. Three turns in swift succession should confirm it—if the scout-car hung on their tail. His eyes narrowed as he saw the headlights coming up fast; they were no longer being followed—they were either about to be stopped or passed. He was starting to turn the wheel to move in from the centre of the road when the car nipped in alongside him to the right and kept alongside him as the man next to the driver flagged him down by waving his hands. Petrie pulled up a short distance from the intersection where there was a closed café on the corner and tables still littered the pavement. The driver of the scout-car called to him in German through Angelo's window. 'Please turn off the engine—we would like to see inside your ambulance.'

'We are going back to the hospital—I only speak Italian,' Petrie shouted back, but he realized it was useless—the demand to look inside the ambulance proved that. The men they had left tied up in the barn must have been discovered, must have circulated the ambulance's registration number. It was the only explanation for their being stopped by a German patrol. The scout-car's driver spoke again, but this time he issued the order in crude Italian. 'You will both get out of the ambulance—and I told you to switch off the engine!' Petrie nodded, released the brake, drove forward. As he expected, the scout-car also drove forward to keep alongside him but the ambulance had a few seconds' advantage and he was pressing his foot down as the bonnet of the German vehicle appeared beyond Angelo's window and Petrie swung the wheel viciously to the right in a wide sweep to take him round the intersection and block off the other vehicle. Angelo saw what happened: seeing the ambulance swinging broadside on to his light vehicle, the German driver swung his own wheel over much farther, mounted the kerb at the corner, drove against the empty tables and rammed the shop window. As they swept round the corner there was a sound of glass shattering and one table bounced past Petrie's front wheels as he straightened up and shot down the side street while Johnson peered out of the rear window and then shouted, 'He's backing into the street—he'll be coming after us!'

Without waiting for Angelo's instruction Petrie swung left again, turning out of the side street into another wide avenue as deserted as its predecessor. The guns were opening up again, the moon had gone, but in the distance the flashes briefly illuminated overhanging roof-lines, balconies, the silhouette of a great church, as the ambulance raced down the avenue and Johnson shouted a further warning. 'It's behind us now!' Petrie shouted over his shoulder for him to drop flat on the floor as he built up more speed, expecting any moment to hear the deadly rattle of the machine-pistol the man next to the German driver had carried looped over his shoulder. The gunfire was becoming a barrage which hammered at their cardrums above the high-pitched whine of the engine; the flashes were becoming more frequent and in the distance he saw flames flare suddenly where a bomb had detonated. They were heading straight into an inferno and by the light of the gun-flashes he saw ahead a line of trucks moving across his path so he swung to the left, headed down another side street in the direction of the avenue he had originally come into Messina along, reached the end of the street and swung left again, taking the corner with a scream of brakes and screeching tyres as Angelo cannoned into him and then straightened up as they entered a large square with trees in the centre. They were halfway round the square when the scout-car entered from the street across from them and as Petrie drove on, intending to circle the square and return the way they had come because at least it was deserted in that district, they heard the scream of the bomb coming down. The scream was awful, a head-splitting noise which clogged the mind with terror during the few brief seconds before it hit a building in the square, detonated with a deafening crack and threw a wall down bodily. The masonry tottered, heaved outwards, fell with avalanche force over the scout-car which had just completed its turn, and inside the ambulance they felt the tremor of the tremendous impact. Pulling up, Petrie stared at the cloud of dust, the enormous heap of debris under which the scout-car lay buried.

'How near the flat are we?' he rapped out.

Angelo was holding his head with shock, and Petrie had to repeat the question before he got an answer. 'Just the other side of this square—one minute, no more . . .'

'We'll take our old clothes with us then—change at your place. Ed! Don't forget the sack! Come on—we're ditching the ambulance here.'

*   *   *

240

Sitting at his desk at the Enna GHQ, General Guzzoni, the Italian commander-in-chief in Sicily, put his phone down quickly and looked up at Kesselring, who had just flown in from Naples. 'There are unconfirmed but reliable reports that enemy parachutists have landed in strength at Piano Lupo and near Syracuse.' He stood up, grabbed a pointer off his desk and tapped twice on the wall map. 'Here and here . . .'

'Send a signal to the *Cariddi* to sail at once for Giovanni! I'm bringing over Rheinhardt,' Kesselring ordered.

'You don't wish to wait for confirmation?'

'No! Just send that signal to Baade!'

As Guzzoni went back to his desk and picked up the phone again Kesselring examined the wall map to discourage any more questions. He couldn't explain that as soon as he had learned that Strickland was commanding the British forces he knew it would be Sicily, but now he had his excuse for bringing over the 29th Panzer. Airborne forces had landed; the confirmation would come through later, and that would give him enough ammunition to talk down Supreme HQ. Not that he expected to have to: nothing was more calculated to silence the Supreme Command after the event than a correct decision taken before it. He glanced at the wall clock above the map. 11.52 PM.

*　　　*　　　*

Angelo's flat was on the first floor of a darkened building and they stumbled their way up an unlit staircase with the aid of Petrie's torch. The Italian had his key out when they reached the top, slid it

241

into the lock and went inside. He checked the two rooms quickly, pulled the black-out curtains over the windows where gun-flashes lit the opposite wall, then ran back on to the landing where Petrie and Johnson waited with weapons in their hands. 'It is all right!'

They moved very quickly, but not so quickly that they wasted time. Angelo stripped off his uniform, collected a bottle of French cognac while Petrie changed into his peasant clothes. Then, because the electric light wasn't working, the Italian made his phone call to the man who would be ready with his boat by torchlight. 'Is Alfredo there?' he asked. Petrie saw his expression tighten as he slammed down the receiver. 'It was someone else—a man who spoke Italian with a German accent.'

'Then Scelba has to get us off that train-ferry or we go up with her,' Petrie snapped. 'Let's get out of this place.'

He was carrying the sack of explosives over his own shoulder as they hurried out of the building with Angelo leading the way through the bombardment, into a dark alley where the warmth of the day—and the backstreet smells of Sicily—still lingered. At the end of the alley Angelo stopped, peered out, and then beckoned to the men behind him to follow. Petrie came out into a large square and his mouth tightened as he saw several batteries of 88-mm guns sited inside a park in the middle of the square, saw Wehrmacht soldiers waiting close to the artillery by the light of distant gun-flashes. 'How far now?' he asked.

'We shall be there in less than a minute,' Angelo replied.

'You hope!' Johnson said under his breath. The

242

gunfire had stopped suddenly and the three men could hear the quickening footsteps of a patrol coming up behind them. Less than a minute to the waterfront, Petrie thought grimly, and we're going to be stopped. Under his jacket his hand gripped the Mauser while the other hand supported the sack, but they couldn't afford a shooting-match here—not with those Wehrmacht troops only yards away to their left. The footsteps behind them came closer as Angelo, still leading the way, maintained an even pace.

The huge square was still intact, its stone buildings untouched by the bombing, and behind the stumps of trees, cut down to make way for the battery, uniformed figures of the Wehrmacht were watching them hurry past. They were almost clear of the square when they heard again the overhead droning of incoming bombers. An urgent order was barked out in German and the square erupted as three searchlights hovered, locked on to a plane, and the guns roared. 'Run!' Petrie shouted, seeing the perfect excuse for them to rush out of the square even though the patrol was behind them. Angelo ran into a side street, darted into an alley, ran a short distance, turned down another alley. With the others close behind him he ran out on to the waterfront and then stopped, panting for breath. 'That will have lost them—there are six different ways you can go inside that maze. And we're here!'

'And look what's waiting for us,' Petrie replied grimly.

The waterfront was a huge open space where dockside cranes towered against the flashes, where a queue led up to a gate, where a ship's slim funnel spired up behind a warehouse. The queue was made up of Sicilian peasants waiting to go on board, men in peaked caps and women in dark shawls who carried all their miserable possessions with them in their flight from the heavily-bombed city, people willing to brave the full fury of a major air raid in their anxiety to leave the island for the more peaceful mainland. 'That's the *Cariddi*?' Petrie asked. Angelo nodded. 'She must be leaving soon for Giovanni and somehow these people have heard. They always do.'

'Well, we're not just going to walk in through the main gate tonight.'

Unable to take over the *Cariddi* dock completely from their Italian allies, the Germans had reinforced the area with their own security forces. A file of Wehrmacht troops surrounded the queue and halfway along it three SS officers were checking papers. The Sicilian at the main gate was merely glancing at documents, more anxious to hurry people through, but the SS examination was painstakingly thorough. It was quite clear to Petrie that probably not everyone would get aboard before the ship sailed, but the SS didn't give a damn. Smoke was curling from the slim funnel as he spoke to Angelo. 'We've got to find Scelba—fast!'

'This way! If I'm not mistaken our villainous friend is waiting for us.'

They hurried along in front of the buildings facing the harbour and paused as they came close to an archway where a heavily-built man dodged under cover as bombs came down nearby. Overhead planes turned to evade searchlights, weaved, sideslipped in their desperate attempts to escape the tremendous firepower thundering up at them from both shores. As one battery paused to reload another would take its place, then another as the gunners spread a curtain of shells to prevent even one bomber breaking through. Scelba, tired and haggard, stepped out of the archway and spoke with his mouth close to Petrie's ear to make himself heard.

'You cannot get through the main gate—for some reason a special check is being made on everyone. Come this way . . .'

The mafia boss led them across to the waterfront about a hundred yards from the gate. Despite the intensity of the raid, one of the cranes was in operation, lifting great crates high up in the night and then swinging them sideways and lowering them to the deck of the waiting ship. Looking both ways, Scelba opened the left-hand side of two great double doors, stood holding the door while they slipped through then closed and bolted the door. They were inside some kind of wharf and the place had a derelict look as Petrie shouted his question. 'That was damned easy— we're on the *Cariddi* dock?'

'Good God, no! Scelba's tone was bad-tempered. 'This wharf isn't used any more—it's sealed off from the main dock.'

'Then why are we . . .'

'Come on! The ship is about to sail.'

The *capo* hurried through a long shed open to the wharf on his right, and then men began to appear, men dressed in working clothes and armed with shotguns. The smell of the decaying wharf filled their nostrils and the edge of the wharf was rotting away, the woodwork soggy and treacherous.

'Keep well back!' Scelba warned. Then they were out in the open again with a breeze off the straits in their faces as the gunfire died and was replaced by a weird silence. They heard water lapping at the wharf base, the murmur of the retreating planes. At the end of the wharf several Sicilians stood round two large crates and they stopped talking as the *capo* came up to them. He tilted his head back to stare upwards as he pulled a torch out of his pocket. 'You go aboard in these,' he said quickly. He was looking at the crane's cab which towered high above them from the next wharf. 'Are you ready? Two of you in the bigger crate, one man in the smaller. When you get aboard one of my men on the ship will rap three times on the lid and you will know it is safe to get out . . .'

'We just lift the lid?'

'No, you operate this catch which only works from the inside.' Scelba raised the lid, showed Petrie how the catch worked. 'And Giacomo is ready with the boat, ready to follow you into the straits. Remember a red lamp is at his masthead. You fire a green light when you go overboard. Is that right?'

'Yes.' Like Scelba, caught by the man's urgency, Petrie was speaking quickly. 'But there will be civilian passengers aboard so I may have to set the charges to go on the return trip and we may still be on the ship—will Giacomo come back with it? In fact, he bloody well must—Angelo's man has been captured.'

'If necessary he will go backwards and forwards until you reach him!' Aiming his torch upwards, the *capo* flashed it four times as the cable of the crane started to ascend from the ship's hold. 'Now, you must get into the crates—who goes by himself?' Angelo took the single crate and while he was climbing into it and the lid was being lowered Scelba took Petrie aside. 'You will tell AFHQ about our arrangement?' he asked.

'Don't worry, I'll tell them. And thanks for getting us here.' He looked up as the whirring sound of the crane's machinery increased. Then there was a muffled explosion from somewhere beyond the high wall which separated the derelict wharf from the *Cariddi* dock. 'What the hell was that?' Petrie asked sharply.

'A little diversion to distract the attention of the guards over there.' Scelba gestured behind to where a Sicilian sat by a phone inside the shed. 'He called my people inside the *Cariddi* dock the moment I signalled to the man operating the crane.' The cable swung outwards high above their heads, crossed the derelict wharf, stopped and then came down. 'Get inside quickly,' Scelba snapped. 'Both of the crates will travel together . . .'

As Petrie climbed inside the larger crate with Johnson the huge hook suspended from the waiting cable swayed a few feet away from him and from beyond the *Cariddi* dock wall he heard a second detonation. My God, he thought as the lid closed on him and he huddled beside Johnson, these people are well organized. Outside he could hear the muffled clump of booted feet hurrying about on the wharf, the bark of the *capo*'s voice.

'Move faster!' Scelba ordered as he watched the operation, but the men were moving quickly without the injunction as they manhandled the crate containing Angelo closer to the cable. By this time the large hook suspended from the cable had

247

already been inserted inside a ring attached to Petrie's temporary home. Scelba flashed his torch upwards, the cable hoisted the larger crate a few feet, stopped, and Angelo's crate was attached to another hook dangling beneath the larger container. Both crates were now linked to each other and both were suspended from the main cable as Scelba flashed his torch for the last time. The crane driver began winding up the cable, the two crates left the wharf, and the three men locked inside their cubes ascended into the darkness. The whole operation had taken less than two minutes.

The space inside the main container was very cramped for two men and Petrie was crouched double, sitting on his ankles with the lid pressing down on his neck as he heard the machinery whining and felt himself being hauled into mid-air. Johnson was equally cramped with his knees pressed down on the sack of explosives, and already the heat of their bodies was lifting the temperature as the cable hoisted them higher and higher and the crate started swaying at the end of its hook, their only support as the endless ascent continued. 'I'm glad Scelba didn't tell us about this in advance,' Johnson muttered. Already he was streaming with sweat from his cramped position, from the gnawing fear of the experience itself, from the temperature inside the crate which was rapidly becoming intolerable as the swaying grew worse and he fought down growing nausea. Petrie was, if anything, in a worse state. Confined inside the tiny wooden cell he suddenly felt weary, unbearably tired, his eyes rimmed with fatigue as pain began pounding steadily behind his forehead. He knew he was going to faint. Ramming his fingernails hard into his whiskered skin he scraped them deep into the flesh and the sharpness of the pain pushed back the overwhelming fatigue, forcing a spark of alertness back into his brain as the cable stopped ascending and began to swing them sideways towards the invisible train-ferry. The movement had just started when they felt a horrible lurch. The crate dropped sideways, jerked, and they hung there, thirty degrees out of true, their weight now supported by the side with the floor tilted under them. The ring at the top of the crate was defective—or the hook was bending. Any second now and they would leave the cable, crashing down scores of feet, hitting the deck of the *Cariddi* or the wharfside—or plunge to the bottom of the straits . . .

Inside the crate the fear was naked and contained, contained within the six enclosing walls of the swaying cube, fear intense enough to stop a man's heart 'The hook's giving way,' Johnson whispered between his teeth. The fear drove back the nausea, chilled his body like immersion in ice. 'Take it easy, Ed,' Petrie said, 'we'll be going down shortly . . .' The American felt suffocated as he interrupted, 'That's what bloody worries me.' Petrie's right arm was going dead but he let the sensation progress because he was scared that any movement on their part might topple the crate off the hook. 'We'll be down in one piece in thirty seconds,' he said. 'Start counting.' Johnson started counting as the cable began to lower them, and Petrie counted with him. Their bodies were so rigid now that they might have been in a state of muscular spasm—without saying a word both men knew that even the slightest movement could be fatal, so tilted sideways in the most awkward positions they held these positions as the cable went on lowering them. But the crane-driver had kept his nerve: he lowered them more slowly than usual and the hand which held the lever was as damp as the hands of the men inside the crates as the cargo slowly dropped and dropped and the train-deck of the *Cariddi* waited for them.

They had counted up to fifteen when the crate sagged a little farther, a slight jolt which sent a paralysing streak of fear through both men. The hook was giving way a little more—the hook or the ring. Petrie blotted out of his mind the futile attempt to diagnose the cause of the trouble and for a moment he couldn't remember where they'd got to. 'Sixteen . . .' he said through cracked lips, and Johnson joined him in the counting. Reciting the numbers gave them something for their sanity to hold on to, so they kept counting as the crates dropped lower and the air inside the tiny room became non-existent. The thud came at twenty-four, the thud when Angelo's crate hit the deck and their own toppled over it; when hands grappled with the crate and turned it upright and something hard struck the lid three times. Petrie released the security bolt and then had the devil of a job locating the catch, then the devil of a job getting it to work. When the lid was opened back and cold night air flooded in they lay inert, unable to move for several seconds until Petrie stirred himself, forced his legs to move again, forced his hands to get him upright, forced himself to climb out of the crate which was surrounded by other cargo which effectively hid them from anyone except the Sicilian who sat him down on a pile of sacks and then went to help Johnson as Angelo's head appeared out of the smaller crate. Petrie looked at his watch. The bloody thing must have stopped. It showed one minute to midnight.

CHAPTER FOURTEEN

Friday—Midnight

The wall of cargo which surrounded them had been dumped by the crane near the bows of the train-deck which rested against the dock, and above their heads was open air, moonlit sky. Glancing round the enclosed refuge they had been dropped inside, Petrie decided it was the perfect place to conceal the sackful of explosives while he got his bearings. 'Ed, hang on here a bit while Angelo and I take a look round . . .' Squeezing his way between cargo and bulkhead, he peered out and beckoned to the Italian to follow him. The massive bows of the vessel were open where the dockside link-span extended a single-track line up a ramp, connecting it with the train-ferry track, and the cavernous interior of the huge vessel was dimly lit with blue lights. But there were no coaches aboard for this trip where the single-track rail went inside and splayed out into three separate tracks, running the full length of the ship to the stern.

Petrie lit a cigarette as he leaned casually against the bulkhead, carefully shielding the match flame behind his cupped hand. 'You can get down into the engine-room from here?' he asked.

'No. We have to go up to the next deck . . .'

'In a minute. I'll look round here first.'

251

Even though time was so short he had to get some rough idea of the layout of the vessel: later, the knowledge could make all the difference between success and disaster. He looked up at the wheelhouse high above them, and behind it where the slim funnel was belching out smoke as the *Cariddi* made ready to sail. As he walked inside the train-deck he had the impression he was entering a great train-shed, a train-shed which floated, and under his feet the deck vibrated with the throbbing of the powerful engines. A little way in under the roof he waited for his eyes to get used to the gloom, then he saw that the interior was crowded with peasants sitting or sprawling over the three tracks, many of them asleep as though in the last stage of exhaustion. The huddled crowd of unsuspecting humanity decided him: the charges would have to be planted to detonate on the return trip, when these people were no longer on board. When he turned round to face the bows again he saw two civilians hurrying along the dock, but his pace didn't change as he walked back to where Angelo waited near the piled-up cargo. 'You see what's coming?' he said as he leaned close to the Italian.

'Gestapo!'

It was written all over the bastards. The standard uniform of belted topcoat and soft hat, one of them tall and thin, the other short and fat. 'Laurel and Hardy,' he murmured, then realized that Angelo wouldn't know what the hell he was talking about. The two men hurried up the link-span, stopped close to Petrie while they stared into the train-deck, then one of them produced a torch and switched it on as he came in under the roof. The torch-beam

252

flashed over the haggard faces of the men and women sprawled on the deck, paused at each one, then moved on. As the torch-beam hit him, Petrie was smoking his cigarette, and blinked in the glare until the Gestapo man moved on to continue his examination. At the dock gate the SS had scrutinized everyone coming aboard, but now the Gestapo was conducting its own security check. 'Angelo,' Petrie said out of the corner of his mouth, 'tell Ed to get back inside the larger crate and stay there with the lid down until we come back. Four raps and he'll know it's us—two long and two short.' He waited while the torch-beam brandished by Hardy proceeded along the train-deck. It was just going to make it that much more tricky— having those two characters on board. When the Italian came back he spoke again. 'More company joining us for the cruise—and you wouldn't ask them to dinner either.' Four SS men ran up the link-span on to the deck and then went immediately up the port staircase behind Petrie.

'This is most unusual,' Angelo, whispered in a worried tone. 'Never before have I seen this on a previous trip.'

'So this could be a special trip. Now, where's the engine-room?'

They climbed the port staircase the SS men had ascended and reached the upper deck under the wheelhouse. The vessel was swaying ponderously as the wind rose and a heavy swell developed out in the straits. An open deck led along the port side where an enormous jetty wall curved northwards to the harbour exit. The Italian left the open deck, stepped over the coaming through a doorway under the wheelhouse into an internal

253

companionway with cabins leading off to their left. The long corridor was deserted as he stopped, tried the door of Cabin Three, opened it into darkness and switched on the light. 'This is the deputy-engineer's cabin,' he explained. 'It would make a good base for us—I know from Volpe that his deputy is on leave so we shall not be disturbed here.' Petrie stepped inside and Angelo shut and bolted the door behind him. The single cabin was small and cramped with a bunk along one wall and a washbasin in a corner. Opening a cupboard, Petrie stared at the deputy-engineer's uniform suspended from a hanger, an ornate outfit with gold buttons. Cap, jacket, trousers. 'How big is he?' he asked.

'About my size and build. Why?'

'I just wondered. Is that the key to the door?'

Angelo took the key hanging from a hook over the wash basin. 'Yes. We can lock the place when we leave.'

'Funny he leaves it unlocked while he's away.'

'He is Sicilian.' Angelo shrugged expressively. 'Now I will show you the engine-room . . .'

'Just tell me how to get there.' Petrie's tone was urgent. 'You go back down to the train-deck and try and fetch Ed and the sack up here right away—before those Gestapo men nose around too much. If they come up here and find the door locked will they be suspicious?'

'Why should they be? I have never seen them on board before.'

They left the cabin quickly and Angelo showed Petrie a staircase farther along the companionway leading down to the deck below. 'At the bottom you turn right and halfway along you will find the entrance to the engine room. I can come with you . . .'

'No! Go and get Ed—I'll meet you back in the cabin. I'll rap four times—two long, two short . . .' He went down the staircase cautiously, pausing at the bottom to look round the corner to his right. Another long companionway extended into the distance, but this one wasn't quite deserted: an Italian sentry with a rifle was leaning against the wall farther along. Without hesitation Petrie went down the last step and started walking along the companionway which was closed off from the train-deck. The air was stuffier down here, the throb of the engines a more measured beat, and as he came closer to the soldier he saw he was leaning against a steel slab hooked back from an oval-shaped doorway. The thump of the machinery became very loud. The sentry glanced at Petrie as he passed, then looked away, bored stiff with being put on guard duty at this hour. The glimpse inside the oval-shaped doorway had been too brief to show much—a glimpse of heaving pistons as the engines built up power, of men working in soiled white vests and trousers beyond a metal platform just inside the doorway. Instead of walking the full length of the lower companionway, he turned right up a staircase, reached the upper companionway which was still deserted, turned left and hurried towards the stern.

The sway of the vessel seemed to have increased up here and he wondered whether another storm was on the way as he opened a door and stepped out on deck at the stern. Below him lay the roofs of trucks at the end of the train-deck and the wind whipped at his face as the ferry swayed again, but it

255

was the view beyond the harbour wall which interested him. A solitary boat with a red lamp glowing at its masthead was moving steadily out into the channel: Giacomo was taking up station in the straits ready for the moment when they went overboard. He went back along the open deck on the starboard side and it was uncannily deserted. As Angelo had forecast, the ship was lightly guarded and the main defences were against air attack, a quadruple of 20-mm guns fore and aft with some singles behind the bridge. The comforting thought had just passed through his mind when a door opened and a *carabinieri* soldier stepped out. A flashlight blinded Petrie for several seconds and was then switched off. 'What are you doing up here?' the soldier demanded.

'I must have come up the wrong staircase—I'm trying to find my way back to the train-deck.'

'Straight along there, then down the stairs.' The soldier went inside, closed the cabin door, and a whiff of smoke and wine which had drifted out dispersed in the wind. Petrie hurried along the deck and then stopped at the head of the starboard staircase as Laurel and Hardy came up it. The short fat brute leading the way glanced at Petrie from under his hat brim. A rounded face with small eyes and a depressed nose flattened against the skin. He appeared to be walking past Petrie without taking any further interest in him when he stopped suddenly. 'Papers!' Against all wartime regulations the torch was flashed on open deck as the restless eyes wandered over Petrie's rags while the thin man stood with his arms folded. So Hardy was one of those, full of little tricks to catch a man off guard. Petrie used his left hand to pull the

256

identity document from his breast pocket while he kept his right hand lower, inches away from the Mauser. As the squat Gestapo official took the papers and started examining them Petrie looked at the thin man who stood chewing while he stared out over the rail. His face had a bloodless look and the eyes were dead. This, Petrie guessed, was one of the trained executioners, one of the men sent on journeys to eliminate those whose continued existence was not healthy for the Third Reich: honest patriots, men who refused to collaborate, anyone who got in the way. A pretty pair to have on board as travelling companions. But it was the small man who worried him most, the man who would restlessly prowl the vessel checking—flashing his torch into people's faces, looking at papers, testing cabin doors.

Hardy returned his papers without a word, walked off along the deck with Laurel following. As Petrie ran down the staircase the *Cariddi* was on the verge of departure. Above him on the dockside a man was uncoiling a rope from a bollard as the deck swayed heavily and the engine vibrations increased. Crossing the train-deck, he went up the port staircase and then waited at the top to see if the enemy was sending any last-minute reinforcements on board. Ropes were cast loose, the uplifted bows of the ferry moved down, locked themselves in a small break between the rails. The ferry began to move. A gap of water appeared between its hull and the harbour wall as several Sicilians came out from the interior to watch the departure while smoke poured from the funnel and the vessel made for the harbour exit stern first. But there was one final point to check. Giacomo. Petrie spotted him again as the train-ferry steamed out backwards through the harbour exit where a tall monument on the jetty wall was a blurred shadow in the night. A red lamp at a masthead swaying drunkenly some distance ahead to starboard. He was back inside the cabin as the vessel turned, swinging its bows through an angle of a hundred and eighty degrees until they pointed northeast for Giovanni, then headed for Italy.

*   *   *

Three men inside the tiny cabin was one too many. 'It's like being back inside that blasted crate,' Johnson grumbled. 'When do we start?'

'Now,' Petrie said, emptying the contents of the sack on the bunk. Johnson and Angelo each took a Luger pistol and spare magazines while Petrie quickly examined the explosive. The charge was a floppy, putty-like substance, cylindrical in shape, and he put it back inside the sack to take up as little room as possible. The four timers he checked cursorily, then rewrapped them in newspaper and added them to the sack. 'I'll have this under my arm and it's damned heavy,' he told Angelo, 'so how do we explain it to Volpe when we get down into the engine-room?'

'You are a stone-mason, so those are your tools,' the Italian suggested promptly. 'With the present shortages it would be almost impossible to buy new ones—so he won't think it strange at all that you carry them everywhere. Probably he'll hardly even notice—he is a very egotistical man.' He picked up a large Very pistol from the bunk. 'This, of course, is vital for signalling to Giacomo, but it's too big to

258

take with us. I suggest we leave it here for the moment.'

'Agreed,' Petrie said. 'This cabin is a perfect base —it's so close to the open deck when the time comes to jump for it. Angelo, how long does it normally take the train-ferry to disembark passengers and cargo and leave Giovanni?'

'Half an hour—but you can never be sure.'

'We'll play it as it comes then. I can't estimate how long it will take me to plant the charges.' He picked up the sack, tucked it carefully under his arm. 'Incidentally, there's an Italian sentry guarding the engine-room door . . .'

'That has never happened before!' Angelo was momentarily appalled. 'But my bottle of French cognac may do the trick!' He spoke of the spirit as though it were a weapon of war. 'If possible we must avoid trouble until you have planted your charges.'

'If humanly possible,' Petrie emphasized. 'Now, you'd better go out first—it might look odd if someone saw a couple of peasants leaving this cabin.' The Italian switched off the light, unlocked the door, stepped out into the companionway, froze as he saw the retreating back of an SS man in the distance. The German went out on deck at the stern, disappeared behind the closing door. Angelo waited a moment to make sure he wasn't returning, then beckoned. He locked the door when they had come out, then led the way. At the bottom of the staircase to the lower companionway he paused, looked up at Petrie in bewilderment. 'No sentry.' Petrie peered round the corner: the companionway was deserted, the engine-room door still folded back against the bulkhead. 'Hurry it up!' he snapped. 'Before he comes back.' The companionway seemed longer than before to Petrie as they walked along behind Angelo, an endless corridor into which the Gestapo men might easily step from one of the staircases. His feet were dragging now and the sixty pounds of high-explosive inside the sack over his shoulder felt more like six hundred pounds. And it was getting so bloody hot and airless at this level. God knew what it would be like down in the engine-room. They halted as the Italian held up his hand. He had stopped close to the oval-shaped doorway and the machinery was pounding away, echoing inside Petrie's head. 'I have come to see Chief Engineer Volpe,' Angelo shouted. The sentry was on the platform beyond the doorway.

'No one is allowed in here,' the soldier said wearily.

'But I am a friend of the engineer's . . .'

'The order is no one allowed in the engine-room.' The soldier lifted his rifle without much enthusiasm. Avoid trouble, Petrie had said. Angelo hauled the bottle of cognac out of his pocket, waved it above his head as he caught sight of Volpe below. The chief engineer came forward closer to the platform, bawled to make himself heard above the din of the machinery, and when the soldier clearly couldn't hear a word Volpe gesticulated vigorously, indicating that the Italian was to come down. The soldier sighed, stared as Angelo beckoned two more men on to the platform, then stepped over the coaming back into the companionway to make more room. The chief engineer knew them, so that was good enough; he wasn't mucking bothered. In fact, he could hardly stand on his feet for lack of sleep.

Petrie came on to the platform with Johnson as Angelo went quickly backwards down a steel ladder. Holding on to the rail, Petrie looked down, saw the entrails of the train-ferry far below, a complex of hammering pistons and levers where men naked to the waist stood among the powerful engines which were driving them closer to Giovanni with every piston-stroke. The heat hit him at once, a torrid clammy heat akin to what they had suffered during their grim journey across Sicily. At the bottom of the ladder Angelo looked up, repeating his beckoning gesture, then turned to thread his way among the machinery. Volpe was some distance away now with his back to them as he talked to a member of his crew. Holding the heavy sack under one arm Petrie swung round to go down the ladder and the nightmare began.

All three men were draining their last reserves, but the strain Petrie had been subjected to was even greater. Without sleep for twenty-four hours, he had driven across Sicily in the heat of the day, and since nightfall he had driven the ambulance all the way from the level-crossing where they had left the little train. To say nothing of the train journey itself and the long walk to Puccio after the Beaufighter had destroyed the mafia boss's Fiat. He had not eaten a great deal, he had been on the alert constantly, and there was very little left as he started the descent, going down backwards, the sack under his arm and a good twenty-foot drop behind him to the metal deck below. He was in trouble at once because the intense heat was making him sweat and he had to go down holding on with only one hand, a hand which was already

261

sticky with moisture as it slithered over the metal rungs. The sack made it difficult for him to look down, to see where he was placing his feet, so he had to move by feel alone, and he had descended only three rungs when he began to feel faint and a wave of giddiness swept over him. Gritting his teeth, his face streaming with sweat, he glanced up once and saw Johnson standing on the platform while he looked down anxiously. Going down this ladder was going to be a real swine. He paused, took in a deep breath of the steam-laden air, felt, if anything, even worse, and decided to keep moving down steadily, whatever happened. Holding on with only one hand stretched above him, he had to let go for a split second every time he descended a rung, whipping his damp fingers urgently down to the next rung, and this was where the greatest danger came of losing his grip, of crashing down bodily to the deck under him—because his fingers always slipped horribly as they grasped at the next metal bar, fingers which were not only wet but which were already aching painfully under the tremendous pressure of holding him up. It was not only the fingers which worried him: his legs were feeling the strain badly, so they were less supple and when he lowered a foot he had to force it forward on to the next rung, and then the muscles would protest at the pressure of his body weight. He had something else to think about as well: the sack was becoming unbearably heavy, as though it were filled with lead bricks, and he knew that if he didn't reach the bottom soon the sack was going to slip out of his cramped grasp. He lowered another foot, panting with the effort, let go of a rung, clutched savagely for the one below, felt his fingers slipping all over the place, then locked them tight until it seemed the bones would break. To hold his balance, to prevent himself swinging outwards and losing all equilibrium, he had to keep his holding arm fully extended and now the forearm muscles were protesting agonizingly, so he was entering into a state of almost complete muscular cramp as he lowered another foot, fumbled around for another rung. God, his whole body was giving way. His right foot hit something and because it was a different feel his heart jumped with fear, then he realized with a shock of surprise that it had hit the metal deck. He was down!

His legs were trembling as he grasped the folded sack with both hands, waited while Johnson descended the ladder, and then gestured for him to go in front. The American edged his way between the machinery, careful of where he put his hands, and the engine-room noise was appalling, a hammering assault on his fatigued brain as the pistons thumped and the deck quivered with endless vibrations. Going round the corner of a high metal cover, he bumped into Angelo, who shouted to make himself heard as he introduced them to a large fat man in his forties wearing dark trousers and a soiled vest. Chief Engineeer Volpe was a fleshy-faced individual with a thin smear of dark moustache and greedy eyes. 'This is my cousin, Paolo,' Angelo said affably. 'He has wished to be an engineer all his life but when he was young there was not enough money . . .'

'Down here we run the ship,' Volpe began at once with an expansive gesture of his large hand. 'The bridge think they run the *Cariddi*, but the passage takes only thirty minutes so what can go

263

wrong? Whereas down here we must watch everything. Now, you see this dial over here . . .'

'Pietro, also a cousin . . .' Angelo introduced as Petrie came round the corner and nodded, but Volpe hardly glanced at him as he went on expounding about the hazards facing a chief engineer. Johnson noticed immediately that Petrie was no longer carrying his sack, that he must already have hidden it in some convenient spot, and then Angelo was producing his bottle of French cognac and Volpe was drinking their health as Johnson gazed round with assumed wonderment. A few minutes later when the engineer's back was turned Petrie caught his eye and winked, and when Volpe swung round again he was holding a hand to his head as though the heat was getting too much for him. 'Pietro,' Johnson shouted quickly, 'suffers from seasickness, but it will soon pass off.' Volpe shrugged, his only comment on the weaklings of this world, and went on showing them his marvels, pausing only to shout an order to one of the crew occasionally. By moving round a little, the American observed there were six other men in the engine-room, and the presence of so many crew worried him: Petrie was going to have a hellish job planting the charges under these conditions. At least two men were close to the engine-shafts and Johnson knew that these were one of Petrie's prime objectives. A few moments later two things startled him: Petrie had vanished and the soldier with a rifle was standing on the platform above them while he peered down inside the room.

Johnson froze, then deliberately relaxed and folded his arms as he wandered after Volpe to

264

another part of the engine-room with Angelo. Pressing back his worn cuff he checked his watch. Christ! Eight minutes to Giovanni: Petrie could never plant the charges and get out of the engine-room before they docked now, and with the guard peering down from above he might be seen at any second. Johnson was sweating profusely in the steamy heat, but he suspected he would have been sweating in any case as he listened to the engineer's boastings and kept an eye on the soldier. For God's sake move, man, he prayed. Go away, get lost! 'Have some more cognac,' Angelo offered genially and Johnson hastily stared at some chomping machinery as Volpe upended the bottle for the third time. The chief engineer seemed to have deputized his duties to another member of the crew who stood watching a lot of gauges and issuing brief instructions. Johnson looked up at the platform again and his prayer had been answered: the soldier had gone. 'We have a very important cargo for our next trip, Angelo,' Volpe said grandly. 'And for the trip after that and the one after that. For hours, in fact. The Germans, you know!'

'Really?' Angelo seemed unimpressed as he raised his voice above the beating pistons. 'I thought Germans were crossing all the time?'

'But this is their big tank division . . .' Volpe belched loudly, stopped in mid-sentence as though he had said too much. 'I like your cognac,' he went on rather superfluously. 'Now this gauge tells you . . .' Johnson stood limply with his arms still folded and an interested look on his face which gave no indication of the shock he was experiencing. 'Their big tank division . . .' The 29th Panzer Grenadier Division was about to start its crucial crossing to

Sicily. The airborne forces must have dropped and Kesselring had reacted instantly, ordering the 29th Panzer across the straits. And the *Cariddi* was still afloat, pushing her way through the swell to meet the waiting Germans on the Giovanni dockside. He could already feel the vessel slowing down and the clangour in the engine-room seemed louder as the engines slowed. Standing on the metal plates, surrounded by machinery thumping like a steam-hammer, fighting the dizziness which the clammy heat and the vessel's movements were bringing on, Johnson knew that Petrie had not yet managed to plant the charges. Volpe returned the half-empty bottle to Angelo who capped it and put the cognac back inside his pocket, knowing that the engineer wanted them to leave. 'If we can't get any transport out of Giovanni we may be coming back with you,' he said amiably and Volpe, remembering that the bottle was still not empty, looked disappointed as he scratched the back of his head.

'I am sorry, but no civilians will be allowed on board from now on . . .'

He broke off and started issuing instructions, bawling at the top of his voice. Angelo turned dubiously to Johnson as the engines churned more slowly and the American started back towards the ladder. He knew what Petrie was planning to do: since there was no chance of planting the explosives while the crew were driving the ship, he had hidden himself away in the hope that the engine-room would empty briefly before her next passage back to Messina. It was typical of Petrie to take this decision, knowing that he might be marooned in the bowels of the vessel, and Johnson was careful not to look for him as he went up the

266

ladder followed by Angelo. And if the sentry was still waiting outside in the companionway there was another problem: he had seen three men go down into the engine-room, but only two would emerge. When he stepped over the coaming into the companionway the sentry was there, leaning against the wall with his eyes shut. The poor devil had gone to sleep standing up. As Angelo came out behind him the sentry stirred, blinked himself awake, then called out to them as they were walking away.

'Where is the other man?'

Johnson went back to him, stared at him closely. 'He came out ahead of us. You must have seen him.'

'Ah! I remember now,' the sentry lied quickly. 'Of course!'

They returned the way they had come; along the companionway, up the staircase, along the upper companionway. But when he reached Cabin Three Johnson walked past it and went out cautiously on to the open deck. It was again deserted and after the heat of the engine room the chill of the early morning wind cut through his shabby clothes as he kept inside the shadow of the wheelhouse and looked down. The view gave him a nasty shock.

On the train-deck below the passengers had moved near the bows, huddled closely together in their anxiety to leave the vessel which was now passing inside the harbour at Giovanni. Already the ferry was rocking less, gliding forward very slowly, and in the distance under hooded lamps which lined the dockside the Wehrmacht was waiting. Trucks, petrol wagons, orderly rows of men seen only dimly in their soft-capped Panzer uniforms. And a train of many coaches, some kind of goods train. The spearhead of the 29th Panzer was ready to come aboard. A nerve-racking sight for the American. Perhaps he was looking at the death of an invasion, the Allied invasion. As the vessel bumped the dockside, shuddering to a halt, ropes were thrown for mooring and the bows began to ascend. This was going to be a damned quick disembarkation, followed by an equally quick embarkation. 'It makes it more difficult, does it not?' Angelo said over his shoulder. Johnson turned and they went back to the cabin, closing and re-locking the door before they put on the light.

'Jim can't plant those charges while the crew's hanging around,' Johnson said savagely.

'They always come up,' Angelo told him. 'I have seen it happen when I stayed on board to give Volpe another drink. Can you imagine them staying down in that atmosphere for hours when they can come up for air while she's in port?'

'If he's not back here inside thirty minutes we'll be making another trip to that engine-room. And this time it won't be so easy.' Johnson put away the cigarette he had taken out from his crumpled pack; he was dying for a smoke but the atmosphere inside the tiny cabin was already suffocating. 'It won't be easy for several reasons,' he went on, staring hard at the Italian. 'The boat will be far more crowded. You heard Volpe say no civilians are being allowed on board, so we'll be spotted the moment anyone sees us. And tight German security will be in operation.'

'Anything else?' Angelo inquired ironically.

'I think that will be enough to occupy us.' Johnson pulled out the three stick-grenades they

268

had hidden under the bunk's pillow and rolled them up neatly in a blanket. But there was something else he hadn't mentioned to Angelo. When Petrie had planted the explosive charges he would also set the timers and the whole fiendish mechanism would start ticking down to zero. And Johnson was pretty sure that the goods coaches waiting at the dockside to come aboard were an ammunition train. The Germans were about to convert the *Cariddi* into a floating powder house.

*   *   *

Forty minutes later they were still trapped inside the cabin by the constant procession of booted feet tramping along the companionway. They had sat in the darkness for what seemed hours, and while they had waited they had listened to the grinding of colliding buffers as an engine pushed the ammunition train up the link-span and inside the train-deck; to the shouting of German voices; to the endless tramp of the Panzer troops' footsteps marching past the cabin. The footsteps were becoming less frequent when, for the third time, an unknown hand grasped the door-handle from the outside and turned it, but the owner of this hand was more persistent. He rattled the door, then leaned against it with all his weight and pushed. The Italian, facing the door as he sat on the bunk alongside Johnson, held his knife pointed at the panel as his heart pumped faster in the darkness. The lock wasn't all that strong and it only needed sufficient pressure to burst it open. Johnson also held a knife ready for use—if shots were fired, if the alarm was raised at this stage with Petrie still imprisoned down in the engine-room it would be a disaster. The handle was turned again, more pressure was applied. Some bastard who wants to travel first-class, the American thought. Well, first-class on this trip meant a knife in the belly. The assault on the door ceased abruptly. They sat in an odour of sweat and animal fear as they listened to footsteps retreating along the companionway. The ship's engines were beating faster when they heard the whirr of the mechanical bows descending, the sharp thud as it met the deck. Only seconds later the vessel started moving, backing stern first out of Giovanni harbour.

'We'll go get him now,' Johnson said hoarsely.

Angelo fumbled for the switch, pressed it, blinked in the unaccustomed light. 'In those clothes, it would be too dangerous for you to come with me, but no one will notice me in this uniform!' He stood up, studied himself quickly in the mirror over the washbasin. The deputy-engineer's uniform he had slipped on earlier fitted him well; in fact, he felt quite pleased with his appearance. He took the marine cap Johnson handed him and tried it on his head. 'A little too small, but it will do. It has to be this way,' he insisted. 'Ashore the postman is never noticed—people accept him. It is the same on board—a man in marine uniform is invisible. I must find out what the position is.'

'All right, but for God's sake be back in five minutes. We've got to get Jim out of the engine room before the charges detonate.' Johnson put down his knife and pulled out his handkerchief to mop his face and forehead as Angelo switched off the light and unlocked the door. The Italian looked both ways, saw the companionway was empty, stepped out and pulled the door shut behind him. A second later the squat Gestapo man Petrie called Hardy walked round the corner from under the wheelhouse. He stared and the Italian knew that he had seen him closing the door, and from the frown on the German's face he also knew it could only be a matter of seconds before he was recognized. The marine uniform was puzzling the Gestapo man for a moment, but he'd get there, Angelo had no doubt about that. Luckily, he seemed to be on his own. 'I have seen you earlier on board ship,' the German snapped. 'What is there inside that cabin?'

'Dirty vests and soiled linen,' Angelo told him insolently. 'None of your bloody business.' He raised his voice so Johnson could hear him and made his reply as provocative as he could. The Gestapo man stared at him again without positive recognition, muttered an oath and grabbed at the handle. Inside the cabin Johnson couldn't find his knife so he changed his tactics as the door opened, a rectangle of light flooded in, and the German entered. Johnson's hands grasped the Gestapo man by the throat, hauling him farther inside the cabin as Angelo lunged at his back with his shoulder, forcing him right inside the cabin. The Italian followed him, squeezed himself past the door and rammed it shut as he switched on the light. By now Johnson had toppled the German on to the bunk, was lying half on top of him as he maintained the pressure of both hands round the thick neck, jabbing his thumbs hard into the windpipe.

Temporarily caught off balance, the German began reacting violently, punching with his left hand at the American's face while he shoved his right hand inside his coat. Angelo grabbed at the right hand, forced it out, tore the Luger viciously from him, grabbed at the other hand. In the confined space of the cabin it was difficult and the Italian held on to the struggling hands, pulling them back behind the man's head as Johnson's slippery fingers tried to hold their grip. The German had his mouth open, attempting to shout, but the thumbs dug into his windpipe stopping him emitting anything more than a strangled gurgle as the fight went on. It can be surprisingly difficult to kill a man and the German had a lot of strength in his short body. Tearing his left hand free from Angelo's grip, he forked two fingers and aimed for Johnson's eyes. The American jerked his head back, still kept his grip on the German's throat as Angelo grabbed the man's wrist and forced the attacking arm down on the bunk. The German's heels hammered frantically and Johnson held on, tightening his grip, then the heels were thudding only spasmodically and suddenly they stopped, felt limp. Johnson waited a little longer before he released his throttling hold and wiped the back of his hand over his streaming forehead. The hand came away smeared with blood where the stabbing fingernails had gouged him. 'Christ! That was rough.'

'We must get him out of here,' Angelo urged, 'put him over the side—it isn't far . . .'

Johnson compelled himself to think, but it took only a few seconds to reject the idea. 'Too dangerous—we'd bump into someone. Leave him here and take a look round. But hurry! And leave the key so I can lock myself in—four raps when you come back, two long, two short . . .'

Angelo left the cabin, heard the lock turn in the

door behind him, walked at a leisurely pace along the now deserted corridor despite Johnson's injunction to hurry: people who hurried drew attention to themselves. He went light-footed down the staircase to the lower companionway, pausing to look for a guard outside the engine-room. The Italian had gone—and in his place stood a German sentry with a machine-pistol looped over his shoulder. As Johnson had predicted, things were deteriorating. Still concealed behind the staircase wall, he took out his knife, fixed it inside the marine cap, then walked towards the sentry while he fluttered the cap as though the heat were becoming a bit much. He walked forward at the even pace a ship's officer would have adopted, knowing that within minutes the alarm would be sounded—after his encounter with the sentry. It had to be quick; it had to work the first time. The sentry watched him coming without interest; as Angelo had foreseen, the uniform was accepted without a trace of suspicion. But there might be another guard inside on the platform. As he came close to the engine-room door the sentry was so uninterested in the new arrival that he looked back through the open door, but then he looked back again as Angelo arrived, stopped not too close to him and spoke in Italian. 'I suppose Engineer Volpe is down there—there's some question about changed landing instructions when we reach Messina and I want to have a word with him.' He ran the words together in a gabble, but the German didn't understand a word of Italian. As he spread his hands to show his incomprehension Angelo let the cap fall, thrust his knife forward. The blade went in deep, the German gulped, and then he was

273

falling. Angelo grabbed him as he fell, struggled to shift him back out of the companionway, but the weight was enormous and the soldier's limp feet caught the coaming. Angelo heaved him half over his shoulder, staggered on to the platform, dropped him and with an effort retrieved the knife, as he scanned the scene below. Volpe was standing with his back to him and the crew was concentrating on turning the vessel's bows through a hundred and eighty degrees to face Messina.

From behind a machine-cover Petrie stood up, ran to the foot of the ladder, came up it fast. 'Charges planted, whole bloody lot,' he said quickly as he reached the platform. 'The crew cleared out when the ship docked, but they came just as I'd finished . . .' Petrie looked gaunt, hollow-eyed, was streaming with sweat. Down in the engine-room, Volpe turned, saw them, shared in astonishment, moved towards the voice-pipe, then stopped as Petrie aimed the Mauser and waggled it. Volpe moved away from the voice-pipe and now the rest of the crew were turning their heads. The moment we leave here Volpe will inform the bridge, Petrie thought grimly. 'Let him go,' he said to Angelo and the Italian released the body which rolled off the edge of its own volition and crashed to the deckplates twenty feet below. 'We'll have to move fast,' Petrie said as he went into the companionway. 'Where's Ed?'

'In the cabin . . .'

'You go first—you're in uniform. Any sign of trouble—take your cap off to warn me.'

Angelo put the cap he had retrieved from the companionway floor on his head, walked rapidly towards the staircase. With Petrie close behind him

274

he ran lightly up the steps, paused at the top, took off his cap and instead of turning right along the upper companionway he went up the next staircase opposite. Petrie saw the warning signal, understood that there was someone in the companionway, and when he looked round the corner he saw an SS man close to Cabin Three. The German was kneeling on one knee, fastening his boot, a task which occupied his full attention as Petrie nipped across the companionway, and followed up the staircase. Pushing open a door at the top, the Italian came out into the open on an upper deck. The chilling wind and the darkness hit him, moonset was at 12.30 PM and the blackness was total. He waited while Petrie followed him up, straining to get his eyes used to the night while the vessel completed its turn and the heavy swell splashed below him. 'We have to go along this deck,' he whispered, 'down a staircase, and then we're near the wheel-house.'

'Keep in front—and keep your eyes open!'

Angelo started walking towards the bows as the vessel headed for Messina. It was so dark that he didn't see the man in the open doorway until he had passed him. He took off his cap, hoping to God that Petrie could see the action. The figure waiting in the doorway was the tall Gestapo officer, presumably searching for Hardy, the man Petrie called Laurel. 'Just a minute! You there! Come back here!' The fluency of his Italian startled Angelo, but only for a moment. Swinging round on his heel, he took a long stride back to the German who was now standing on the deck, ramming his knife hard into the man's stomach. Petrie's knife entered his back as though the movements had

275

been synchronized and the German sagged with only a gasp. 'Get him over the side!' Petrie snapped. 'We don't want anyone finding this yet.' Between them they hoisted the body up to the rail, shoved it over the edge, and the distant splash could have been a wave meeting the vessel as the *Cariddi* steamed forward and the body drifted back towards the thrashing twin screws at the stern. Angelo leaned over the rail, but there was nothing to see, only the shadowed heave of the sea. 'He'll be mincemeat for the fishes,' he said cold-bloodedly, and started walking again along the deck. The incident hadn't occupied more than twenty seconds.

Near the head of the staircase he slowed down, then stopped. From the deck below near the wheelhouse he could hear people talking in German. He tiptoed forward, looked over the rail, saw a blur of soft-capped heads below. There were anything up to half a dozen Panzer troops gathered under the wheelhouse while they killed time gossiping. He went back to where Petrie had halted. 'German troops just under the wheelhouse—so we can't get down that way. They must be pretty close to Cabin Three.'

'We'll go back the other way. You've seen Giacomo's out there, thank God.'

As they went back the way they had come a red light was bobbing in the night some distance away to their right as the *mafioso* took his craft on a course parallel to the *Cariddi*'s. There were other vessels' lights also in the straits so Giacomo's was conspicuous only by its colour. Leading the way with his cap on his head, Angelo turned down the staircase to the upper companionway. To his relief he found the corridor deserted. 'Run!' Petrie whispered behind him. They ran, pulled up before they reached Cabin Three which was close to the wheelhouse where the Panzer troops were chatting, then walked up to the door. Angelo rapped quietly with his knuckles, praying the Panzer troops wouldn't hear him, that Johnson would. The key turned at once and the American stood in the doorway with a knife in his hand. Pushing inside, the Italian grabbed the Very pistol from under the pillow on which Hardy's head rested. Johnson reached over him to pick up the blanket folded round the grenades as Petrie looked over his shoulder, saw the dead Gestapo officer and wasted no words on comment. 'The alarm will have been given, Ed, so expect trouble—a heap of it. . .'

In the short time since they had arrived at the cabin Petrie had released the wooden holster from round his waist, snapped the holster on to the Mauser butt, and now the weapon was ready for long-range use. Fast fire. Johnson thrust one of the stick-grenades in his hand and he pushed this down inside his belt, then he glanced out both ways and left the cabin, running along the companionway towards the stern. They had to get up that staircase again on to the upper deck where they would drop off the side after Angelo fired his Very pistol. Petrie was halfway to the staircase when two SS men came down it with pistols in their hands. He fired as he ran, one short burst, and the Germans had dropped when he reached the bottom of the staircase. He was on the first step when the door opened at the top and two more appeared. He fired upwards, stopped, fired again to discourage anyone else up there. A figure appeared, darted back out of sight as he raised the muzzle again and then didn't fire. 'No good!' he warned the others, then he jumped over the crumpled bodies of the two SS men and ran at top speed towards the stern. The situation was definitely getting difficult: they should have been off the ship before the alarm was raised. He reached the door at the end of the companionway, pushed it open with his gun muzzle and heard feet running along the upper deck towards him from his right. No chance of diving off that side—they'd be shot as they jumped. He went the only way he could—down a staircase leading to the train-deck.

Angelo followed behind him with Johnson bringing up the rear. As they came close to the door the American looked back and saw a soldier standing well back along the companionway, lifting his rifle. Aiming down the corridor would be like firing in a shooting-gallery: he couldn't miss. With the rolled blanket under one arm, Johnson swung round, aimed the Luger, fired one shot. He had taken prizes for shooting moving targets but this was the process in reverse: the marksman was moving, the target stationary. The soldier was falling as he turned and went through the doorway, and as the door swung shut behind him a bullet came through it. Johnson went down the steps to the train-deck three at a time and then he ran out of space. The three tracks were fully occupied by the ammunition train.

'This way!'

Petrie called out from behind a coach on the middle track and Johnson followed them down a narrow corridor dimly lit by the blue lights with his shoulders brushing the coaches on either side. It

278

felt weird—walking through what was apparently a goods yard with the floor under you heaving and falling while the couplings rattled gently with the motion and the coaches creaked. At the front Petrie walked with the Mauser gripped in both hands, a fresh magazine inside it while he watched for movement ahead. There had to be guards down here—this was the Wehrmacht for Christ's sake! His earlier fatigue had gone, his faculties were keen and sharp-edged, and his eyes were growing accustomed to the gloom as he walked forward at an even pace, not dawdling, not hurrying. There was shouting somewhere above them, but down here on the train-deck it was surprisingly quiet, so quiet he could hear the lapping of the water against the vessel's sides. They had one chance only of getting clear—they had come deeper into the vessel, which was probably the last place the search parties would expect them to run for. He was walking past another coach with the door half-open when a uniformed figure stepped out from between two coaches ahead of him and the man started addressing him in German. He hadn't expected any trouble and Petrie didn't want any noise, so while the soldier stared at him dull-wittedly Petrie raised his gun muzzle and brought it crashing down on the soft cap. The force of the blow jarred him up the arms and the German collapsed without a sound. Three more coaches brought him close to the bows and he slowed down as he heard a clatter of feet coming down a staircase, then a voice giving orders in German. 'Hans! You take a file of men between each line of coaches! Check carefully between each coach! Use your torches to check the roofs . . .'

Petrie pushed the other two further back the way

279

they had come with his hands. When they reached the open coach he gestured upwards and they scrambled inside noiselessly, then he followed them. There wasn't much damned room—on this trip he seemed to be specializing in confined spaces like crates and one-man cabins. Now for the real tricky operation—closing the door. His heart was pounding so loud he felt the others must hear it as he eased the door sideways inch by inch, but the only sounds he heard were the shuffle of feet as the Panzer troops commenced their search of the train-deck. The door closed silently on its well-oiled runners. Wonderful German efficiency! When it was shut he used his torch to drop the handle into the locked position and then he flashed it on the piled-up boxes which three-parts filled the coach. On one box was stamped the legend 7.5 cm LK 70 PK 41. This was definitely an ammunition train. 'Wonder how long it will take?' Johnson whispered in the darkness. No one replied. No one knew as they waited and listened to the muffled sounds of the Germans searching, rattling at the handles as they checked each coach.

*   *   *

The search was quicker than Petrie had expected as the unseen men moved along the tram-deck, and when he judged they had moved some distance away from the coach where they hid he unlocked the door, eased it open a few inches and listened. He heard faint sounds above the slap of the water against the ship's hull—voices, the clink of metal against metal—but he wasn't prepared to stay aboard any longer. The charges were timed to

280

detonate any time from now on. Dropping to the deck, he looked both ways and saw nothing. He beckoned to the others and went towards the bows of the vessel. This area, at least, should be safe: it had just been searched.

The bows were a vague silhouette looming against a starlit night and here several petrol tankers, brought on board after the train, were parked close together. He climbed the port staircase slowly, step by step, and when he came under the wheelhouse he saw beyond the port rail a red lamp swaying in the distance. Giacomo was still there, still keeping a course parallel to the train-ferry as it drew closer and closer to Sicily. The others crowded up behind him as he reached the deck and peered along its darkness. Had a shadow moved there or was it simply strain—the nerves expecting something to be there? 'Send the signal,' he whispered. Angelo pushed past him, went to the rail, raised the Very pistol high above his head and fired it. High over the straits a green light exploded, flaring brilliantly. 'Get over the side!' Petrie rapped out. 'Both of you! Head for that red light fast!' A German soldier came round the corner from the companionway with a rifle grasped in both hands. He stopped, splayed his legs, aimed the weapon in one action. Petrie fired a short burst and the German sagged as Angelo went over the side. All hell was going to break loose now. The sound of a racing engine was coming closer from out at sea as Johnson dumped the blanket on the deck, unrolled it. 'Grenades!' Petrie swore at him. 'Get over the side!' Johnson was poised on the rail when bullets began spattering all round him and a wood splinter ripped across his forehead. As the

281

American left the rail Petrie fired a long continuous burst straight down the upper deck where the shots had come from, arcing the gun slightly from side to side. He thought he heard thuds on the deck as he reloaded and the shots ceased. Then he picked up one of the grenades Johnson had left, went to the archway under the wheelhouse and threw the grenade blind as far as he could. That should clear the companionway for a moment.

The racing engine from the sea was a roar now. A searchlight came on, almost blinded him for a fraction of a second, then it dropped to sea-level. An E-boat was alongside, attracted by the strange Very signal. The craft was close to the train-ferry as it swivelled its light over the water, passed Angelo's head, then swung back to hold him in its glare as the manned machine-gun began to chatter. The Italian took a deep breath, dived under the water as Petrie ran to the rail, measured the distance, tossed the grenade and dropped flat on the deck close to the last grenade Johnson had left. He didn't see it happen, but the missile landed amidships, detonated before the crew knew what was happening. The explosion reached the fuel instantly, there was a dull boom and the E-boat disintegrated as flame flared and debris rained down on the deck of the *Cariddi*. Something hot seared the back of Petrie's neck and then it was quieter, quiet enough to hear the clatter of boots coming up the port staircase from the train-deck. Still sprawled on the deck, he saw a jostle of movement on the staircase as he grasped the last grenade and threw it. His face was buried in the deck when the crack came and when he looked up the staircase was empty and there was a strong smell of burning in his nostrils. He stood up with the Mauser and emptied the magazine along the upper deck which must be clear if he was to have any chance of survival when he went over the side. Hoisting himself up, he sat on the rail, pushed off, and the sea came up to meet him out of the darkness with a splash and a thump, then he was swimming furiously away from the ferry to get clear of the twin screws.

Hitting the sea was a shock; the water was horribly cold, probably felt colder than it was in his fatigued state, and swimming with his boots on was damned difficult. It was also incredibly dark, utterly black, and there was still a heavy swell as he swam forward with strokes growing in power. Once he thought he heard shots, but when he glanced back only the ferry's stern showed as it headed at top speed for Sicily, its own motion taking Petrie out of the firing line. The red lamp he could see but it seemed to be changing position and he hoped to God Giacomo wasn't puttering about trying to find them. All the Sicilian had to do was to stay put and they'd find him. With luck and the strength to reach him. The waves jostled his face, bounded under him, so it was like swimming on a sea of rubber as odd sensations began stirring inside his head. It was an illusion, of course, this dizzying whirling sensation as the waves gyrated round him, but it was no illusion that he was on the verge of fainting. The steady beat of the *Cariddi*'s engines was fading away and the only sound he could hear was the sloshing slap of waves as he forced his weary arms and legs to continue the rhythm, to continue swimming towards the swaying red lamp which he now believed was stationary. And he was becoming waterlogged: the weight of his sodden clothing was pressing his body lower in the water as the red lamp came closer with painful slowness. The dizziness became worse as he felt a powerful current pulling at him, sucking at his exhausted body to carry him away from the waiting red lamp. He had a moment of rebellion against this last enemy—the current—as he took an enormous breath of the cold night air and thrust out with all his remaining strength, trying to break free from the current's clutch. Then he felt something scrape his shoulder, hook deep inside his sodden clothes, graze the bare flesh under his shirt, a boat-hook which held him only because his clothes were so sodden since dry clothes would have torn apart under the pressure. The boat-hook held by Giacomo hauled him steadily forward and then hands were grasping him, lifting him, hauling him aboard as Johnson and Angelo heaved him over the side and deposited him in the bottom of the boat.

'Are you all right?' the American asked anxiously.

'Fine . . .' Petrie gasped out as he flopped for a moment, staring up at their faces, at the red lamp beyond, at the brittle stars beyond that. The fainting feeling was coming back. 'Get me upright . . .' They sat him up with his back against the mast, a tall structure with wooden pegs like rungs projecting from the pole. Petrie had heard about these strange craft somewhere: the rungs were for the captain of the craft to climb to the masthead and direct operations from his elevated position when he saw the swordfish approaching. 'Thanks,' he said to Giacomo, then remembered that the man was a deaf mute. Short and squat, the Sicilian was large-bellied by the lamp's glow, and it was to the lamp he was pointing now as he picked up a shotgun and waved to them to keep their heads down. They waited with huddled heads while he aimed. The gun barked, the lamp shattered, showering glass into the boat. Giacomo had just used the most effective method available for putting out the lamp which could locate them.

'Those charges,' Johnson called out hoarsely from the stern near the outboard motor. 'You planted them where you wanted them?'

'Just where they ought to be—all of them,' Petrie assured him. 'Two ten-pounders in the propeller-shaft tunnels alongside the first bearing—and they're connected up, so both shafts should go at the same moment. The big job—the forty-pounder—I put inside a lubricating drum against the starboard side.'

'They'll all go together?'

'They're set to, but there'll probably be a thirty- or forty-second gap between them.'

'What will happen?' Johnson rested his bare feet on a rope coil as he dabbed at his blood-streaked forehead with a cloth the silent Giacomo had provided.

'At a guess the engine-room should flood inside thirty seconds, the next compartment inside a minute. I reckon the ferry will go down about five minutes after the first detonation.'

'The Germans will be searching the whole engine-room,' Johnson pointed out soberly.

'They will, and I expected the charges to detonate before now. But an engine-room is a

285

complex place to search.'

Giacomo went to the stern, indicating with gestures that he wanted Johnson to move. Crouching low over the outboard, the Sicilian pulled at the starter cord and the motor growled into life as Petrie glanced anxiously around. There was no sign of other craft in the vicinity but the straits crawled with E-boats and he was counting on the expected detonations to distract them. The motor built up power, the boat began to move south down the channel towards distant Malta as four pairs of eyes stared in the direction where the train-ferry had vanished in the darkness. They were staring in the same direction when the first detonation came, a gigantic hollow thump like a single blow against a giant drum. There was no flash with this detonation, no immediate smoke as the searchlights of three E-boats came on and roamed over her, only the hollow thump which seemed to make no difference to the ferry's progress until Petrie noticed a change in direction as the silhouette of funnel and high bridge and superstructure became foreshortened.

'She's altered course!' he shouted.

'She's heading for Paradiso Bay,' Angelo said.

'Her steering's smashed!' Petrie blinked to get a clearer view. 'The next charge will get her.'

The E-boats' searchlights remained focused on the train-ferry as she continued to turn, her steering mechanism smashed beyond repair while more E-boats scudded across the water towards the stricken vessel. The second detonation, the forty-pounder, made its predecessor sound like a tap on a door, and the straits seemed to shake as the detonation's thunder swept across the water and

286

into the mountains so that in Messina and Giovanni it came to them like the crash of a whole battery of six-inch naval guns firing at the same moment. Seconds later there was a great flash, more illuminating than dawn, followed by another and then another. In the stern Johnson stared in awe. A whole ammunition train was starting to go. The explosive power confined inside the train-deck was unimaginable. Another detonation came and they felt its blast as it was followed by two more and the fire took hold, fire such as Johnson had never seen before, as enormous tongues of flame leapt over the crippled ferry and lit the straits with a glow which reflected redly in the grey waters. Then a fresh detonation of appalling violence, erupting like a minor Etna as flames soared and wavered in the wind and the smoke came, great belching black clouds so that soon the ferry was shattered from end to end, a floating furnace burning to the waterline as petrol flooded out, spread over the deck, engulfing men and materials as it ignited in a terrible combustion while the E-boats scurried about the doomed vessel like distracted ants, taking care not to speed in too close to the inferno. As the ammunition coaches jammed close together on the train-deck exploded with a continuous crackle they began to send debris in all directions. Part of the vessel's superstructure was already gone, exposing the train-deck beyond, outlining the ferry clearly in the flames—the silhouette of a petrol tanker, the crumbling bridge, the still-intact funnel, shadows against the red glare which itself was brilliant against the curtain of black smoke behind it. The petrol tanker burst, vanished, and now the funnel and the high bridge

287

were going, heeling over as they were consumed by the flames and the vessel became a floating platform of burning petrol and exploding ammunition. Another detonation came, hurtling up white-hot debris which travelled a vast distance and showered down on patrolling E-boats which suddenly fled away from the disaster area in panic. Then the ship settled stern first, raising its bows briefly so they pointed skyward, their plates red-hot and glowing, and went down slowly. Despite the distance Petrie fancied he heard a hideous hiss as the water closed over the ferociously heated remnants.

No one spoke for a moment as they sat dazed by what they had witnessed, then Petrie stirred himself and went to the bows of the boat to keep watch. Johnson found him there an hour later as they proceeded steadily down the straits through the darkness, found him crumpled up, fast asleep. 'This I won't let him forget,' he told Angelo with a weary grin. 'Caught asleep on watch duty?'

In the early morning when the glowing disc of the sun climbed above the eastern horizon to roast Sicily afresh they were becalmed, out of petrol, out of sight of land as they floated on a gentle undulation of pale blue sea which caught the sun's reflections. Only Johnson and Giacomo were awake, and appropriately enough it was the American who had climbed to the top of the mast and hung there while he waved his shirt madly. Appropriately enough because the US flag was fluttering from the mast of the PT boat roaring towards them across the peaceful sea, the PT boat which was to take them southwest to Malta, away from the coast of Sicily where Allied troops were

288

pouring on to the beaches prior to driving inland and conquering the island in thirty-three days.

EPILOGUE

Sometimes it is what happens later which is significant.

After the invasion Don Vito Scelba received his reward, largely on the strength of the bald but accurate report which Petrie felt obliged to submit to AFHQ. He did not become mayor of Palermo; instead he was given a more powerful post in the Allied administration which took over the conquered island. And while he used his position to increase his influence, Scelba was secretly organizing large-scale raids on Allied supply dumps, looting them systematically for the black market which plagued first Sicily and, later, Italy.

One thing led to another. The huge profits from the black market operation helped to build up his political power; by the end of the war he had linked up with the mafia in Naples, with the criminal underworld of Marseilles, and with the most powerful of the five families controlling the New York mafia. He had re-established an international mafia. Gradually it extended its operations over half the globe, operations involving prostitution, currency manipulation—and the drug traffic. It was this organization Scelba built up which years later directed the drug traffic which threatens the vitality of so many western nations—a system made possible because the Allies approached the Sicilian mafia for help in the middle of a war.

The ambush which eventually closed round half the western world was sprung in July 1943.

The death of Don Vito Scelba was ironic: he

291

died of the dreaded *lupara* sickness. An ageing man, still travelling round Sicily in shirt-sleeves and braces, still peering at the world through his tortoiseshell glasses, he walked out of a Palermo hotel one hot July morning and found his car wasn't waiting for him. Ten years earlier he would have been instantly suspicious, but Scelba was no longer the *mafioso* who had stabbed a fireman to death one night at Scopana Halt. Instead, he lingered on the pavement edge while he wondered what had happened. Then a car came, a car driven very fast by four young men in dark glasses who, as they passed him, emptied their shotguns at point-blank range. When he fell on the pavement no one ran to help him. Don Vito Scelba had outlived his time.

Chivers Large Print Direct

If you have enjoyed this Large Print book and would like to build up your own collection of Large Print books and have them delivered direct to your door, please contact **Chivers Large Print Direct**.

Chivers Large Print Direct offers you a full service:

✰ **Created to support your local library**

✰ **Delivery direct to your door**

✰ **Easy-to-read type and attractively bound**

✰ **The very best authors**

✰ **Special low prices**

For further details either call Customer Services on 01225 443400 or write to us at

Chivers Large Print Direct
FREEPOST (BA 1686/1)
Bath
BA1 3QZ